DEAR READER,

The human experience is an adventure. We're born, we live, and we die, but for those left behind, the journey can sometimes feel too short. Life comes with a lot of WTF moments, and I want you to know there are quite a few WTF moments in these pages. While life is magical, it can also be an absolute shit show from time to time.

Things I'll Never Say is a story about loss. Specifically losing someone to a drug overdose. And even more specifically, to an opioid addiction. Casey Jones turns to drugs to numb the pain of grieving before she finds a way out of her own addiction. This story is about living with rage, anxiety, panic, depression, and ADHD. There are a few biphobic and internalized fatphobic moments addressed and worked through on the page.

There is also light and love and laughter here, because sometimes in our darkest moments, that's when we need to laugh the loudest. I'd like to think that by the end, we find Casey healed in a multitude of different ways.

Lastly, there is no right way to mourn. I have learned through my own losses that the cycles of grief are like the motions of a tide. Sometimes the pain comes rushing in and eats away at you grain by grain, until you're full of holes. And other times it rushes in with memories and fills the holes it created in the first place. Ride the waves of grief, keep their memory alive, and eventually, you'll find yourself healing along the way.

I hope that Casey's story helps you heal, or at the very least, lets you know you aren't alone.

Kindly—

Cassandra

For my family—always be the ripple in still water.

—C.N.

Published by Peachtree Teen
An imprint of PEACHTREE PUBLISHING COMPANY INC.
1700 Chattahoochee Avenue
Atlanta, Georgia 30318-2112
PeachtreeBooks.com

Text © 2023 by Cassandra Newbould
Jacket art © 2023 by Hokyoung Kim

Edited by Ashley Hearn
Design and composition by Lily Steele

Content Warnings: opioid addiction, drug and alcohol use, death by drug overdose, anxiety, panic, depression, ADHD, internalized biphobia and fatphobia.

Printed and bound in April 2023 at Lake Book Manufacturing, Melrose Park, IL, USA.
10 9 8 7 6 5 4 3 2 1
First Edition
ISBN: 978-1-68263-596-4

Library of Congress Cataloging-in-Publication Data

Names: Newbould, Cassandra, author.
Title: Things I'll never say / Cassandra Newbould.
Other titles: Things I will never say
Description: First edition. | Atlanta, Georgia : Peachtree Teen, [2023] |
  Audience: Ages 14 and up. | Audience: Grades 10-12. | Summary:
  Seventeen-year-old Casey turns to journaling to cope with her twin
  brother's death and the complicated, romantic feelings she develops for
  both her best friends, Francesca and Benjamin.
Identifiers: LCCN 2022056444 | ISBN 9781682635964 (hardcover) | ISBN
  9781682635971 (ebook)
Subjects: CYAC: Interpersonal relations--Fiction. | Bisexual
  people--Fiction. | Friendship--Fiction. | Diaries--Fiction. | LCGFT:
  Novels.
Classification: LCC PZ7.1.N4854 Th 2023 | DDC [Fic]--dc23
LC record available at https://lccn.loc.gov/2022056444

things
I'll never
say

CASSANDRA
NEWBOULD

PEACHTREE
Teen

DEAR SAMMY,

That's how these things always start, right?

I pretend you're still here, spill my guts on the page, and hope one day you'll understand the meaning behind my words.

Except you won't.

Because to understand, you'd actually need to read what I'm saying.

And we both know that will never happen again.

Seventeen.

That's the number of journals I've written to you since you died. One for every month you've been gone. Well, almost. I skipped last month. Let's just say there were a few days where I was . . . on vacation. A brain break, if you will.

Life has been super overwhelming lately. To be honest, I'm starting to hate these journals because no matter how often I write, or what I say, or how hard I wish we could talk about it later, you never respond. Which is probably why I blew you off last month.

I can't win. Even though I sorta hate it, I also *need* to write to you to function.

The worst part is I can still hear your voice in my head when I try to imagine what you'd say. It makes me want to cry and scream and break things (which I often do) because I'm terrified one day I'm going to lose that part of you too.

That's all I have left. A memory of your voice. It's not enough.

I miss confiding in you. I even miss your bs answers that never made sense until, like, three weeks after the fact. Or your bored two-word texts in response to a freaking paragraph of my grief (you always reminded me it wasn't *that* deep in the first place because me and drama go together like PBnJ, and I've got the attention span of a gnat). Or how you used to fill up an entire note during fifth period with your horrible stick-figure drawings while I waited impatiently for your advice on something serious.

That shit used to make me so mad. Now? I would literally sell my soul for one word from you. One stupid stick figure.

I cannot grasp the fact that I'll never get your opinion about anything in my life ever again. Especially because there is *SO MUCH* we need to talk about *RIGHT NOW*.

All of my journals have been important in one way or another, but I promise you eighteen is going to be the Mount Everest of them. Like this one is gearing up to be a level seven on the WTF scale. And the absolute worst thing about it is a part of me *still* expects an answer from you. I *really* need your advice, and I have no one else to turn to. Not even the Scar Squad.

Especially not the Squad.

I don't know if I can forgive you for this, Sammy.

But I'm going to keep making these journals because if I stop it means I've stopped mourning you. Well, I've never been a quitter, so I'm not quitting you.

Over and out—

~~Your sis~~

Casey Jones

DEAR SAMMY,

It's been four days since I saw the sun. And before that, the only kind of light I had last week were those harsh fluorescent monsters that won't let you sleep no matter how tired you might be. You know the ones. The kind you find in hospital rooms. The kind that leaves no shadows for hiding . . .

I can't seem to find the energy to crawl out from under the covers. I told Mom I might have the flu, but I don't think she's buying it. She hung up my graduation gown on the back of my bedroom door so it's the first thing I see (and the last thing I see) and I hate her for it.

And you.

Low blow, I know, but I don't want to do this without you here.

That first day last week when I refused to come out for dinner, Dad snuck in while I was sleeping and put this journal on my nightstand. I know I skipped last month and I'm sorry. There's a lot to say right now and it's hard to find the words, but I'm trying.

It's a screwy situation because my therapist says writing should be encouraging or uplifting or whatever, but sometimes all I feel is guilt instead of the *you-can-do-it, you can survive* vibe.

When I look at the empty pages it's hard to see past all the things I'll never say to you. All the moments we're never going to have together.

Once I walk across that stage, I will have officially moved on. I can't.

I just . . . can't.

Over and out—

Casey Jones

OPI.OID CRI.SIS

Pressed pills
Pressed for time, life, love
They take it all away
Stealing, always stealing
Time, life, love.
You swallow them down, one by one
Two by two
Until you can't count anymore.
They sell you a belief that you'll find relief
Off those pressed pills
But you'll only find they are the source of your pain
Dragging you under until you drown.
You swallow them down, one by one
Two by two
Until you can't breathe anymore.
They'll leave you lying on the floor
Dying, while your survivors cry why?
You're giving them nothing in return but
Pressed pills

Pressed for time, life, love

They take it all away

They took you away.

You swallowed them down, one by one

Two by two

Until they were the only thing

left . . . of you.

Over and out—

Casey Jones

DEAR SAMMY,

Three a.m. is a strange time. Everything is so still. Except for the frogs. They won't shut tf up. I promised myself I'd only take one of your pills to stop the pain, and I broke it. I'm sorry. All my life I wanted to be like you. I mean, obviously a much cooler, prettier version of you. Ha! You know what I mean.

I wanted to find the light you gave off. Bottle it. Save it for a rainy day.

Wow, it's *reeeeally* hard to write in the dark. The words keep dripping off the paper. What I'm trying to say is, I do still want to be like you in all ways—except for this one.

I'm sorry.

The countdown has begun. Six more days until the end of an era. A new future: without you.

Remember that one time when you promised me nothing would ever change? Breathing is underrated.

Under

Rated.

Under debated.

A shadow keeps moving up the wall, and sometimes I think it's you. The way it creeps all stealth-like. It's got a purpose. You had one too. I just can't seem to remember what it was. . . . Fuck, I think Mom's coming.

Everything's so blurry.

You know what's heavier than you'd expect? A pen. It holds the weight of the world in a tube of ink, just waiting to explode and spill nonsense across every surface. Gonna go, I can't keep my eyes open.

I'm sorry

Over and out—

Casey Jo

DEAR SAMMY,

First, I just wanted to say I'm sorry I fell asleep in the middle of my last entry.

Okay. That's a lie.

I passed out. But I am sorry nonetheless.

This whole graduation thing's got me twisted because it was always something I planned on doing *with* you. So that's big. Epic, right?! The culminating event that takes us into adulthood with the entire world waiting for us to explore it afterward. Except now *we* can't. No matter how hard I wish otherwise.

And trust me when I say there's no way to prevent the inevitable. Believe me, because I almost failed like three classes last semester trying to do just that, and even though my grades were shit, they still passed me because I'm grieving or whatever.

So here I am, on the second-worst morning of my life, confessing how much it's killing me, *and* along with the other million reasons why graduation sucks, the cherry on top is that I'm about to break my last promise to you. No, not just the one about not taking pills.

The *other* BIG one.

Unacceptable. I know. But maybe now you can see why I got so sloppy the other night. The pressure is overwhelming. Remember when we used to play KerPlunk, or Jenga, and we'd get to the part in the game where we *knew* we were about to lose but there was no turning back? That's how I feel 24/7.

All eyes are watching and waiting for the last piece that's going to destroy me. The timer is set, the bets are placed. It's just a numbers game from here on out.

And sure, I may have broken a couple of promises to you, but you broke a lot of promises to me, so I'm going to consider this blip a free pass. Just in case you were wondering, it's incredibly difficult to keep my word about *all the things* when we can't re-negotiate the terms, like, ever.

I'll be honest. I don't know if I can stop the pills completely. I want to, though.

As far as the *other* promise, well . . . as much as I'd like to believe you only had my heart in mind, I know you were scheming—it's so obvi. I just don't know why. But regardless, I haven't told Ben I like him. Not even a little bit.

You made me swear on the life of Boscoe I'd tell Ben I'm crushing on him, or you'd make my life a living hell for being such a *punk bitch.* I think it's safe to say you're doing that already, so your threat is preeety hollow. *Anyway,* I have a plan. It's just delayed, and has become a bit more complicated since last year. Before I can open up to Ben, there's someone else I need to talk to first. Luckily there's this massive grad party coming up, and I'll talk to both of them then.

Also, in case you're wondering, Boscoe is alive and well.

Who'd have thought a cat would outlive my own twin.... It's so weird to think about shit like that.

Crap, there's a lot more I want to say right now but Mom really is calling me this time. I wish I could stay in my bedroom forever. It almost feels safe here. Maybe I could set my gown on fire—then I wouldn't be able to walk.

Hey, it's about to be hurricane season, maybe a freak storm will blow down the entire school in the next three hours. Or maybe I'll just run away when shit gets tough.

That's always been our specialty. Right?

Gotta go, but I promise I'll return. Tomorrow. Swear.

Over and out—

Casey Jones

DEAR SAMMY,

Okay, so I'm back. Let me just say you didn't miss anything. Why don't people warn you about how boring the actual graduation ceremony is? I mean, come *oooon*. Four hours of people getting up onstage and talking about all their dreams and goals and . . .

Fuck. I can't breathe. Gimme a sec, okay?

Breathing is underrated.

That's my observation of the day. You'd think it'd cross people's minds more often considering we'd all die without oxygen, but nope. I've realized I am in the minority when it comes to my obsession. And I hate it. It's not fair. All my focus revolves around my chest tightening and closing in. The squish and soft bits that protect my skeleton become a vise—a torture device—and it's squeezing every single bit of oxygen out of my existence.

If you were still around, you'd understand because you were the only person who knew me better than I know myself. You had this magical way of making me forget about breathing altogether. But you aren't here anymore. I won't lay the blame entirely on you, promise, but who am I kidding? Life was a lot easier with you in it.

I miss you, Sammy. I literally miss you with every breath I take. When do we—the ones who are uncontrollably obsessed with breathing—get a chance to forget ~~about you?~~ about our lungs? Are we malfunctioning humans? Has my warranty already expired because yours did?

If so, then I want a refund. Honestly, because this sucks. I only need to forget for a little while. Just a few Sammy-free breaths.

Before you died my anxiety was like a pebble in my shoe. When I noticed it, it super sucked, right? But it wasn't *always* there. Now there's a goddamn boulder in my shoe and it's stuck with superglue. I feel it in EVERY step. This constant panic is now my NORMAL. My body is a sellout and my brain is an asshole, and because of you, I end up concentrating on breathing all the time.

It's like I'm walking underwater against a tide that just keeps coming in and I'm pushing, crawling, fighting my way forward and never gaining a single foot of ground.

That first month after you died I was lost. A goner. I couldn't find my way back to the surface no matter how hard I tried. In the first session with my therapist, I mentioned how we always used to write to each other whenever one of us was having issues, and now my issues have multiplied about a gazillion times, but I can't tell you any of them.

My therapist said, *Casey, when the world feels overwhelmingly huge—like it might swallow you alive—there's a trick to shrinking it back down to a comfortable size.*

I remember looking at her skeptically. There's no universe I, Casey Jones Caruso, know of in which such a trick exists. And if it does, why has it eluded me for eighteen years?

But then she solemnly gave me some stellar advice.

She said, *When the world is swallowing you whole, put all your fears in a journal. Then burn it. Set your fears free. Let the smoke pull all your anxieties up into the ether until you're able to inhale.*

So I did. And for the most part, I haven't stopped. Sounds like an easy way out. I know.

It doesn't always work, sometimes the anxiety even gets worse, but there's a reason why our parents built a massive fire pit in the backyard last year, and a bigger reason why we have bonfires all year long now and probably always will.

Burning my journals is the only way I can still talk to you. Even in the dead middle of June.

I believe when the ashes rise into the sky somehow all those unheard words find their way to you. Those small flecks of carbon smash into your stardust and you can absorb what you're missing. In those moments I can inhale. It's magnificent.

Frankie and Ben write to you too. Not journals. But they do write notes now and again. On the last day of every month, we get together and watch our words burn in your tribute.

I know you're laughing at the thought of us sitting around a fire in our washed-out turquoise Adirondack chairs, sweating buckets while flames torture us from below and the sun beats down on us from above. You know we're missing you a lot because who in their right mind would purposely sit around a bonfire for hours during a Florida summer?

Trust me, we're doing everything we can to carry on. And if this gets me closer to you, then all I gotta say is Burn Baby, Burn.

Usually I can cope, with a little wishful thinking and a lot of lighter fluid.

This time, though? I don't think a fire at the end of the month is going to cut it.

Today has been one of the shittiest days in my entire life, and it's only about to get worse. I'm writing this entry down in vain, because it's my last chance of reclaiming my calm. If I don't figure out a way to breathe again, I'm going to fade away.

I thought I knew tragedy. I thought I knew pain.

I was wrong.

So unbelievably stupidly wrong.

Love is *never* easy. You said so yourself when I first told you I caught the feels for Ben. But what if I told you I'm actually crushing on *both* of our best friends?

Yup.

That's my star-exploding secret. Told you it was a massive one.

I still like Ben, but holy shit, Sammy, I like Frankie too.

What should I do? These are people who know who I was before . . .

People I love . . . more than myself.

Love is never easy. But dude, both? At the same time?

Well, let me just say here and now, it's an absolute nightmare.

Over and out—

Casey Jones

DEAR SAMMY,

One of the things I am thankful for is that Mom and Dad have never questioned the fact I'm bisexual or that Frankie is gay.

Can you imagine having to hide yourself from the people who are supposed to love you most? I can name three of our friends off the top of my head who are closeted at home, and it's not fair. Parents should have to sign a contract that states: *Since we're bringing this kid into the world, we swear we will love them and protect them—unconditionally—forever.* I mean, that's the bare minimum. Love your child unconditionally. And yet so many kids are put through hell.

I think I was eleven when I realized I like girls as much as I like boys. I don't remember a time when Frankie even considered liking boys. And I cannot describe the relief I felt when I opened up to Mom and Dad.

Remember?

We were in the seventh grade and I was totally crushing on Lila Simone. During art class I asked if she could eat with us at lunch because I wanted to talk to her about something important. She smiled and said, "Sure!"

As soon as that bell rang I ran straight for the cafeteria. I wanted to make sure we had time to talk before y'all sat down. When I told her I was crushing, her eyes widened and then narrowed. She looked around like she was worried someone could hear.

Then she said she didn't feel the same way about girls.

About me.

She stopped talking to me after that. Got up from the table and went to sit with someone else without looking back. Y'all were still in line, I think. And I was all alone at the table. I'd messed up big-time. I was unlikable and always would be, I thought. Which hurt more than I can explain in a journal. I hoped I wouldn't lose her just because she didn't feel the same way, but she never did talk to me much after that day. I guess our friendship wasn't important enough to her.

I wasn't important enough.

Now I can say it's her loss. But man, I was devastated back then. My first heartbreak. I didn't say a word the rest of the day. My lip probably has permanent scars from biting down on it so hard to keep the tears from falling. When we got to Ben's later, I couldn't hold it in anymore. I confessed how embarrassed I was—said I'd never let another person into my heart. Never ever. Frankie offered to kick Lila's butt. I said no, and she settled for giving me a hug. Y'all reminded me I totally was important enough. And that one day I'd feel differently. That Lila sucked for walking away, but you can't choose who you love, so that part wasn't her fault.

Which I knew.

I was crying because of how ready she was to end our friendship over it, ya know? Nobody warns you how life isn't just about the relationships you form along the way. It's also about the ones you lose. That part is so important and everyone expects you to navigate them as easily as if you were given a damn handbook.

Sorry, lost my train of thought for a moment.

Do you remember how we spent the entire afternoon vegging out on Ben's sofa eating all our favorite foods while I took turns crying and talking shit? I felt like I was wrong for liking Lila. Even though I'd never felt Frankie was wrong for liking girls. Maybe I felt like that because I couldn't make up my mind, but if liking both girls and guys feels right, who can tell me it's wrong?

I knew in the deepest spaces of my mind and heart that what I was going through was real. At the time, everything was *So. Overwhelming.*

Gotta hand it to the rents, though. They didn't try to talk me out of it. Or say it was a phase. Dad said it was Lila's loss and one day I'd meet someone who cared about me the way I cared about them. Because that's how attraction is when it's reciprocated. It just makes sense to those who are involved and fuck the rest of the world and what they think.

I hugged Dad while you were behind me, laughing about how Dad said *fuck the rest.* Mom just smiled with tears in her eyes.

I don't think I understood back then how much our parents can hurt when we're hurting. *Because* we're hurting.

Believe me when I say, I know all too well now.

Before that conversation, it was like someone had sculpted me out of clay and broken sticks and random discards, and the second our parents said, *We love you for you, Casey, not who you love. That's for you. Not us,* it was like I'd turned into a whole human being made from the ocean and the sun, and this heated rush of relief that felt like the most epic wave traveled from my head to my toes.

I didn't have to hide from those I loved most. I could be myself. My true self.

Except now I sorta *do* have to hide from those I love most. Because I am crushing on Ben *and* Frankie. And you aren't here to help, and you suck *sooo* bad. I can't talk to Mom and Dad either because they've been going through so much lately, and I don't want to burden them with my troubles.

The tears are always there now. They don't always fall, but they are there. Waiting.

Over and out—

Casey Jones

DEAR SAMMY,

Here it is. A list of pros and cons because that's what my love life has boiled down to. A list. Ugh. Shoot me. Since you can't add or subtract any items, I'm going to pretend you approve of them. Maybe I'll add more if any pop into my head later on.

I'll start with Ben—

PROS

—I've liked him half my life so I'm sure the feelings are solid (at least on my end)

—He smells SO good

—Kind

—Easy on the eyes

—Says I'm beautiful. And I believe it when he says it

—Is a badass soccer player so can you imagine his stamina in um . . . never mind, not gonna go there

—Has drive and goals (going to also put this in my cons tbh)

—Was your best friend (that's got to count for something)

—Puts me first

—He's hot

—He listens when I talk. Like actually pays attention

—He understands me

—Can *almost* surf as good as me. Almost

—Makes a good pillow

—Doesn't mind when my snot gets on his shirt because I've been crying so hard, also, great shoulder to cry on

—He loves nachos

—Is a night owl and the best person to have late talks with

—I miss him when he's not around

—I can't imagine a world without him in my life

—Makes me feel ALIVE!!!

CONS

—I don't know if he *likes me* likes me

—If I tell him how I feel I could ruin our friendship

—His drive and goals, which got him accepted to Harvard, so he'll be leaving in the fall

—He likes roast beef and turnips. Ew

—Sometimes he's a bit too quiet and I don't know what he's thinking

Now Frankie—

PROS

—She literally knows all my secrets and still loves me

—She's hella cute when she wakes up

—She makes me happy even when I don't want to be happy

—She probably *is* as good a surfer as I am but don't ever tell her I said so

—When she smiles her dimples make my heart beat faster

—She was also your best friend (and that's got to count for something)

—She never pushes me to be anything but myself

—She's one of the most creative people I know. Her clothing designs blow my mind

—She understands me

—She loves mashed potatoes

—Is a morning person so we'll never miss a morning surf session or sunrise

—Would pretty much kick anyone's ass who fucked with me

—Sleeping next to her makes me feel completely safe

—We can talk for hours and there's no awkward silences

—I miss her when she's not around

—I can't imagine a world without her in my life

—She makes me feel ALIVE!!!

CONS

—I don't know if she *likes me* likes me (sensing a pattern here?)

—My crush on Frankie is so new, what if I'm confusing attraction for something more?

—She's also got a crush on Raine (Ugh. Gross. I can't even with this)

—Most of the girls she's dated only date girls, I dunno how she'd feel about dating someone who is bi. Knowing Frankie she probably wouldn't give a fuck, but still . . .

—She's going to the Fashion Institute in New York next year, and even though she deferred a year she's def going, so that's something to think about

—Sometimes her temper is a lot to handle but it's never directed at me, so I'm not too stressed about that

—She lives for leftovers and I can't hang. Dunno why old food skeeves me out so badly? (Probably because I got food poisoning that one time from eating that two-day-old pork chop Mom made)

... Okay, so on first observation there are quite a few matching pros and cons. But that's to be expected, right? I mean, they are my best friends, so naturally there's going to be some overlap. Taking that into consideration, I'll focus more on the differences and how they'd affect our relationships (or lack thereof) going forward.

I'm freaking, dude. The more I write about opening my heart to them, the more real it's becoming. Like daydreaming about Ben was never scary because I knew it was only a dream. I was safe. Now here I am, about to spill my guts to my besties and risk it all.

What if I just broke my promise instead? Then all this internal drama would disappear. *Poof.*

Maybe.

Ugh.

Honestly, what the hell would you do?

This isn't even all about my dumb promise. There's a finite amount of time before Ben leaves for college, and I want to take control of my life for once. To allow myself a sliver of happiness in all this chaos. However, if I *truly* want a chance at happiness, I owe it to Ben (and to myself) to acknowledge that I like Frankie too. Yeah, this train of thought could completely blow up in my face. But your sis has never been a pussy, and I don't intend to start being one now.

With that in mind . . . I'll hit you back soon. Promise.

Over and out—

Casey Jones

DEAR SAMMY,

On the way home from work today a song came on that reminded me of our first week of eleventh grade. I don't know if you'd remember, but Frankie was blasting it to cover up the sound of Jackson farting when he hit the joint too hard. First and last time we ever picked him up for school.

It feels like yesterday. Ben made us roll down all the windows so he wouldn't smell skunky or funky (thanks, Jackson) because he wanted to make a good first impression with his new teachers. You purposely kept blowing smoke on him just to piss him off, but he never even batted an eyelash. I don't think you were ever able to get under his skin until you left us.

Everyone else? Daily.

But Ben had this magical zenlike quality when it came to you. Hard as you tried, you never did figure out how to push his buttons. Maybe that's why you two were so close. Did you ever notice you were like three shades calmer whenever he was around? I sure did.

He misses you terribly. I've seen him crying a million times when he thought I wasn't looking. Like uncontrollable bawling.

It happens out of nowhere sometimes. To all of us. I never know what to do when Frankie or Ben breaks down, because I'm afraid if they notice me noticing them they'll pretend they aren't falling to pieces to protect me.

They deserve to mourn you without guilt.

We've cried enough to fill an ocean. A fitting tribute to a surfer if you ask me, but as much as I've cried over losing you, believe me when I say I'm still salty as fuck about you overdosing. There aren't enough tears in the world to take that kind of salt away.

Even though I don't know how to comfort them, they always know exactly what to do when I break down.

Before you get the wrong idea, it's not like we're embarrassed because we're crying over you. We're proud of the love we shared. Scar Squad for life!

I think it's more that those moments where only one of us loses control are supposed to just be between us and you. They're meant to be private. We share the big ones. Like all of our birthdays, or the anniversary of your first-place win at the spring surf contest. Those are the days when everyone smiles through the tears. Or sits in puddles of sadness and pain.

Anyway, do you recall how the air was exceptionally humid on our first day of junior year? Ben was driving, I was sitting shotgun, and you and Frankie were the ends of a Jackson sandwich in the back. I remember leaning against the window frame with my head on my arm, my hair whipping in the wind as I stole glances at Ben's profile. Picturing what it would be like to run a finger over his jaw. Was his skin still smooth, or was it spiky like yours when you were too tired from partying and would go a few days not shaving?

I thought I was being sneaky about it until you punched my arm. When I turned, you gave me a look. The one that said, *I know exactly what you're thinking.*

I wanted to sock you for it. But I couldn't because then Frankie would've called dibs since she never passed up a chance to beat your ass, and Ben would be wondering why we were both beating you up when he was the one getting mids blown on him.

Besides, I was already overheating, and the last thing I needed on the first day of school was armpit stains on my brand-new shirt from working up a sweat while kicking your ass. So instead, I just smiled a super-lazy smile and proceeded to let my hand catch air as it rode the sweltering currents outside the window.

You're lucky it was too hot to fight.

Was my response surprising or something? At the very least I can safely say it wasn't the reaction you expected, because you sat back with your mouth twisted to the side like you were thinking real hard.

I don't remember a single class from that day. Not one assignment. Not what we ate at lunch or what we talked about with Mom and Dad at dinner. But what lingers still are the moments after we got home. When it was just me and you eating a bag of popcorn and talking about how next year we'd be seniors.

"Did you see that asshat Peter Owens is putting up posters for class president? Fall quarter's barely started and he's already trying to stake his claim. I could win . . . if I wanted to." You leaned back as you said it, arms tucked neatly behind your head, so sure of yourself and what you could accomplish . . . if you wanted to. But I wasn't buying it.

My lip curled as I asked, "Dude, since when do you give a fuck about student government?"

"Since Kiley told me she's running for treasurer."

"Ha. Didn't know they let stoners handle the finances."

"*Pfft.* She's smart. You'd know that if you gave her a chance. Anyway, I think we'd look good together. Class prez and moneybags. Maybe we'd even fix a few things. In fact, betcha five bucks I'll be valedictorian by the time we finish this shit school."

"You might as well just pay me now." I threw a kernel right at your eye and barely missed. God, you hated when I did that.

But that night? You didn't even try to swat the popcorn away. Instead you leaned forward, brows furrowed like you were deep in thought arguing with yourself about something. And then your face relaxed, as if the answer had worked itself out, and you said, "Seriously, though, before we graduate you gotta promise me one thing."

You were never serious. About anything. But by then we'd been chilling less and less and it was nice having you all to myself. Felt like old times. I would have promised to hang the moon if you'd asked. In retrospect, you almost did ask the impossible.

"Well," I pressed, "are you gonna leave me hanging or what?"

You grabbed the popcorn bag and put it on the ottoman so I'd only concentrate on you. "Promise me you'll tell Ben how you feel before we graduate. It's not fair for you to go your entire life being a pussy."

You snickered but your eyes remained serious. Probably the only reason I didn't immediately get up and walk away.

"We've talked about this a million times," I said. "I just don't think the Scar Squad could handle the shakeup. What if he laughs? What if he freaks and never speaks to me again? Also, like, why are you pushing so hard for your best friend to date your sister all of a sudden?" I crossed my arms, waiting for the other shoe to drop. "Daydreaming about me and Ben running away together, far far away from you, and living the most epic lives ever has always skeeved you out."

"Dude, I'm not saying you need to run away and get knocked up and drop out of school. Just tell the guy you're crushing."

"Dick."

"Ho."

"You realize I'd actually have to be screwing people to be a ho."

"I don't want to think about it. Just chill. What I'm trying to say is we've got a finite amount of time left before our lives become more than just the four of us hanging in Auggie, catching glass, fucking around, ya know?"

"More than the Scar Squad? More than surfing? *Pfft.* Impossible."

"Very possible."

"*Annnnd* that's why you want me to tell Ben?"

You jumped up from the couch like a fire ant bit you in the ass. Arms flailing as you said, "I just don't want you to wake up one day wishing things had been different. You know he's applying to Harvard?"

"Since like the fifth grade. It's always been his dream."

"Well, when he leaves—and he will—what are you going to do then?"

My mouth opened and closed. I'd never really thought that far ahead.

Finally, I admitted, "I dunno."

"Exactly. Look, the Squad's got two more years together and then who knows? Scott and I are thinking about taking an epic road trip after graduation, and I'm not sure when I'll be back."

"You don't have to remind me." I picked up the popcorn and took a huge handful. "Seems like every time the Squad tries to make plans with you you're always fucking off with Kiley and Scott."

"And?" An edge crept into your voice. It did anytime I complained about them. "Casey, we're allowed to have our own lives, you know. Our own friends. There's no rule saying just because we're twins we've gotta do everything together forever and ever, amen."

"I know."

"Do you?"

The room got quiet as I contemplated your question. The rational part of me *did* know that, of course. At times we'd each be on our own and have friends the other might not like. But the part of me I'd never admit out loud to you wanted it to be just the four of us forever. Scar Squad for life. That was our pact. I intended to keep it.

You never let me answer. Maybe because you didn't want to know. Maybe because you already knew. Maybe that's why you were pushing Ben so hard. So I'd be so caught up in him I'd forget about you leaving.

I really, really wish you would have let me answer.

Over and out—

Casey Jones

DEAR SAMMY,

If wishes were fishes, then we'd live in the sea. Since that's not a thing, and I can't wish you back into the world—my world—then I guess I'm stuck with this awful condition forever.

I'm experiencing an entirely new species of anguish. It rolls along my bones, pecks itself into my brain, and keeps me up at night. It's making me unbearable. Like, to the point I'm worried Frankie and Ben are going to ghost me because I keep having panic attacks and I can't explain to either of them what they're about.

What would you have done if you knew I also liked Frankie? Would you still have made me promise to tell Ben what was in my heart? Would you have pushed me toward Frankie instead? Would you have told me I was walking on a tightrope to big-mistake-ville and better jump off quickly?

Over the last year I've hated you for a lot of things that you've missed. Or will miss. But not being able to confide in you right now? Not being able to get your advice about the people we both love most in the world? This tops the rest. It's almost unforgivable.

There are a lot of reasons I didn't tell Ben how I felt over the last year.

Biggest one? You died.

Don't mean to put all the blame on you, but maybe you deserve it.

For the longest time I felt nothing. I was afraid to feel at all. Because if I allowed myself to feel, even a little bit, then I'd drown in the grief of losing you. I *STILL* drown if I let myself think about it for too long.

So I closed up completely to save myself.

Frankie says for that first year it was like I died too.

On the worst days, I couldn't move. I could barely breathe. Ben and Frankie never left my side. Even when I'd scream and yell. Or go hours . . . days, without saying a single word. They were my pillars. But my heart was shattered, and the very last thing I could think about was loving anyone, not even myself. I especially didn't want to think about loving someone else.

What I'm going to say next, though, scares me more than you'll ever know.

For the last six months or so it's like my heart has started beating again. I can't place a finger on the exact moment it began, but I went from being a cold fish floating on an endless tide to swimming my way back into the current.

If you could just see what happens to me when I concentrate on Frankie's face, you'd understand why I'm freaking. When the dawn light rolls over her cheekbones and highlights every single freckle, it sets my heart to beating like I've just finished running the mile in under ten minutes. And then I seize up and hold my breath like a complete toolshed for staring at her when we're supposed to be sleeping . . . in fact, I haven't spent the night over at her place, or vice versa, for over a month, except for the night before graduation. Which is pretty much unheard of. And she's bugging. I can feel it in her texts.

But in those moments, the remember-forever moments, I lose control of myself.

Like when Ben's hand brushes against mine and electric shocks heat up my entire body. There was this blip in time the other day when we were both paddling out for a wave, and on our overhead arch, the edges of our hands slid against each other. Nothing between our skin except for the salt and sea. I stopped paddling. Midstroke.

Just so I could savor that moment.

When he looked back at me, his face all scrunched in confusion? Well, I lied and said my foot was cramping up. It's not like I could blurt out the truth. How could anyone? I doubt even you would have, and you were the most confident person I knew.

Maybe I'm confused by my attraction to Frankie. Like I've crushed on about thirty different celebrities and that doesn't mean I actually *like them* like them. But when she chews on her lip in the middle of sewing one of her outfits, you can see the wheels turning as she creates. It's the most magical thing and . . . I'm sure it's nothing.

It's gotta be.

Besides, how can it be anything when my whole body is so attuned to Ben? I swear it's like we're secretly made from magnets because we can be across town without having talked at all, and suddenly I am being pulled by this invisible force, my feet moving of their own accord until inexplicably, there we are. Randomly showing up at the beach at the same time, or the library, or Burgr Shack, like we made plans. Except we didn't. And it feels so right. You know when you've got an itch in the middle of your back and no matter what way you twist and turn to scratch, you just can't reach it and it's about to drive you mad but then, out of nowhere, you find the spot and BAM. Total bliss. Absolute ecstasy.

Yeah. It's like that.

No matter what, I need to at least tell Ben and Frankie how I feel, right? After that, who knows? There's a really good chance these are one-sided feelings and I'm torturing myself for nothing. Yes, I do that constantly anyway because I'm a drama queen. Whatever. You used to live for drama too, you big dummy.

And if I'm being completely honest, here's another thing that's tripping me out: If I'm able to sense all these feelings again—an excitement for living—does that mean I'm forgetting about you?

I made you a promise and I won't break it just because I'm scared. Or even because I like them both now. Besides, if I'm not forgetting you by moving on (and I still don't know if I can), it's not like I can date both of them . . . right? No matter how much I like them—no matter how much I want to keep my promise—if it means giving you up? Well . . . sorry, dude. It's not worth it.

I can't move on if it means you'll fade away. I refuse to let that happen. I may not have power over a lot of stuff in my life, but I'd rather shut down than shut you out. I can't choose between you and them. What if I *do* end up with one of them, and the more we grow together, the more you dissolve?

I'm not ready to lose you, Sammy. Not even for Ben's or Frankie's love. However, if I spend my entire life worrying about who I'll hurt with who I choose, when do I choose myself?

I can't.

I just can't.

I think I need to go on a walk. Even writing this down is overwhelming. The truth is that every step into my future is a step farther away from you. It wasn't supposed to be like this.

Right now, we should be fighting because you're taking off on your graduation road trip.

You know what? Fuck you. No matter what future I try to imagine, with you alive or dead, I'm always left behind.

You suck, Sammy!

Casey Jones

DEAR SAMMY,

Mrs. Rodriguez, my therapist, suggested when I've got writer's block (like what happened before graduation when I had that breakdown), I might find solace in poetry again. I haven't written too many poems since you died. And that used to be my thing. I love how you can get so much emotion into such a compact space, and let's face it, your death is *preeetty* much an infinite pool of material for poems, right? But I don't feel compelled to create anything anymore. It's difficult to look at the world in wonder when all you see is ruin.

Still, I'm going to give poetry another chance. That way I'm communicating with you in some form and not keeping everything bottled up inside.

Apparently, bottling everything up makes my panic attacks worse, and we all know what happens then. I think you'd be happy to know I haven't touched the pills I hid under the bed in over two weeks. Sometimes they scare me. Sadly, that fear never stops me from taking them when I'm using, just stops me from taking too many at once. Hopefully I won't go looking for them again anytime soon.

I think the reason I'm afraid is because they're like the ones I found in your closet after . . . and I don't know for sure if that's what you OD'd on, but you had so many of them in your closet . . . Anyway, once those ran out I found Flynn—he's a senior who transferred to our school last year from somewhere in central Florida. Can you believe he never saw the ocean before he moved into town? Can you imagine?! Scott and Kiley hate him because he's invading their turf or whatever, but screw them. I can't forgive them for taking you away from us. I'm not saying it's their fault, but I'm not *not* saying it either.

Anyway, I started trading Flynn surf lessons for some of his grandma's stash. I don't think they're the same kind you . . . well, you know.

But if they are, I sorta get it now. They do help numb the pain.

I promise, I don't eat them a lot. Just when I feel like I'm drowning. Mostly on the days I can't write to you. When I miss you the most.

No, I don't think Frankie and Ben know what I'm doing. They'd probably kill me. They don't even know I *like* them, so how can I tell them about my pill problem? Yeah. It's not like I take them all the time or anything. Not anymore, anyway.

I doubt you're listening to these entries anyway, but just in case you are somewhere in the universe waiting for my next installment or whatever, I guess I'll give poetry another shot right now. Maybe it will help. Here's one about the Scar Squad. The four of us. You, Frankie, Ben, and me. Or, I guess, this is me trying to come to terms with the idea that you're not a part of the Scar Squad anymore. I don't know. Anyway . . .

SOMETHING YOU SHOULD KNOW

dawn

And

midnight

those were always the times

When the world was ours

even when nothing made sense, it never mattered

because we were together.

Our afternoons were spent daydreaming

about becoming our best selves

Hopes that

our deepest wishes

Would come true . . .

Put in motion

Us Against the World,

Together,

We would conquer anything that

Stood in our way

United

Forever and always

until the day it felt like something was missing

Because you were missing

gone

Foolish

it never occurred to me that those

Obstacles about to get in our way?
Might be each other
no one warned me our dreams of a future,
Never a story for one,
would become my nightmare
Even while we waited for something to
Happen.
when we were little
You turned the page
while I read aloud
and we were
in perfect harmony
Complete
Us.
Friends, forever
The Best,
Lifers.
never once did I recognize
that all those wishes
We created together
Were Unreachable.
then, the world took you away
I
Know now how smart we were
at calling ourselves the Scar Squad
Cuts run deep
the pain is unbearable

Will never go away

Not in my lifetime

Heal is the worst four-letter word.

My heart is screaming

Head

Is betraying me

Full of lies.

i can't shut it out

and the secret is killing me

oh no

I want to hide I

Fear those dreams now

The ones where we imagined a future

Four of Us

Together

Because I Finally Understand them

they, no, We Were Meant for So Much More . . .

Over and out—

Casey Jones

DEAR SAMMY,

You always bragged about what a good judge of character you were, but I'm here to say that isn't entirely the case. I know you think I didn't like Scott and Kylie because I was jealous or whatever, but it's not that. At least, not one hundred percent that.

Honestly? I think Scott sucks and always has. I'd tell you that to your face if you were here. Even knowing you'd be pissed and try to blame it on my "jealousy."

Before, I couldn't pinpoint a reason as to why he seemed like bad news, beyond the fact that he partied *waaaaay* too much, but I finally can. It's too late to do either of us any good, but I still think you should know what kind of dickhead you were hanging out with. Not trying to have an "I told you so" moment *buuuuuut*...

A few months ago I did something I can never take back. Now, before you go and say something like *of course you did,* let me just say this is far and away worse than my usual stupid decisions. I mean, this is like you'd-kill-me-if-you-caught-me kind of dumb—and I know how ironic that statement is, considering your condition and all, but it is what it is and there's no going back. Believe me, I'm cringing as I'm writing this, but hear me out.

My dumb decision happened right after third period. I remember because Lani Tinskey asked Mr. Rollins for a hall pass because she was surfing the crimson wave, and he said no and that she'd have to go to the restroom after class—because he's the absolute worst.

Lani's face turned bright red and she sank so far down in her desk I honestly thought she might fall out.

A few kids giggled, but most were staring at Mr. Rollins's back since he'd already turned around to walk to his desk. They were probably wishing him the grand experience of shedding your uterine lining on a Wednesday morning in the middle of a bland world history lecture. Or maybe they wished him something even worse.

I won't lie, I was totally wishing him something worse. And let's face it, getting your period and not being allowed to go to the bathroom is pretty fucking awful, so you can only imagine what I was picturing would be fair retribution.

You could feel the tension in the air. Lani was screwed, and there was still fifteen minutes left before class got out.

I glanced at her again and saw her head tucked into her arms on the desktop. Every few seconds she'd sniff like she was holding back tears.

That's when I knew I had to do something.

"*Psst*, hey." I tried to keep my voice low.

Lani lifted her head ever so slightly until I could make eye contact.

"Here, catch."

She held out a hand.

I tossed her a tampon and then stood up and pointed at the window, shouting, "Oh My God, I think Mr. Walker is having a heart attack. Somebody do something, quick!"

I'm not certain, but I don't think you ever got a chance to meet Mr. Walker. He's one of the upperclassmen deans. Since he's a complete drunk and doesn't let school get in the way of that, I'm pretty sure you at least heard the rumors about him. He's also the superintendent's uncle, and word around town is that he is untouchable even when he's day drinking during school hours. Yay nepotism!

Last year a senior's parents went to the school board with an official complaint because Mr. Walker kept nodding off during a discipline conference "involving" Josh Chapponi's disruption of the pep rally right before homecoming. Something to do with the pantsing of our school mascot (which honestly makes no sense since we've got a shark as a mascot and sharks don't wear pants, but still, the de-finning maybe? I don't know).

Regardless, someone ran up and pulled Eddie Cullen's suit down. Which, in my opinion, is pretty messed up. The dude already has to deal with having the name Edward Cullen (no relation nor resemblance to you-know-who, and you can take that whichever way you want, because I'm not here to judge). And then on top of his unfortunate name, he gets pantsed at a pep rally. Good thing he was wearing clothes underneath his costume. Can you imagine? I'd fucking kill Josh.

But here's the most screwed-up part.

Mr. Walker totally claimed it was Josh who was the culprit, right? And in a way, I suppose he wasn't wrong, only that he messed up on the most important part of the situation.

He pulled Josh Chapponi in for a discipline conference when really it was Josh Schroder who attacked the mascot. To make matters worse, Mr. Walker completely ignored Josh's parents while they tried to tell him he had the wrong Josh. Mr. Walker slept through their entire defense, then woke up and suspended Josh for four days without ever getting the *right* Josh in trouble.

By then, he had moved on to his next screw-up. Gotta love authority figures with a God complex and a Jack-and-Coke liquid diet.

Well, of course Josh Chapponi's parents were pissed. Spent half a school board meeting complaining about Mr. Walker and still nothing happened.

I heard that when you get in trouble and you're sent to Mr. Walker's office, you should never inhale when he leans in to yell, because you're bound to catch a full blast of whiskey breath. And Frankie swears she heard Jasmine say she's seen him topping up his Hydro Flask before the first bell. I mean, I dunno if that's true, but why would she lie, right?

Well, it's also public knowledge that Mr. Walker likes to catch some quick shut-eye beneath the willow tree in the lower field during third period, and it just so happened that Mr. Rollins's classroom's west-facing windows have a pretty good view of the willow tree. Should anyone be looking, of course.

I was looking.

And it's not my fault Mr. Walker likes to nap with one arm flung over his head and the other wrapped over his chest with his hand on his heart. Or that he sleeps with his legs spread out all wonky so he actually looks like he just fell.

But it is my fault that I completely used it to my advantage in this situation.

"Mr. Rollins, I think he might be dying!" I raised my voice, then screamed for good measure. Other kids joined in. Eventually, even Mr. Rollins looked up from his desk, once he realized we weren't stopping anytime soon. He was a sight to see as he lowered his glasses down the bridge of his nose. His perpetually cranky face went slack, eyes growing wide.

"Stay in your seats, everyone!" Mr. Rollins rushed out of class.

I've never seen the man move so fast before or since.

I leaned into the aisle and said, "Think you're good to go, Lani. Sorry he's such a douche."

Lani stood up, tampon in hand. "I won't forget this, Casey."

"No biggie." I shrugged off her thanks and stood up too. "I doubt Mr. Rollins will make it back before the bell. Look." I pointed around us. Kids were leaving the classroom in twos and threes. It seemed everyone else had already come to the same conclusion.

So there I was, walking down the hall, pretty proud of myself for coming up with such a genius escape, and who happens to be standing by the door to the parking lot? Only the biggest burn-outs in Shoreline High—Kiley Richards and Scott Hill, of course.

"Hey, Casey. Surprised to see you round here." Kiley's smile was unsure, like she was afraid I'd yell or something.

I paused. I really hadn't spoken to either of them since . . . well, not in a long time. They were always people *you* spent time with. It wasn't even that I was unfriendly with them, it's just . . . I dunno. Sometimes it hurts to be reminded of the past.

Of you.

With people that weren't a part of us . . .

"Heya. Where are you two headed?"

"To the lot. Want to join?" Scott held up a joint while Kiley waved me over and pushed open the door.

For over a year I'd managed to avoid them. Most of the time it was easy. Without you around it's not like there were many reasons we'd cross paths. They weren't a part of the Scar Squad. Still . . . at one point we'd been . . . well, not friends, exactly. Friendly, I suppose.

"Come on, Case. It's been ages and we rolled up some skunky nugs." Kiley clasped her hands together when she begged.

Her sincerity was hard to resist. My foot bounced while I contemplated my next step. The now-empty hall felt spookily still. There really was no place I needed to be at the moment, and honestly? As nervous as I was about talking with Kiley and Scott alone, I didn't fancy the idea of lingering around the hall with the chance that Mr. Rollins might show back up at any moment.

After a few more awkward seconds of us just staring at each other, the joint waving in the air like a wand about to cast a spell of devious intent, I stammered, "S-sure. Why not."

We quickly walked to Scott's car, weaving in and out of everyone else's while also trying to look like we were supposed to be there. Scott stopped in front of an old ragged-out Subaru and we piled in.

"I'll take backseat," Kiley said softly.

I nodded my thanks.

Scott turned the key in the ignition just enough so the engine didn't turn over but the AC and stereo came on. The windows were rolled up and it was already blistering hot. Even though I was still uncertain about my decision to join them, I was grateful we weren't about to melt away completely.

"Guests first." Scott lit the joint and passed it my way.

"Sure, thanks." I held it between my fingers before I brought it to my lips. *How many times did you sit in this exact seat doing exactly the same thing I'm doing now?*

I squeezed my eyes shut as hard as I could. Trying and failing to banish all thoughts of you. Failing miserably.

I inhaled like my life depended on it, wanting so much to make all the noise in my head disappear. And then I immediately regretted it. My lungs screamed. I probably coughed for five minutes straight. To their credit, Scott and Kiley didn't even crack a smile. In fact, Kiley leaned forward and passed me her water.

I chugged some down and then sheepishly grinned. "Lifesaver."

"No worries, it happens to me all the time." She winked.

For a few heartbeats everything felt normal. I could almost pretend it was. We passed the joint around in silence mostly. Reggae floated out of the speakers, sending me even further into the zone. The seat's sun-baked vinyl stuck to the backs of my thighs where my shorts ended, so I moved my legs to the beat in an attempt to unstick myself without looking like a tool. Once I accomplished that, I leaned my head back, letting my thoughts and worries drift away to a place they couldn't reach me. My eyes unfocused as I tried to decipher the shapes of animals in the clouds floating by.

"A giraffe," I whispered to no one in particular.

"Nah, a narwhal," Scott said with seriousness.

"No way."

"I dunno, I sorta see where you both may be right," Kiley, ever the peacemaker, said from behind.

"Maybe," Scott conceded.

"Doubtful." It was definitely a giraffe.

"Hey, Case, um, I know it's been a really long time, but I was wondering if we could talk about—"

"No." I sat up.

I knew I was being rude, but it didn't stop me. The cloud animals vanished, and the cacophony of my thoughts returned—as loud as an eighty-piece orchestra without its conductor.

Why did Scott have to go and ruin a good time? It's too early. A year since you'd been gone. Still too early.

"Thanks and all, but I've got to go." My fingers played with the lock as I tried to make an escape.

"I've got it." Scott pressed a button and the car unlocked. "Look, I'm sorry . . . We tried to talk him out of going to—"

"Nope. I don't want to hear it. I can't. Not now. Maybe not ever. Sorry." I jumped out of the car, trying to avoid looking back, because I didn't think I could handle seeing whatever emotions were plastered on their faces.

I shoved my hands in my pockets and forgot to shut the door as I tried to make my escape. Even though I managed not to look back, unfortunately I could still hear them just fine.

Kiley said, "For fuck's sake, Scott, did you really have to bring it up now?"

"I don't know. Shit. I miss him."

The sadness in his voice almost broke me. "So do I, Scott. So do I," I whispered to myself.

I was so busy paying attention to what they were talking about, I didn't notice someone standing in front of me until their shadow fell over my feet. I stopped dead in my tracks.

"And where do you think you're going?"

Can you fucking believe it was Mr. Rollins? Like, dude, why am I the unluckiest person in the world? I can't figure it out.

Anyway, I totally thought I was being slick when I said, "Um, I forgot my chem book in my car and thought I'd grab it before fourth period?" I hoped I didn't look as stoned as I felt. Knowing I didn't have my chem book on me, or a car for that matter.

"I see. Forgotten about Mr. Walker and his unfortunate near-death experience already, then? In case you're wondering, I think he'll make it. However, you? Well, I'm not so certain."

Oh man. He's pissed. My stomach sank. I had a feeling I wasn't getting out of this mess easily.

I put on my most sincere face. "That's awesome he's alive! I mean, wow, he really looked like a goner there for a second and, um, you're like a hero, Mr. Rollins!" I glanced around and things went from bad to worse. Smoke was still spilling out of Scott's car. Any second, Mr. Rollins would figure out what we were really doing out here, and then we'd be totally screwed.

So . . . I ran.

I don't know why. Like I said, I was super stoned and I knew nothing I had to say would convince Mr. Rollins to get off my back. In retrospect, running probably wasn't the keenest idea I've ever had either.

But! At least my attempted breakout took all of Mr. Rollins's attention and allowed Scott and Kiley a chance at a clean getaway.

I made it to the north end of the senior parking lot before my flight to freedom ended for good. There, by the gate, Mr. Walker waited for me, walkie-talkie in hand. I could hear Mr. Rollins's voice crackling through. Wherever he was behind me, he wasn't pleased at all.

"Do you see her?"

"Yeah, thanks for the heads-up. Over and out." Mr. Walker dropped his hand to attach the walkie-talkie to his belt loop like it was a Smith & Wesson. He leaned forward until he towered above me and said, "So I hear you're the one who's been so concerned with my health today. Why don't you come along with me and we'll have a nice chat?"

Frankie was right. Whiskey breath was kicking something awful. I tried to lean back and inhale some fresh air, but before I could, his hand clamped on my shoulder.

"You wouldn't be thinking of running again, now would you?"

My high was fading fast. At least I'd saved Scott and Kiley. At least there was that. Mr. Walker broke into a smile, his eyes focusing on something behind me.

"Mr. Walker." I didn't even need to turn to know who was behind me. Mr. Rollins sounded so smug, I could've kicked him. I stiffened when he said, "Before you go, I think you might be interested in bringing these two along. I found them in the parking lot. They claimed to be lost."

Bro, this entire day sucked. But it was especially bad in the moment when Mr. Rollins thought he was about to destroy my world. And there I was having to think about what you'd do in this situation . . . and then try to do the exact opposite. (Because we both know you never figured out how to talk your way out of trouble :P)

Mr. Rollins actually sneered when he said, "You might want to hang on to this too. This one here said he thinks Miss Caruso may have dropped it."

I turned around to see Mr. Rollins passing a baggie with at least an eighth in it to Mr. Walker. Scott refused to meet my eye. Kiley mouthed, *"Sorry."*

That dick. After everything I'd just done for them and he was going to try and blame me for his stash? *Oh, hell no.*

It occurred to me that maybe they hadn't even seen me trying to distract Mr. Rollins from discovering them. Still. What kind of jerk goes and tries to pawn off their stash on someone else? He should have hidden it better after we smoked.

I held up both of my hands, hoping my red eyes wouldn't betray me, and said, "No flipping way is that mine. Think about it, how many times has Scott been caught? Right? Now what about me? If you don't know, the answer is never. Because I don't even smoke. Come *onnnn.* You know that's his." I narrowed my eyes, daring Scott to even try to think about saying I was wrong.

"We'll find out who is responsible for what. My office, now. Come along," Mr. Walker said as he herded us back to the main building.

In the end, when we got to the office my counselor, Mrs. Hargreaves, saw us walk by. She flagged Mr. Walker down and whispered something. Not sure what it was but I'm guessing it was about you, because I only got a week of after-school detention.

Both Scott and Kiley were suspended, but since Mr. Rollins only found the weed on the ground and couldn't one hundred percent prove it was theirs, it was only for two days.

So much for trying to do a good deed.

When the Scar Squad found out what happened, Frankie offered to kick Scott's ass for me, and Benjamin of course had to jump in and talk shit. He said *he'd* do it because he didn't want Frankie to break a nail. She said she wouldn't waste a good manicure unless it was worth it, and my honor was worth it. Then they started wrestling until I let them know we were going to miss the prime parking at A Street Beach because the waves were hitting hard.

It's so strange to chat shit together without you around to interject. Like I think that's why Ben is so extra with Frankie now. That was always *your* job and now he's trying to pick up the slack. I can tell she's grateful. The silence is so deafening in the moments where you still belong.

The worst.

So anyway, we grabbed our boards and took off to ride our frustration out on some nice glassy rollers.

On top of the peak of a set as I was riding into shore I decided to let the entire day's events go. Even if Scott was a complete dirtbag for trying to throw me under the bus, he still used to be your good friend and that counted for something. I guess.

Suffice it to say, I've avoided them ever since.

And because of that, Scott never did get to say whatever it was he tried to tell me back in the car. Who knows, maybe it was something I needed to hear. Another grain of a story to keep your memory alive. Or it could have been another one of those inflated apologies you get when it comes to people dying. *You know.* The ones that always make the person apologizing feel better about the situation while they make you feel infinitely worse? Not on purpose. But it happens all the same. What are they sorry for? It's not like they killed the person?

At least . . . I hope not.

Regardless, he is an asshole. Thought you should know.

I don't think I'll make an attempt to find out what he wanted to tell me. Not anytime soon, anyway.

Does that make me a dick?

No, don't answer that. I already know the answer.

Over and out—

Casey Jones

THE RISE AND FALL OF BEGINNINGS, AKA AN OLD FRIEND MEETS A NEW LOVE—

The shortest distance between two points

is the line that runs between me and you

Do I take the road less traveled to find

a path we can walk together

Or do I stay on the well-worn track

safe secure and a little bit boring

Friends to lovers

Fairy tales and sweet nothings

Are we a storybook

Do we get our happily ever after

The rise and fall of your chest

as you breathe life into me

Makes me want to fight the battle

Am I your chosen one? I volunteer as tribute

Again and again until we get this right

DEAR SAMMY,

I wish we were sitting on the pier like we used to when one of us needed to decompress. That was our judge-free zone. Where we could tell each other what was inside the deepest vaults of our soul. Where we gave each other our most honest opinions. Even when we didn't want to hear them. *Especially* when we didn't want to hear them.

Remember last time we went there and I said I thought you were an addict?

You told me to fuck off.

You said I was wrong. Stupid. Jealous.

You screamed and denied.

And then, after a really long silence, you told me I was right.

You were *sooo* pissed I made you admit it. You got up and ran off. How was I supposed to know that would be one of our final conversations??

Would I have called you out still if I knew? I'd like to say of course I would have. I'd probably be lying. We both know I'd lie a million times over if there was a chance it could change what happened the night you . . .

Since we can't go there anymore, I'm gonna pretend. I'm getting really good at that.

So here's the deal. I need you to give me some advice. Some honest truth. Because I feel like if we were on the pier right now, you'd be telling me I only have surface feelings for Frankie. You'd wanna know why after a gazillion years of professing my love for Ben I'd go and muck it up in the fourth quarter.

But here's the thing. I really do like both of them. Maybe if I tell you more, you'll see why I'm in such a pickle.

. . . Am I really asking my dead brother for love advice right now? Yes, yes I am. Mrs. Rodriguez is going to have a field day at our next session. I can feel it.

Anyhoo, I can tell you the exact day Frankie went from being someone I felt completely at ease with to someone who gave me the cold sweats. One morning—April fourteenth to be exact—we were getting ready for work together, just like we'd done every Saturday morning for the last two years.

Typically, on weekends we crashed at her place because she's the one with a reliable ride, and she'd drop me off on her way downtown. In January, my New Year's resolution was to resolve being broke *and* depressed, because I was exhausted from being both. So I got a job at Animal House Veterinary Clinic as a kennel girl, and Frankie works part-time at this little clothing boutique in downtown St. Augustine called The Goods.

As you know, this is a girl who's seen me naked a million times, heard me cry a million more, knows all my bad habits, and accepts me for every one of them, as I do her. We've laid bare our deepest and darkest secrets, and somehow have managed to not scare each other away. That's true friendship. Or at least, I assumed so.

And before April fourteenth—which is forever burned into my mind as the Day the World Turned Against Me—I thought that would never change.

Before that day, we'd spend hours with our heads against each other's while we read out of the same book in bed. Or stay up all night watching disaster movies. Or talk on FaceTime about everything and nothing until my voice felt raw. There were so many moments (it might actually be impossible to count now) we'd sneak out to rage at a spodie on a school night and sneak back in with the dawn before our parents caught us. (And if you're a parental unit reading this then you should probably stop because I'm almost one hundred percent certain you cannot ground a child when you've stolen their journal, so don't say I didn't warn you. This isn't for your eyes.)

Anyway.

Lucky.

We always thought we were lucky.

HA.

What if there's been something more between us this entire time and I just didn't see it? I do now and it's anything but easy. I can't concentrate when we're around each other and that's a huge problem. Instead of paying attention to our conversations, I find myself fascinated at the way sunlight catches the auburn streaks in her hair. How the rays turn it into a faux-halo. The girl glows. Something I never clued in to before, but it makes sense since it's pretty much the feeling I get inside when we accidentally touch now. Light. Warm. Soothing. And I won't lie, it's completely terrifying.

Before, we could literally talk about anything for hours without ever getting bored with each other or running out of stuff to say, and lately I get tongue-tied at the most casual of conversations.

Sorry, I totally lost my train of thought. See? I can't even write about her without rambling.

Anyway, the Day the World Turned Against Me was an *EPIC* fail. I don't think it's going to get better anytime soon either. That morning the conversation went a little something like this:

"Hey, Casey, want to hit up the beach after work?" Frankie asked, pantomiming jumping on a surfboard as her abuela yelled out to us, "If you do, make sure you get your butts back here by six! You know I've got bingo tonight, Francesca Graciela Romero!"

"Ooo, she just dropped the three-punch takedown, *Francesca Graciela Romero*," I repeated as I stood up from my spot on her abuela's orange-and-brown art deco sofa.

"Ten-four," Frankie yelled back. "Bingo is her lifeblood, *Casey Jones Caruso,* what can I say?"

I stuck out my tongue, but I couldn't deny how nice my full name sounded coming from her lips.

Frankie lazily ran a hand through her short curls before asking, "So are you in, or are you out?"

I blinked, averting my gaze to something neutral, and landed on the three-legged glass-and-wood coffee table between us. It didn't help to slow down my heart. Frankie throwing her hair back kept playing in my mind on repeat. Little zaps of electricity traveled my arms like I'd just slid my shoes along her abuela's shag rug. Abuela Shirley is all about maintaining a midcentury-modern vibe, something Frankie had resisted at first when she moved in with her, but now, ten years later, it was starting to make an appearance in her personal belongings, like her bedroom decor.

Just last month we picked out a new platform bed to replace the twin daybed she'd had since we were seven. The sleek teak-wood frame fits the room's look perfectly. You wouldn't recognize it.

"Yo, Earth to Casey . . ." Frankie waved her hand into the space between us.

I blinked away thoughts of her bed and tried to focus. "Um, you—you want to go surfing today? L-like we'd have to be in bathing suits?" I stammered.

If her eyebrows could've gone any higher on her face, they would've totally become a permanent part of her hairline. Her face scrunched up in a very confused way as she said, "I mean, if you want to wear your scrubs, that's certainly a choice. Rock that shit."

"*Yeeeeeah*, no. I don't know what I was saying. If you want a quick sesh after work I'd be down, I guess." My tongue hit the back of my teeth like my body was making an effort to stop me from saying anything else incriminating.

"You *guess*? I know you checked the wave report at dawn. Are you coming down with a fever?" Frankie closed the gap and leaned in to put the back of her hand against my cheek. "Oh, you are a little warm. Hey, Tita, come here, I think Casey's getting sick."

Her face was only inches from mine, so close I could see her pupils dilating. My gaze traveled along the freckles on her nose.

Funny. I'd never noticed how cute they were before. At least, I'd never allowed myself to notice.

This time, though? There was no going back. I hyperfixated on this stray lock of hair hanging in her face and the urge to reach out and tuck it behind her ear became so overwhelming I actually let out a sigh of frustration.

"You okay?" The concern washing over Frankie's features killed me.

I backed away, holding both of my hands up. How could I say, *I'm fine. Totally fine. It's just, well, the idea of you seeing me in a bathing suit, something you've done every week since we were seven, is now sending all the blood in my body rushing into my face and it's not a fever, it's the touch of your hand that's making me blush.*

Well, I couldn't.

So I didn't.

In fact, instead of just telling the truth, I leaned into the lie. Grabbed my stomach and really played it up.

Tita Shirley walked over to us, a bottle of vapor rub in one hand and a cup of steaming tea with slices of orange and lime floating in the other. She passed them both to me and said, "Here. Put some of this on, drink this down, and then I think it's best you run along home, nena. I can't risk missing out on bingo tonight. They've got the grand prize up to four hundred dollars for Sizzling Saturday!"

"I think you're right. I'll call Mom and my work. Actually, I might just go lay down until she gets here if that's okay with you."

I turned to hightail it into Frankie's room, but Frankie called out, "I can drop you off. It's not a thing. Seriously."

Except it was. And I had no clue what to do with these new feelings. So I waved her off and pretended to take a nap until Mom got there.

That was the day I just knew keeping my promise to you would be . . . complicated. Because things were so much bigger than they used to be.

It's one thing to find yourself crushing on your bff. Like there are no rules for it. If there are no rules, how do you play the game? And if you can't play the game, how do you win?

You don't.

In retrospect, I should have seen it coming. There were definitely clues I could have tapped into if I'd only paid a little more attention. But how was I supposed to recognize my feelings when over the last four years I'd been secretly harboring a crush on our right hand, the square to our pegs, the dawn to our night, Benjamin Dean?

Finally figuring out I liked Frankie felt like getting a bucket of ice-cold water dumped on me when I least expected it. Shocking. Left me gasping for air. My fight-or-flight kicked in and all I wanted to do was run. And yet, at the same time, it was exhilarating. Refreshing. I felt more alive than I'd been in a really long time.

With Ben it was different. A slow burn. From the start of our friendship, anytime he laughed, I'd get this weird feeling right where my neck and shoulders meet. He could be clear across the room and the moment the sound hit my eardrums, bam. Tingles. The pleasant kind. But still.

It was hard to hide that from you in the beginning. Especially because it always seemed like you guys had a bit of a rivalry going on behind the scenes. I know you loved each other like brothers, but whew, when you two would fight?

Well, to be honest there were times when I was surprised you made up in the end.

Here's the deal. I never expected my heart would turn on me, but life seems to keep flipping the script. The worst part of all of this is I know you'd have an answer to this problem. It might not even be one I wanted to hear, but it would be a start to a solution.

Last time I checked, the universe still refuses to send me a single reply to any of the journals I've burned, so I guess it's up to me to figure this shit out.

Like I said, this is a no-win situation, so consider me forever a loser.

ONE IS THE LONELIEST NUMBER BUT THREE IS THE MOST CONFUSING—

First it was you plus me
And then somewhere
between the rising vapors of the cracked asphalt court
And the bounce of a ball as it scuttled away
We crashed together
A twosome
now a threesome
and then a foursome
Forever the Scar Squad
Us against the world
We're writing our own future
And now I'm torn
like a well-read page
Dog-eared and saved for later
For the reader to decide our fate

Over and out—

Casey Jones

DEAR SAMMY,

Remember the epic grad party I mentioned earlier? The one where I would uphold my final promise?

Well, hang on to your board shorts 'cause here's how that went. You'll never be able to call me a puss—

Fuck.

Never.

It's such a long time. Every second is a forever that you'll never be a part of again. Do you know how tiring that is?

I feel it bone-deep. And somehow, I still have to go through the motions of life while you're dead. I'm aware I'm broken, but in between the cracks, I find seeds of who I used to be. In those fleeting seconds I can even forget for a little while. The party two nights ago was one of those times. I almost felt normal. Until it went to shit.

Natalie Haggins's graduation spodie off the backroads south of Crescent Beach was a banger. It had been more than a month since I'd suffered *the* panic attack about the possibility of Frankie seeing me halfway naked. She'd called a few times without me answering and when I finally did pick up a few days later, I chalked my silence up to dealing with the stomach bug of all stomach bugs.

Since that freak-out, we'd been so busy getting ready for graduation I was able to pretend like nothing was wrong. Then I went dark and Mom told Frankie and Ben I needed some rest. Which they've given me over the last few weeks—although they still came by every Wednesday for family dinner.

But I knew there was no way I'd get out of the upcoming spodie without Frankie cluing in to something happening between us (or at least between me and my thoughts of us), so I got my shit together and put on my game face. This night would be the chance to come clean to both of them. I'd let the chips fall where they may, and *maybe* everything would work out somehow. I *had* to believe that. Otherwise I totally would've chickened out.

I've gotten really good at compartmentalizing my feelings if you haven't noticed. It's the only way I can get through the day without falling apart. What was the harm of creating another cubby to stuff in the grand scheme of things, right?

As far as parties went, Natalie usually made them pretty epic. This night was no exception. A huge vat of spodie—the highly alcoholic punch such parties are named after—was flowing freely. You see, all spodies are parties, but not all parties are spodies. *We* never got to go to one *together* because by the time *we* could go to spodies *you* were always with Kiley and Scott.

Dick.

You would have *looooved* them . . . or maybe you did love them. Maybe y'all went to spodies on the nights you never came home for all I know.

I wish I understood who you really were in the last few months of your life the way I've known you since we were born. I feel like I missed out on so much in such a short time span. Important parts. The most important parts. The kind that would drive you to . . .

Anyway, this particular spodie also had three kegs, a massive bonfire, a live DJ set, and no cops in sight.

We piled into Frankie's Camaro along with Terah and Milo Simmons. And we managed to pick up an eighth of mid-grade from Benjamin's older bro for a pretty decent price. By the time we got to the party I was mellow and ready for anything. About two beers in, I found myself saying way too much about my feelings to anyone who would listen.

"Hey, Casey, do you want another beer?" Jackson Radcliffe tilted his red Solo cup to pour out the last foamy dregs before refilling.

I considered his question. Did I? *Probably.* Should I? *Maaaaybe not.* Instead of answering, I asked with a hiccup, "Have you ever crushed on someone you knew was going to be trouble but you couldn't help it?"

I blinked a few times to battle the extreme crunchy feeling in my eyes as I waited for his answer. Earlier, Benjamin had claimed the buds were only mids, but my eyes were definitely acting toastier than a junk joint. Oh well, I wasn't complaining.

"You could say that." Jackson looked past me to a group of kids hanging out by the fire. It was hard to tell exactly who he was focusing on. Especially since my eyes were already somewhat out of focus. But at least my attention was on point thanks to the joint.

Thing is, when your mind wanders as much as mine, it's hard to keep a steady line of thoughts on track. I wish it was something I could control, but usually I can't. First, I'll be talking about my plans for the day, then I'm wondering if they'll ever allow people into Area 51 for tours of alien spaceships, then I'm asking if biscuits and gravy sound like they'd hit the spot for breakfast. All the while, our parents are looking at me like I've lost the plot and saying, *It might be time for her to start Adderall again.* (No, the answer to that is always a no for me because I will undoubtedly abuse it.) Or they're wondering if it'd be a good idea to increase my therapy sessions (yes, the answer to that is always a solid yes), and I'm just sitting there next to them still trying to figure out what's the plan for breakfast so I can either discover the secrets to the universe or at the very least get on with my day.

You know what's super messed up? When we were little, Mom and Dad had no issues getting you tested for ADHD because Dr. Rowe thought you might have it, right? But not once did they ever even think to test me. I hate that just because girls' signs and symptoms are different from boys' no one thinks we could have it too. Daydreaming and not being able to concentrate, looool. Sound familiar?? I got so bad with finishing my schoolwork last year, Mom finally found me a doctor who took me seriously, and guess what? When they tested me for ADHD all signs pointed to yes.

Knowing helps, but it doesn't fix it by any means. Especially since I am not to be trusted with the meds that help me focus. It's a fine line I walk and I haven't quite figured out the correct path.

Speaking of which, I am totally getting off subject. So! In moments like the one I was having with Jackson, where my mind slowed down to one train of thought, I stupidly decided: *Hey, maybe tonight won't be so bad after all.*

Ha! Spoiler alert . . . Epic fail.

I was ready to fulfill my promise to you. I even practiced what I'd say as I walked over to Ben. "Wanna know a secret? I've been in love with you since we first met." *Nooo, too intense.* "What would you say if I asked you out on a date?" *No, that gives him a chance to say no and laugh at me.* "Know that feeling you get when you catch a wave and you almost fall but then you find your balance and it's just you and the ride and nothing else matters in that moment but the rush? That's sorta how I feel about you . . ." *Yeah, that's it. He'll understand completely if I say that.*

So I did.

You know what's funny? All this time I was afraid my feelings were one-sided. More than anything else, that's what kept me from telling him. But when I finally did, it felt so natural, so normal, that when he said, "Feeling's mutual," I could have cried with happiness.

You were right all along, fucker. I really should have just listened to you last year. But wait, there's more!

A few seconds later, Benjamin kissed me.

Right behind a souped-up Jeep Wrangler with lifted wheels. And when he leaned me up against the rear windshield and spare tire, my legs hit the bumper hard enough to cause a bruise.

"Is this okay?" His voice wavered with indecision, pupils dilating, whether from booze or anxiety, I wasn't sure. "Can I kiss you, Case?"

The fact he actually asked permission to touch me had to be the hottest thing I'd ever heard. So much so, I temporarily lost the ability to respond in actual words, apparently.

He leaned in until his face was just inches from mine. "Well?"

"I'd like that. A lot." I slapped a hand over my mouth. My cheeks were burning. I think it was better when I couldn't find words.

But all my worries about talking dissolved when his hand cupped my neck and drew my head to his with a passion I didn't even know he possessed. I felt like I was in a movie. His other hand began to travel from my waist to my back and I almost flinched as the pressure of his fingers gliding over my stomach sent warning bells of embarrassment through me. A feeling I wasn't used to at all anymore.

Usually, I'm completely confident in myself and my body, but right then I was feeling a bit like I had on the first day of sixth grade. Wondering if everyone was going to point and laugh. It was an awful feeling to experience on what was turning into one of the best nights of my life, and I tried my hardest to squash all of the self-hate because in this moment there was nothing more I wanted to feel than alive.

Whole.

And absolutely perfect.

He must have sensed my unease because his hand stopped moving and he leaned his head back until we were looking straight at each other.

"You're so fucking beautiful, Casey Jones." His voice was soft and low.

The affirmations sent my self-doubt fleeing back to the dark hole in my mind it had tried to crawl out of. My confidence returned like a tidal wave washing over me until I felt renewed and I grinned.

"I know," I responded, the hint of a laugh in my reply.

"Humble too."

"Never."

"And that's why I lo—" Dimples formed as he bit off what he was about to say.

My heart sped up. The Scar Squad was forever saying we loved each other but it never felt like this before. Maybe that was why he couldn't say it now. It would mean something different. Something more.

We stood there, facing each other as the world continued on without us, curiosity bouncing between our stares. In the end, we left the unsaid-word-bomb ticking. I think we were both ready to put off the inevitable explosion a confession like that would cause.

Instead he bit his lip and asked, "Where were we?"

Before I could answer, his hand continued to travel along my body with a confidence that made *me* feel confident and I pushed any lingering threads of self-doubt away because that wasn't my style.

His fingers softly scratched my back in just the right way, sending electric waves down to my toes, making them curl inside my trainers. And when his fingers tangled in my hair, I swear there was a moment where I almost asked him to pull harder, but instead I just leaned into it before I totally turned into Jell-O in his arms.

His lips were soft and questioning and undoubtedly powered by liquid courage, or that's what I assumed from the taste of his tongue as it grazed mine. I peeked mid-kiss to see if I could find answers in his eyes to what was happening between us, but they were closed. Squeezed shut with fear or fascination. I'd like to believe it was the latter.

My fingers twined into his curly brown hair and I pulled him even closer because this was what I'd been waiting years for. I'm not sure if the kiss lasted five hours or five minutes but when we broke apart, his lips curled into a lopsided grin that pulled at my heartstrings in all the right places. Especially when he quietly said, "Wow," in a silly surprised way and the grin grew until his entire face was beaming.

It was everything I dreamed it could be. Believe me, there's been a hell of a lot of dreams about this over the last few years.

I was a marshmallow on a cloud of rainbows and the world was spinning like a confetti-colored top. A perfect moment in time. As we walked back to the keg I felt his pointer finger curl around my pinky, his thumb rubbing the outside of my palm like we'd done this forever.

That touch was more intimate than anything I've ever experienced. Made the kiss seem like a silly kindergarten clay sculpture compared to the Statue of Liberty.

We kept stealing shy glances at each other in the glow from the bonfire. People around us melted away to a background soundtrack, the buzz and laughter muted until we were the only two people in the world.

This was big. Humongous. I needed to tell Frankie stat!

I needed to tell *you*.

I'm telling you now. You win. You knew it all along.

I promised Ben I'd be right back and he nodded, happy to wait for my return.

But then everything came crashing down and the moment that I'd just claimed to be the perfect night, a night to remember forever, fell to pieces.

Pieces that could never be put back together again. Because when I went to tell Frankie what just happened, I saw her making out with Raine Silverton.

Raine was some senior skank who liked to talk shit under her breath whenever she thought I wasn't paying attention for fuck knows why. Maybe she was jealous of my relationship with Frankie or maybe she was just a basic bitch.

But when I saw her standing in the shadows holding on to Frankie tight enough you couldn't tell where one ended and the other began, their mouths pressed against each other like Raine was claiming Frankie for her own, a fiery heat lit up in my chest that traveled through my arms and down into my fists. It took everything I had in me not to pull Raine off Frankie and take her place.

That was when I knew, there was no turning back.

Nothing would ever be the same again.

And then, on the way home, after I'd spent the remainder of the night hiding by the keg with Jackson talking about why feelings suck so bad and avoiding both Benjamin and Frankie, I got a call from Mom that Nonno had suddenly passed away and we were taking the red-eye to Asheville day after tomorrow. We wouldn't be back for a while.

I wish I could lie and say I was absolutely heartbroken and destroyed by the news, and I was. A little. But when I understood I wouldn't see Frankie or Benjamin for weeks, relief washed over me in a way that made me hang my head to hide the fact I was smiling through my tears.

Yes, I am a monster. Or at the very least, a questionable friend. Maybe a bad grandkid too.

And so, dear Sammy, my query to you is, what am I going to do now? Because I'm on a plane to Nonna's in two freaking days and I have NO CLUE who, if any, of our friends I should take a chance on when I get back home. The reality is that I can't hide forever. Especially after that kiss. *Both* kisses.

There's no turning back. I opened Pandora's motherfucking box and look what it got me.

So screwed.

This is sorta your fault, so you better help me figure it out.

Over and out—

Casey Jones

DEAR SAMMY,

Do you know what my least-favorite moment of the spodie was?

When I cringed from Ben touching my belly.

How screwed up is our society that in a moment so intimate, so *perfect*, the very first thing I did was wonder if he'd care that I've got a belly? That's how ingrained my own internalized fatphobia is. Even when I actively fight it. I'd like to say at this point in my life that I am proud of my self-confidence. And for the most part, that's a true statement.

But it *KILLS* me that in the unforgettable moments I will cherish for the rest of my life, the doubt comes sneaking in like a viper. Striking, making me freeze. Even if I feel unworthy for five seconds or five hours it's too much!

I hate that we're brought up by the shows we watch, the books we read, the people we talk to, to believe we should have to wait for our happily-ever-afters if our bodies don't fit the standard. Whatever the heck that implies. That eventually, if we change ourselves to fit a certain narrative, we too can have a life of happiness.

Well, fuck that noise. I don't want to wait. I want it now. In the body that I'm in NOW. We all deserve the satisfaction of our lives happening *now* because nobody is guaranteed tomorrow. We deserve to be the heroes of our own stories from day one. I can't put into words how disappointed I am in myself for letting that confidence slip. Especially because I know in every fiber of my being that Ben adores me. All of me. Exactly as I am. As does Frankie. So why would I ever allow doubt to shadow that love?

Because I'm human. And until the world raises kids of all sizes to love themselves as they are from the beginning we're set up to fail.

I refuse to fail.

I swear it to you right now, right here. The person I end up with won't love me in spite of my body. They will just love me. Period.

I remember the first day I realized I was "different." Yes, I know everyone is *different*. I get that we're all snowflakes blowing through this blizzard of a life hoping we don't melt too soon on the journey. But back then? When we were still kids? I really did think I was just like everyone else. Until I understood I wasn't.

We'd been halfway watching TV, some sitcom we only watched when nothing else was on, while we played a round of *The Resistance: Avalon* board game. It was the weekend before summer ended and middle school began.

Of course the entire Scar Squad was in attendance. Remember how we always had rotating end-of-the-summer sleepovers? I loved being the host. Mom would help me set up the living room floor with blankets and pillows and *all* the snacks. The best. Remember how they even let us drink in there because this particular night was a special occasion? We were leaving elementary-school life behind. Growing up. And they knew we knew if we spilled our Kool-Aid we'd be toast, so we all silently agreed to make the most of our new privileges.

Anyway, there we were having the time of our lives. I had a slice of double pepperoni in one hand and a powdered chocolate donut in the other, because I was really into savory-and-sweet combos back then, when I heard the words *Nothing tastes as good as skinny feels* echo from the TV.

I turned my head to see this waif of a person on the screen smiling as she admired a fashion magazine and sucked in her gut.

For some reason the words made me feel awful. I looked at my hands and the food that only seconds before had been nothing more to me than tasty nourishment. Now they were weapons of mass destruction and I was target zero.

I placed both of them back on the plate. Everyone else continued snacking, gobbling down pizza and donuts and all the rest, oblivious to the revelation I'd just had. Maybe you hadn't heard what I heard because y'all were skinny.

I peered down at my body. Yeah, I was curvy. My belly jiggled when I ran. And I couldn't fit into Frankie's clothes. Which sucked sometimes because we were always watching movies where girls shared clothes, and Frankie had always had the most amazing outfits, even back then.

The more I studied my body, the angrier I got. All these new feelings I couldn't describe swirled in me, and my thoughts changed from hopeful to harmful. I'd been looking foward to the first day of school for the last month. Now I wished it would never come.

What if everyone felt like that actor did about bodies? What if they all hated me because I wasn't skinny? What if y'all started to leave me behind because I didn't look like the rest of you?

"Case, you gonna finish that?" you asked as your hand grabbed for my abandoned slice.

"No. You can have it." I let out a sigh and leaned back against the couch.

"Weird. You feeling okay? You never give in that quick." Your hand hovered over my plate, my answer pausing you mid-snake.

"I'm just not hungry anymore." I tried to keep emotion out of my voice but I could feel the tears coming. They were creeping at the corners of my eyes. I needed to get out of there quickly. If any of you saw me crying you'd want to know why. I didn't think I could explain. I barely can now.

Not without completely embarrassing myself.

"Gotta go to the bathroom, be right back."

By this time both Frankie and Benjamin had stopped the game and were looking back and forth at me and you.

"Want me to go with?" Frankie asked.

"Naah, I'm good." I jumped up and hopped over pillows and blankets until I'd made it to the hallway. By then the tears were flowing. Luckily my back was to the Squad so no one could see. I shut the bathroom door, slid down its hard surface, and buried my head in my knees. Sobs poured out of me as I thought about what might happen on Monday.

What if I didn't make any new friends?

What if y'all realized you didn't want me around either?

That thought stopped me crying. I couldn't imagine a world where we'd ever turn on each other. I slowly lifted myself off the bathroom floor and took a good look in the mirror.

I dunno what I expected to see there, but all that reflected back at me was the girl I'd always been. Sure I might be curvy and sure I might be tall. I also had a big smile, curly hair, tan skin, and big brown eyes. None of the other things I observed made me feel bad or good about myself. It was just part of who I was. So why would the shape of my body be any more important?

I turned sideways and sucked in my gut, trying to see if I felt any different. Beyond a bit of an ache from trying to hold my muscles so tight, I felt nothing. Not better. Not worse. When I let my stomach go the air rushed out of me.

And you know what I immediately felt when that happened? Relief.

Because I wasn't trying to hide who I was.

No. I was me. And I was okay with the person staring back at me through the mirror. I promised myself there and then that I'd try to never hate my body again. It didn't matter what the person said on that show. There was a chance I'd never know how good skinny felt because I just wasn't built that way, but I refused to let anyone take from me again what I already knew. I felt good in my body too. Exactly as I was.

I swiped the tears away and straightened my shirt. I still looked like I'd been crying so I turned on the faucet and splashed my face with cold water until the redness faded. Then I left the bathroom. When I got back you were all playing the game.

Frankie looked up and patted the empty space next to her.

"Here, saved you a slice. Cootie-free, don't worry." She held up a piece of pizza, waiting for me to grab it.

I looked around at my friends and you. You all were exactly the way you'd always been. Ben fiddled with his glasses and gave me a grin. You pretended to snatch the pizza out of Frankie's hand. And Frankie lifted it up so it was out of your reach.

Before I could change my mind, I grabbed the slice and took a bite. It tasted good. As soon as I sat back down we all started playing again. Our game talk peppered with casual conversation about what we thought might happen on the first day of sixth grade. I knew deep in my heart that whatever was waiting for us on campus, we'd get through it together. Because we were the Scar Squad and nothing would ever tear us apart.

And for many years that was the truth.

I can't say I've always felt good about my body since then. I'm only human, after all. But I am so thankful I chose to not follow the voice hinting I might not be good enough for everyone else.

Did you know that about me? How sometimes it was hard to be in this body next to the three of you? I didn't like comparing myself to y'all but I will admit that sometimes, every so often, I did get jealous. Especially when we'd go clothes-shopping.

I wonder if you would have understood. I hope so. I'm glad I'm in a good space with my body now.

The only person you should ever need to feel good enough for is yourself. It's the longest relationship you'll ever have with somebody so why make it a toxic one?

Sammy, why couldn't you love yourself enough to stop? What were you afraid of?

A BODY IS—

Skin, bones, hair, nails

Cartilage, blood, water

A body is forgiving

It flexes and bends to your will

Ready for any test you put it through

Waiting for you to rise each morning

And begin again

It is the only thing you'll have at the end

Of your journey

And yet

It's the easiest thing to abuse

To hate

To despise

And even when we are the worst

Wishing that we were in the body of another

Someone else

Anyone's but our own

It is still there waiting for us

Loyal, dependable, constant

A body is

So much

And yet

We give our brains the power to destroy

That which keeps us alive

And sometimes we find out
Too late
That
our body is
not
Eternal

Over and out—

Casey Jones

90,000 POUNDS AND I'M STILL THE HEAVIEST THING IN THE SKY—

up here

the air is thin

and so are the seats

they Dig, Bite, Scrape

Skin against Metal

A battle of flesh and the false promise of

Stillness

stillness of the Mind, Body, and Soul

as an internal struggle wages war with the external to fit in

to conform to the space that was never ours to begin with

Never intended for bodies like mine

so we make ourselves smaller

Painfully

Glances and glares say more than a million words ever could

as I connect an extra piece of cloth around my belly

My judge jury and verdict

a claim that I do not belong

that I do not fit in

90,000 pounds flying between clouds of light air and water
and somehow I'm still the heaviest thing in the sky
a metal bird built of dreams and imagination
yet sometimes?
I'm the most unbelievable part of the experience

Over and out—

Casey Jones

DEAR SAMMY,

Up here the world seems like such a romantic notion. Cities of clouds with soft spherical curves and not a sharp line in sight.

I fit in up here. Where round shapes make sense.

The sky is infinite and for the first time in a long time I feel so dang small, like my problems are only ants on the giant redwood tree of life. A line of ants that started well before me and stretches farther than I can see. We carry our struggles together as we move up the trunk. And knowing that I'm not alone, that my sadness is not some great unique experience, is freeing.

The way the moonlight reflects off the clouds makes me feel like I'm tripping. Remember the day we discovered a doorway to the universe? I remember. Sophomore year. February fourteenth. The day the Scar Squad shared our greatest dreams with each other. And our greatest regrets. The answers to an epic life sat on our fingertips. All we had to do was trust in each other to make them come true. We really believed it would be that easy.

And then?

The cops showed up. Wasn't the first time, *definitely* wasn't the last. In hindsight, would you have done it anyway? Don't need a Magic 8 Ball to tell me all signs point to yes.

God, remember how impatient you were at the beginning of the night? I'd give anything to have you bitching at me right now. No one ever warns you how much the small shit matters when someone dies. How grief can make the most annoying traits important. The very things you hated about a person you now miss ferociously.

And Sammy? Lemme just state for the record, you were exceptionally annoying that night . . . until you weren't. Let me remind you just in case you forgot.

"Come on, Case. We're going to be late."

"Dude, five more secs. Swear." Obviously you didn't realize how vital it was to pick out the perfect outfit for the night. Everything needed to be foolproof. You only get to trip for the first time once. And everyone said the most important part of pregaming was finding a comfortable outfit. Nothing too tight. Last thing you wanted to be focusing on while tripping balls was a bad fit.

I grabbed my favorite tank top and slid it over my lucky bikini top, buttoned my shorts over my bottoms, and then stuffed some underwear and baggy jeans in my backpack for later. At the last minute, I threw in a hoodie and flung the bag over my shoulder. If we were having a night surf sesh there was always a chance it could get breezy later on.

As we walked down the hallway, I checked myself in the mirror for the final time. When Ben's older brother Ronnie found out what we were doing that weekend, he warned us to stay far away from mirrors once the acid kicked in.

I planned to follow that advice.

"Big night for V-Day, kiddos?" Dad reached an arm overhead from his spot on the couch and waited for the ritual high fives.

You got to him first. "Not really. Hitting up the beach. Maybe Burgr Shack after."

Then my hand connected with Dad's palm. "Yup. Nice and mellow. What are you and Mom up to?"

"Think we're going to take advantage of an empty house. Maybe even stay up and finish a movie, ain't that right, babe?" Dad spread his arms wide, encouraging us to observe the space around him.

Mom called out from the kitchen, "Yup. You see, the movies try to sell you on all these big romantic notions but nothing beats a night snugged up on the couch with some pizza and a bottle of wine. You'll understand when you're older."

"I don't know. I mean, a big romantic gesture wouldn't be so bad if you asked me." Before I let myself picture Ben, I kneeled and grabbed my flip-flops from under the couch.

"Romance is overrated. I don't have time to concentrate on anyone but me." You tapped your foot impatiently, more than ready for us to get out of the house before Mom and Dad asked more questions.

"That's because the only person *you'll* ever be in love with is *yourself*, Mr. Ego." I bowed, waving an arm in the air with flourish.

"And that's a bad thing why?"

"Ugh."

Mom poked her head into the hallway. "Is it Frankie's or Ben's tonight?"

"Frankie's," we responded at the same time.

"Well, tell Shirley I said hi."

"Ten-four." You grabbed your surfboard, which was leaning against the door, and motioned to me to come on already.

"Have a good night, y'all." Mom turned back into the kitchen. In her mind, if the Scar Squad was together there was nothing for her to worry about. We liked to keep it that way.

"You, too, Mama," I called to the empty hall, then grabbed my board and shut the door behind us.

As soon as it closed, a blast of humid, hot air hit me in the chest. So much for the possibility of a cool breeze. *Might be different at the beach, though. One must be prepared for the unexpected.* And since that typically could describe any event including the Scar Squad, I was consistently prepared.

Your head dipped from view as you climbed into the back of Milo's mom's minivan. Frankie sat shotgun. Half her body stuck out the window while she yelled, "Took you long enough!"

"One must prepare for the unexpected," Sammy answered as if he'd just been reading my thoughts. I swear, sometimes that twin telepathy really was on point. And we weren't even tripping yet.

"Motto of the night," I mumbled.

Frankie slapped the roof, urging me to hurry. "Y'all ready?"

Ben, forever the worrier, asked, "Is anyone ever ready for an experience like this?"

"Better fucking believe we are. *Come ooon,* Case!" you yelled.

"Dude, chill. We've got all night. Hey, Case." Ben leaned around you and waved me over. "Here, let me get that for you."

"Oh, it's all good. I've got it."

"I insist." Ben stepped out of the van and grabbed my board to stick it with the others on the roof.

Speaking of romantic gestures. Mom really has no clue. I blinked away thoughts of Ben grabbing my hand next to profess his undying love. *Idiot. He's just being nice. Just like every other day we've been together since the fourth grade. Stop trying to make this a thing.* My cheeks heated at the thought of the rest of the Scar Squad catching on to my feelings. Especially Ben. Or even worse, you.

Ugh. I was certain back then that if you ever found out, I'd be destined to a lifetime of teasing. I thought you'd be relentless. Except you never once were anything but supportive of my feelings about Ben. Did you know even then how much I'd need him? Was that when you started planning your departure?

Before anybody could call me out, I climbed in and Milo took off for our favorite beach spot.

"Where are we meeting Scott and Kiley?" Frankie turned to face us. Her cheekbones highlighted by every passing streetlamp. She had this glow about her. The excitement was palpable.

You had this shit-eating grin on your face when you said, "The usual spot. Told them we'd be there by seven. So if they're already gone you can blame Case's slow ass."

"Dude, get off my dick with that already. Fashion takes time."

"She's not lying." Frankie high-fived me.

"Yeah, well, all I'm saying is if they're gone then I hope you have a backup plan."

Your feet landed on my armrest as you stretched out to make yourself comfortable. I elbowed them off. "Such a toolshed."

Ben's soft whisper hit my ear: "Don't let him get to you. It's too early in the night to let him win."

I looked up. He was already staring out the window from the seat next to me as if he hadn't said anything at all. But I knew I hadn't imagined it when I noticed his mouth turned up into the smallest of smiles.

Right. Not letting you win. Besides, I needed to stay in the Zen Zone. And brother dearest, you weren't going to take me out of it.

When we got to the beach and unloaded our gear, Scott and Kiley pulled up alongside us.

"See, we weren't even late," I said under my breath.

You chuckled. "Could've been, though. 'Sup, Scott." Then you walked away to talk with your friends without a backward glance. I don't know why, but that irritated me. You'd been spending a lot of time together at that point. More often than not, you were ditching Scar Squad plans to chill with them. Which was a total killjoy and just a little bit rude, imo.

I tried my best not to get jealous. Even though jealousy's what I do best. Not exactly something I like to admit about myself. Frankie always blames it on the fact that I was the younger twin.

It's inevitable, she once said. *Whenever Sammy's done something first, you're held to his standard. And if he miraculously does it better, your green monster comes out. Your parents biologically set you up to be a jealous beast. It's in your DNA.*

And though she was joking a little bit, there was a kernel of truth in her words. Even when nobody else was comparing me to you, I was. And that's when the jealousy would rage hardest. At least I can admit it now. It doesn't solve a single problem from back then. But I'm not hiding it from you anymore.

Funny thing. At that moment, I wasn't jealous of you making new friends. I was jealous of them taking up your time. The four of us had been exclusive since the fourth grade and I didn't like the idea of that changing. It's like I knew deep down somewhere the end was near and I was trying to hoard every minute. Every second.

The most fucked-up part about it all is that sometimes I feel like me needing to spend more time with you drove you away. You reveled in those moments where you got to be a singular you. Not part of a pair. I get that now. I understand. I wish I could tell you how much I understand. Here. Let me try.

That night you showed me how beautiful life can be.

Remember?

I grabbed my board and took off for the sand. No point waiting around. Not when there were swells to ride. Whether we tripped or not, I was going to enjoy the night.

The moon made her appearance just as I finished waxing my board. You made your appearance a few minutes later. Jumping between the rest of us knees-first and landing in the sand with a thud.

"You guys ready?" A clear baggie hung between your fingertips.

Inside I could make out what seemed to be miniature paper squares. Paper that opened the doors to the universe, supposedly. So weird.

"I'm sitting this one out." Milo had already suited up and was ankle-deep in the froth onshore.

"Good. You can be our driver later on." You opened the bag like it was full of gold.

As if on cue, the rest of us held out our hands, palms up.

Carefully you dropped a small square into each.

I took mine between two fingers. A red rose was stamped right in the middle of the paper.

"Down the hatch," Frankie murmured.

"Bottoms up," Ben said.

You dropped your hit on your tongue, swallowed, and said, "See y'all on the other side."

I looked around at my favorite people in the world. "Remember to buckle up, kids, it's going to be a bumpy ride." And then I cringed as the paper touched my tongue and melted away to nothing.

"Man, don't jinx us." You grabbed your board and took off for the ocean.

Into the water we followed you and had one of the best night sessions ever. The water was glassy and smooth as silk. Remember how the moon lit up everything, surrounding us in a warm glowing orb, pouring its energy into our pores until we felt infinite? Every single moment of our lives was amplified. Salt droplets hit our mouths like bullets, exploding onto our taste buds, briny and sharp. Waves passed through our hands while we paddled as our fingers curled into the arches, letting them ride through like they were digging into melted glass. The crash and hiss as the sea inhaled and exhaled, breathing us back into life with every wave we caught, filled our souls with a comfort that could never be found on land.

We couldn't stop laughing.

The world was inexplicably beautiful.

I can't recall how long we stayed out there but by the time we got back to the beach we were well and truly tripping balls. Milo herded us back to the van like he was wrangling cats. Every time he'd get the majority of us in, someone would pop back out for a reason that made sense to them and them alone.

Once he had us safely in the van we took off for our next destination. While it was true that we were going to Frankie's for the night, what we'd failed to tell Mom and Dad was that Mrs. Romero was out of town. Plus, Frankie's abuela thought we were staying at Ben's. You loved it when we did the switcharoo. I was always afraid we'd get caught, but you? You thrived on the possibility.

"Look, no one's raiding Tita's liquor cabinet, k? Last time she almost caught us." Frankie was now sitting beside me, you were up front with Milo, and Ben was in back.

You looked over your shoulder and said, "I call bullshit. No way could she tell I added water. I tasted it after."

"Okay, alcoholic. I'm telling you, she knew. She just couldn't prove it." Frankie playfully swatted you and then moved her hand back and forth like she was seeing trails. Probably because she was.

Your grin was so easy. I can't recall a single time you ever actually got mad at Frankie. And what was even weirder is that I never felt jealous about it at all. I suppose deep down I knew your closeness didn't detract from ours. The Scar Squad was a unit. Enough love to go around. Maybe more than enough. I snuck a quick glance over my shoulder at Ben. His eyes were open wide, mouth ajar, as he tracked passing cars, drawn to their headlights like a bug.

"Hey there, buddy. You okay?" I tapped his knee.

"It's like we're in a *Space Invaders* game. Everything is so pixelated. Duck! There's another spaceship." Ben jerked to the left. "Whew. That was a close one."

"Wish I could see what you're seeing." I strained to visualize whatever he had going on but except for the lights wrapping each car in a fluorescent glowing cloud, I couldn't. Besides, all the pink giraffes running around would make it absolutely impossible for any spaceships to get by.

"Spaceships, huh? Hang on to your seats," Milo said in a sinister voice. With one hand on the wheel he cupped the other to his mouth. "Passengers, the seat belt sign is on for your safety. Please buckle up, as we'll be infiltrating the Xenu Armada and we have minimal artillery. Sammy, you've got the front guard. Ben, you've got the rear. Frankie and Case, you need to protect the sides. Everyone in position?"

We all started laughing, wondering what Milo was cooking up. Of course you took it all in stride, immediately getting into character, rolling down your window and pretending to aim a cannon at a passing Taco Bell sign.

Then Milo revved the engine and began to swerve in and out of traffic, narrating the entire drive, letting us know when our missiles hit the enemy and when they missed. At some point I remember thinking it was a good thing he'd stayed sober. How else would we have flown through such crowded traffic? Nobody expects a space jam.

I patted my backpack, certain my hoodie would save us all should we get taken down by an alien invasion.

"See, that's why I said you've got to prepare for the unex—"

"Oh fuck." Milo stopped talking and slowed the van to a crawl.

I didn't understand. Obviously the invasion was fully under-way because the lights were growing brighter and brighter. There was even a warning siren going off. Good. The citizens needed to know.

"Why are we pulling over?" Frankie leaned forward.

"Sit back. Everyone just . . . just sit back and don't say anything. Okay?" Milo pulled over and turned off the van, mumbling *We're so screwed* over and over.

"Sure thing. Not a word." I pretended to zip my lip. He was the general, after all.

A ray of light pierced through the open driver's window. Holy shit, we were about to be beamed up.

"Excuse me, son. Do you know you're driving with expired tags? License and registration, please."

"Uh, no, Officer. Um. This is my mom's car. Here, I know it's here somewhere." Milo reached across you for the glove box.

Dude, you were *sooo* trashed. Remember how every few seconds a giggle would slip out and you'd hold out a hand like you were trying to pull the laughter back in?

Milo's hand trembled as he passed something to the officer. "Is this it?"

The officer took a folded piece of paper and Milo's license and said, "Could you step out of the car, please?"

"Yes, sir." Milo bent over like he was unbuckling his seat belt and whispered, "Dudes, just remember, don't say a word until I get back." Then he was out of the car and into the night.

"I think the aliens got him," Ben said from the backseat.

Frankie shook her head. "Liar. He's on a secret mission."

"Bro, look at the lights. It's totally an invasion. There must be millions of them." Your hand kept sneaking to the space beyond the open window like you wanted to test your theory and see if they'd take you too.

Blue-and-red lights bounced on the concrete wall of the closed mini-mart. A part of me still believed it could be aliens, but a stronger part of me definitely felt I'd seen these lights some-where on Earth.

"Shhh. Milo said we need to stay quiet," I whisper-yelled.

"Think they can hear us? I bet they can hear us," Frankie whisper-yelled back.

"I don't want to die." My voice pitched higher. All of a sudden, I didn't feel so good. It was like my body was about to explode. Like my tongue was swollen and my throat was closing up.

Next thing I knew, Frankie was gone and you were sitting next to me, your hands cradling my face. You stared straight into my eyes with determination. "Easy, Case. Everything's all good. Just look at me. Nobody's dying tonight. I'll always protect you. Swear." You let go of my face and pointed behind us. "Besides, we're just pulled over. No alien invasion. Nothing bad. We'll be okay. See?"

Through the rear window I could make out a police car. Milo sat on the curb, head in his hands as the cops talked to him.

The more I stared at what was happening the less I felt like we were floating in outer space. Yeah, everything was still bright and shiny; however, the world didn't feel so upside down. My chest wasn't about to burst open anymore.

Just because we weren't being invaded by aliens didn't mean my heart stopped racing. There was a good chance we weren't dying right now, sure. But if those cops found out we were tripping? We definitely would be dead, 'cause Mom and Dad would kill us.

"Can everyone stop screaming for a second?" Frankie glared. "They're going to hear us."

"I don't think they can hear us," Ben whisper-shouted. "They've got no idea. Besides, Milo is sober."

"Just chill, y'all." You grabbed one of my hands and squeezed. "Remember, it's all good, Case. Easy like Sunday morning."

"Yup. Easy-peasy." I nodded and started thinking of the way the world melted anytime I was on the lip of a good wave. All my problems disappeared for those ten seconds. I imagined myself surfing and my body relaxed.

Right until Ben said, "Oh no. They're coming back."

"Just act natural." Frankie, now sitting shotgun, buckled up and tried to smooth the flyaway curls surrounding her face.

Two hands landed on Milo's open window frame and an officer leaned his head in. "Good evening. As you may know now, we've got a situation underway and I need your complete and total attention or there could be serious consequences."

We all nodded.

Oh man, this was it. We were screwed. I bit my lip to keep from crying. And also to keep myself from blurting out that the officer might want to pick his face up off the seat because it was melting.

"Nobody can leave." He let his gaze travel slowly over us. His features were set in a frown.

Why did it feel like an hour passed with every stare?

When he made eye contact with Ben he reached for something by his belt. Holy crap, was he going to shoot us? This was it. The end. We were goners.

"You can't leave, you see, until every one of you puts one of these on right *meow* and promises to make it home before curfew. I doubt your parents know you're out at two a.m. But if you don't make it inside before two-thirty I plan to tell each and every one of them. Understand?" He then passed something to Frankie.

She visibly gulped as she accepted the items.

The officer dipped his head and then said, "Okay, Milo. You're good to go."

As Milo got back in the car, peals of laughter rang from outside. Somebody said, "God I love fucking with kids," and then all I heard were tires screeching as they pulled away, the strobe lights leaving with them.

"What the hell?" Frankie opened her hand.

The rest of us rushed to the front, leaning in to see what the officer had given her.

"Are those . . . stickers?" Ben blinked.

Frankie started laughing hysterically. "Junior Deputy badge stickers. Here, have one."

She passed them out to each of us. I gripped the gold-and-blue vinyl, tracing the words *Saint Augustine Police Department* with a finger, wondering if I was hallucinating this too.

Milo turned the key in the ignition. "Yeah. About that. Remember how my uncle Vinny is on the force?"

You nodded. We had all experienced more than one run-in with Uncle Vinny. It was a small beach town, after all.

"Well, when they ran our plates, Vinny heard and I guess he told them to fuck with us. So . . ." He shrugged. "At least we didn't get in trouble."

You sat back, dumbfounded as the rest of us. "Do you think they knew?"

Frankie rolled her eyes. "They *had* to. How could they not?"

"Well, good thing I was driving, then," Milo said.

"Bro, do you know how fucked we'd be right now if *this* boricua was the one driving?" Frankie pointed to herself and then leaned over Milo and whispered, "They don't let brown girls get away with a *Whoops, my bad*."

"Damn, I didn't even think about that."

Frankie leaned back. "Well, let's not make that a habit. I got nothing but love for you, buddy—however, some of us don't get to carry around their privilege so easily, ya know?"

Milo nodded. "True."

"Don't stress it, for real." Then Frankie pointed to you in accusation. "Especially when *Sammy* was the one basically screaming 'We're tripping balls' out the window. If *I* was driving around with *his* dumb ass we woulda been locked up for sure . . . or worse."

"Shit. Says you, Ms. I-Whisper-at-the-Top-of-My-Lungs Romero."

"Not the point, dick." Frankie playfully slapped the back of your head. "Dude, your skull is made of Jell-O. Look, Case, he's like one of those bobbleheads." Frankie snorted.

I giggled. You totally did look like one.

Ben nodded to himself. "Frankie's right. But I also think Uncle Vinny or not, they totally would've brought us in if they had a clue we're on acid."

I looked back and forth between all of you. There were SO MANY of you in the car. I swear there weren't any doubles of us before we got pulled over. "Yeah. We're lucky Milo was driving. Regardless, I think it's probably better if we don't go back into battle anytime soon. Besides, there's too many giraffes on the road, anyway."

You gently punched my shoulder and laughed. "You're stupid."

"Back at ya," I replied, letting my forehead rest against the glass. No matter what else happened that night, I knew everything would be okay because YOU were by my side and YOU wouldn't let me come to harm . . .

Up here in the sky it almost feels like I could reach out and touch you. Especially now, at night, where the stars don't seem so far away. Stardust and daydreams. That's all we are in the end. And you're so close and yet, an eternity away.

Why did you leave us, Sammy? You promised you'd always protect me. Now you can't keep your promise, and I'm afraid.

I can't even put into words how bad it sucks but let's just say it's worse than an entire fleet of aliens trying to blow us off the road.

So much worse.

Over and out—

Casey Jones

THE LONGEST ROAD—

A million steps we've walked together
And we'll walk a million more
But the steps
for now
are doomed to falter
Stumble, trip, I'm going under
Hang on, while I catch
my breath
I will not slip
and I cannot lose you
So
Let's pause
Breathe
The air is choking
Is it too late to find my stride?
Wait for me
Patiently
As I try to understand my heart
Do not give up

I know, I'm so confused

I fear the cost of losing you

might be stronger than the prize

Of winning

You

And I cannot lose

No, I cannot lose

So please

Forgive

My lies . . .

Over and out—

Casey Jones

DEAR SAMMY,

Did you know you can text when you're on a plane? I didn't until we flew to Nonna's the other night. Dad let me order the in-flight Wi-Fi in the hopes it would distract me from having a panic attack.

Easier said than done. Especially because even something simple—like discovering you can text on a plane—sets my anxiety to overdrive. Those disposable, unremarkable moments remind me there's an extraordinary amount of life left that you will miss. That we'll never discover together. When I try to imagine the knowledge I'll gain in five, ten, twenty years that you won't, it wrecks me. So I don't picture myself in the future anymore. It feels like a betrayal.

I have all these painful revelations swirling in my mind constantly and on top of everything else that's going on, I won't lie, I downed a painkiller on the flight. And a Xanax.

The reminder rocked me and being in a tin can way up in the air isn't the best place to lose your shit, ya know? Plus having to come here, to comfort Nonna, to go to Nonno's funeral . . .

I don't know if I can handle going to the service. I'm not sure I even know how to talk to Nonna about it.

So I've been dipping into my stash since we arrived and I'm sorry, I really am. I mean it. You can't get mad because it's the only way I know to get through this. Don't be mad, k? I feel lost. All alone. I can't tell Ben and Frankie, and I can't tell you. I can't even burn this journal like I was supposed to at the end of the month because I'm not even home. So what am I supposed to do? Tell Mom and Dad?

Yeaaaah, no.

I've decided it would be blasphemous to light it on fire without the Squad so I'm just going to keep writing in this damn thing until we can all be together again or I run out of space. Anyway . . .

Essentially, while I was floating through the sky in the middle of that foggy haze my phone buzzed and this is how it went down.

P.S. I am a coward.

Ben:
U ok?

Me:
Depends on your definition of ok I suppose.

Ben:
Fair. Where are you?

Me:
I'd say somewhere between Georgia and NC

Ben:
Oh shit you're still in the air?
I didn't know you could text

Me:
Magic!

Ben:
. . . ☺

Me:
:p Dad splurged for wifi.
Why are you awake?

Ben:
Well, I couldn't stop
thinking

Me:
?

Ben:
about kissing you again

Me:
O Rly?

I pulled the hood of my sweatshirt down over my face to hide my blush. It smelled like him. Probably because he'd given it to me only a few hours ago. (And you can just go ahead and shut up right now because I'm not whipped. I swear.)

Anyway, the rest of our conversation went like this:

Ben:
. . .

Me:

Ben:

I'm happy that we're going
to give this a shot.

Me:

(I am too but I'm confused)

Me:

(Your lips are the softest thing I've ever)

Me:

(you were everything I've ever
needed until I realized I needed
more than everything)

Me:

(yesterday I only wanted you
but today I'm not sure)

Me:

I am too.

Ben:

I'm sorry your granddad died.
If you want someone to talk to,
I'm here. Anytime.

Me:

Thanks duder. Going to try and
get some sleep before we land, k?

Ben:

Night, Case

Me:

Night

. . . Can you believe it? I completely wussed out. Why can't I just tell him the truth, that yes, I do like him (of course I like him) but I like Frankie too?

The safe bet would be to forget my feelings for Frankie and stick with Ben. I've got no clue if Frankie likes me at all. But I can't fight the fact that that doesn't even matter. Not when I physically wanted to snatch her out of Raine's arms after watching them make out. That's gotta mean something, right?

The night we left for the airport, Ben came over right after dinner to say goodbye. I was equal parts happy and nervous, wondering if he could read my indecision in the way I avoided his gaze.

We walked to my room, he stayed behind me, holding something behind his back, and when we sat down on my bed he said, "I won't be there to hug you when things get rough and it kills me that I can't be there for you. But!" He held out his arms. Sitting in his hands in a big messy tangle was his good-luck gray-and-blue soccer hoodie. The one he wore to every game. To every celebration we had after each win. Or loss.

His favorite piece of clothing in the world.

"Here. When you feel like it's all too much I want you to put this on and pretend I'm hugging the shit out of you."

I carefully grabbed the hoodie and brought it to my face so he couldn't see the tears forming. Without thinking, I inhaled. It smelled so much like him I couldn't help but close my eyes. The smells of grass and dirt, board wax, salt and seaweed and sweat, and over all of that, a layer of the Jean Paul Gaultier cologne that you gave him on our last Christmas together filled my nose in the most pleasant of ways.

(Okay, okay, you win. I might be a little bit whipped. I am only admitting this because it's not like you can tell him or anything so stop gloating, dick.)

I could have left my face buried in that hoodie all night, no lie. "Mmm," I mumbled.

"That good?"

"I suppose."

"Well, I considered washing it first but I didn't want to risk missing you before you dipped."

"I'm glad you didn't. It smells like home."

It got so quiet in the room all I could hear was the sound of us breathing. I looked over at Ben. His cheeks were flushed and his eyes were bright. The dimples I've loved for forever deepened when he bit his lip.

It took all my self-control to not reach out and grab his hand. Then it hit me that I could, so I did. Our fingers laced together, fitting so perfectly I knew there'd be an ache when we let go. So I squeezed, just to feel the warmth of his touch while I could.

"I smell like home?"

"Yeah, I guess you do." I ducked my head again, my hair falling around my face, and inhaled once more.

A PRAYER—

Now I lay me down to sleep
I pray for dreams that I can keep
Wishes granted wishes lost
Answered at enormous cost
How do I say yes, when I really don't know
We've only just kissed,
Now let me go

Just wait, dear brother, there is more to this evening.

So after we'd said our goodbyes and I was a puddle of mush, I threw on his hoodie and finished packing. Mom kept bugging that we were going to be late. You know how Mom starts circling when she's impatient? Well, amplify that by a hundred. I think she was just stressed because she didn't know how to cheer Dad up and one thing I've noticed is that Mom doesn't know how to sit in sadness very well.

Maybe that's her way of coping with loss. By moving and making sure those of us that are still breathing are happy functioning people. Maybe if she slowed down, the grief would find a way in, and then she wouldn't be able to move again. So she keeps moving all the time.

I get that. I've been there. The not being able to move part. Maybe that's why she was pushing me to hurry because she knew if I really let it sink in that Nonno was dead and we were about to go to his funeral I'd be so frozen by fear I wouldn't leave my bedroom. She's good about things like that. Like a sixth sense or something.

So there we were, rolling our luggage down the hall. Dad's face was so low it almost touched the ground. Mom held his hand, turning her head over her shoulder to chirp at me to come on, and then the doorbell rang.

"You've got five seconds, that's it." Mom grabbed the doorknob and swung the door open, saying, "Frankie, we're super behind schedule so Casey can't chat long, but I left a list of instructions on the fridge and some money in case of emergencies. Casey, pass me your bag."

I let go of my carry-on handle while Frankie wrapped Dad in a hug. "Give Nonna a big squeeze for me and send her condolences from me and Tita. Wish I could be there with y'all."

Dad smiled sadly. "I'll make sure to tell her. Thanks for taking care of the house while we're gone."

"Of course. It's the least I can do. Tita says not to worry about stopping at the store on your way home. She's gonna fill the fridge."

Mom gave Frankie a hug. "Tell Shirley I owe her one. Take care, darling, we'll see you soon. And make sure Boscoe only gets the wet food in the morning." She passed the house keys to Frankie.

"For sure."

Mom and Dad made their way to the car. I picked up my backpack and moved out of the doorway. Frankie was in her pj's and had her overnight bag slung over her shoulder. She planned to go back and forth from our place to hers while we were out of town. Thinking about her sleeping in my bed made my heart race.

"I swear your mom is psychic."

"Is she, though? Who else would be dropping by at ten p.m. on a Wednesday night?"

Frankie tilted her head and eyed the hoodie I had on. "You tell me."

I couldn't help but blush and then my thoughts started ping-ponging off each other because I still hadn't told Frankie about my kiss with Ben, much less that I liked him.

"Well, of course he stopped by. Duh."

"*Of course.*"

"It's nothing. Just a parting gift. To make sure I'm warm on my trip or whatever." My words trickled away as I tried to salvage this conversation without admitting to Frankie that there was anything going on between me and Ben.

The screwed-up part of this entire scenario is I wanted to tell her from the very beginning, ya know? Like, if I couldn't tell *you* then at least I could confide in *her*. We never hide anything from each other. She even knows some of the stuff I never figured out how to say to you. Like once I whispered to her in the darkness of night that I think our parents will always be disappointed in me because I am not as good as you.

And I never will be. Because how can you live up to a memory?

Sorry, but it's true.

Sammy, if I could bare my heart to her about shit like that, then I needed to speak my truth in its entirety, right? But she kissed Raine and feelings got involved, and until I managed to work them out, I just . . . Ugh. So I lied.

She wasn't buying it, though. Go figure.

Frankie frowned. "To keep warm. In June? What—" A light sparked in her eyes. "Shut the fuck up. Spill. Now!"

"I didn't say anything."

"You didn't need to. I can just tell."

"Tell what?" I ducked my head so she couldn't read me. Wrong move. That was exactly what she was looking for to confirm her suspicions, apparently.

"Holy shit. You and Ben? I fucking knew it. I always had a feeling there was something going on between you two." Frankie was vibrating with energy, her words moving as fast as her body as she jumped up and down. "*So obvi.* I mean, look at what you're *wearing.* Ben wouldn't give that hoodie to just anyone for nothing. You little slut." A shit-eating grin pulled across her face as she laughed. "I'm proud of you. But *Ben* of all people?!"

"Okay, nothing is obvi except for the fact I'm taking too long and Mom is going to kill me, and then you'll never know if anything happened between us or not."

"Fine. Go. Go. But you better call me as soon as you land and then? You need to tell me *EVERYTHING.*"

"Promise."

Frankie leaned in for a hug and kiss. I met her halfway, but instead of kissing each other's cheeks like we usually did, at the last second I turned my head because Mom started yelling and our lips touched . . . it was for the briefest of seconds but *OHEMGEE,* when they touched it was like I'd just been electrocuted. Frankie hugged me harder but my arms dropped.

"K, gonna go. See ya, wouldn't want to be ya." I started walking backward. My face was on fire.

"Dude, you alright?"

"Uh-huh."

Frankie put her hands on her hips, brow furrowing as she tried to figure out what was going on.

All I could do was picture us lying in my bed. And then I started imagining her inviting Raine over and I couldn't help but blurt out, "Do not, under any circumstances, invite Raine over."

"What?"

"Nothing. Nothing. I'll call you when I land."

"Casey Jones Caruso, I swear to all that is holy if you don't get your butt in the car—" Mom's voice rang out into the night, and for the first time in a long time I was thankful she was so impatient.

Frankie shrugged, waving me away before Mom totally lost the plot. "Yeah, you better call because you're acting sus."

"I swear. I'm not. I just . . . I'll call. Bye."

"Later." Frankie turned and went into the house. But before she closed the door she blew me a kiss.

I blew one back because that's how we always say goodbye. Except this time it felt different.

So I've been at Nonna's for two days now and I still haven't called Frankie. Hope you've got some room up there because if I keep ignoring her she just might kill me.

Over and out—

Casey Jones

DEAR SAMMY,

Why is it when someone dies you can't stop thinking about the past? Sometimes getting lost in the memories feels more real than what's happening now. Safer somehow. Is that weird? The future is terrifying so I retreat into thoughts of all of us together, when the world was our oyster. When we were invincible.

Never in a million years did I ever imagine that the Scar Squad wouldn't last a lifetime.

It's not fair. Can we even call ourselves that anymore? Remember the day that changed our lives forever?

I mean the first one . . . not the day you died.

Fourth grade, during PE, on the south end of the basketball court where a very serious game of HORSE was taking place, was the moment Benjamin Dean stumbled into our lives. Literally. It was his second day as he'd just moved into town from sunny San Diego, California. But I noticed him immediately.

He'd been playing four square with kids from Mrs. Langley's room, the only other fourth-grade class of Winston Elementary. And as he dove to hit the ball back into play, he tripped over a scooter and slid right into you, me, and Frankie, sending us all sprawling into an awkward pile of bony knees, elbows, and embarrassed faces.

The spill stopped both games. Some laughed around us and others rushed to help, but when kids saw how fucked up we were, the entire court became spookily still. There are moments to this day I find myself wishing for that magnificent stillness. It was like time slowed down to nothing and everyone was waiting for some signal that they could all start breathing again.

For once, I wasn't alone.

In the end, the four of us were sent to the nurse's office. Can you still hear the way all the adults freaked out when we walked in?

I can.

Ben's face had slammed into my knee, resulting in him chipping his front tooth and gaining an impressive black eye and bloody nose. I was left with a tooth-sized hole right above my kneecap that would not stop bleeding; a gash that apparently needed to be washed out with peroxide, which was not fun At All; and a hairline-fractured right elbow, which ended with me in a cast for the next eight weeks.

At some point during the collision, your face made out with Frankie's left elbow and you got a broken nose—which probably served you right—even if you didn't actually deserve it, because you were always teasing Frankie about something back then. :P

Frankie survived the event mostly intact compared to the three of us and escaped with only a significant stretch of road rash along her left hip and two scraped and bleeding palms.

Suffice it to say, our injuries were more than our elementary school nurse could handle at 10:05 on a Tuesday morning and so while our parents were called into the office to come bring us to the hospital and Mrs. Romero was called out of her kindergarten class to comfort us until they could take us, the four of us held our broken and bleeding bits together to form a blood pact that consisted of us never, ever, playing on that dumb court for the rest of fourth grade.

And we didn't either.

Scar Squad for life!

For the last five months of the school year, our coach held PE on the soccer field. I don't know if it was coincidence or if they just didn't want to risk another skin explosion on the basketball court, but either way, we were thankful.

Since Ben was forced to sit on the sidelines with us while we healed from our various wounds, we ended up spending class getting to know each other better. You were super stoked for another boy to join our crew since Frankie and I had been pretty tight since kindergarten when Tita Shirley was our teacher. I even remember the day she brought Frankie to class as a transfer student. And then she put Frankie at our table! That stroke of luck gave us the seeds to grow the best friendship in the entire universe. Even when Frankie's parents moved her away for first and second grade.

Remember our freshman year when Frankie finally admitted to us she was tired of telling her parents she was fine living with her abuela? That whenever they called to check in she had to put on a show and pretend to be happy even when she was crying on the inside?

I can't imagine living far away from Mom and Dad. Especially now . . . considering, well, *you know*. And it's obvious Frankie loves Tita Shirley with all her heart, but she hates being an army brat. Even now. When she was a kid all the moving from city to city and place to place with every assignment her dad was given really fucked her up. Even back then it was easy to see she'd eventually pick stability. Is it shitty of me to admit one of the best things to ever happen in my life stemmed from one of my best friend's worst moments?

Don't tell me, because I already know the answer.

Besides, now she gets to make all the right choices for *her* best life. She's taking a gap year, don't remember if I told you that. I think Frankie imagined going to the Fashion Institute right from get, but they didn't offer her a free ride and since her family can't afford it, she's going to keep working and then go next year.

Fuck. She must be so pissed that you don't know this about her. I wish you knew how many people you've screwed up. God that's an awful thing to admit. I'm sorry . . .

Where was I? Oh yeah, remember how well Shirley and Mom hit it off? Especially after Mom joined Tita's knitting club. Then they started taking turns babysitting, especially when Frankie was in town visiting for the summers, and then one day. Bam. Frankie declared she was moving in with Tita permanently. We became a lifelong trio, since you and I were basically Velcro already—thanks to Mom and Dad never letting us do *anything* alone.

But by spring semester of the fourth grade, our trio became a foursome. We always sat together at lunch. By fifth grade, we were all in the same class and entirely inseparable and unstoppable. And the rest, as they say, is history.

Forever each other's Band-Aids. Except now? Now it feels like y'all are turning back into my wounds. Cutting and scraping me bit by bit until it's like I'm inside out. First you. Now Frankie and Ben.

Do you know how long I prayed for Ben to kiss me before that spodie?

For exactly three and a half years. Morning, noon, and night. When we were studying in biology, doing labs in chemistry, on the peak of a swell on a six-foot day with the gulls overhead and starfish underneath, sprawled out beneath the vast array of a star-studded sky during one of our epic backyard sleepovers.

All.

The.

Time.

And not once, not for a single minute in all of those three years, did I ever believe or hope or expect that Ben wanted the same thing.

So when he finally kissed me?

And when he gave me his hoodie?

And when he texted to see if I was okay?

How in the world could I find the words to tell him he wasn't the only one who claimed my heart? Maybe some daydreams are better kept in the spaces between, because I'm terrified of reality.

I've closed my eyes while running my finger over my bottom lip and imagining the weight of his kiss. How it felt. How I felt then. How I feel about it now. I've done it like a bazillion times since we arrived at Nonna's and lemme just say, I can totally remember the pressure of his lips on mine. And it was . . . no . . . *is,* every single thing I imagined it could be. Wanted it to be. Soft, sweet, and a little bit urgent. Like we were about to be pulled apart forever and this was our last moment to declare our love—all sealed into one kiss.

I've slept in his hoodie every night too. It really does feel like he's hugging me when I put it on. I feel safer. Protected. I really thought I had this all figured out. I'd forget my feelings for Frankie and concentrate on building something with Ben. But I can't lie to myself, there's no way I can forget Frankie. Not when I got so ragey over seeing her with someone else.

How do I choose?

The memory of Ben's kiss makes me want more. And there's no denying I felt something with Frankie when we kissed goodbye. I want more of that too.

But I can't have them both, right? So how do I give up something I want, even if I know I just want it a little bit less now than I did before?

Can I have my cake and eat it too?

I wonder . . .

Over and out—

Casey Jones

DEAR SAMMY,

Gentle guitar riffs floated through the hallway and hit my ears with the comforting reminder that while those in the living room were mourning, life was still happening, and I should probably get out of bed and go be a good daughter and an even better nipote. Nonna needed us now more than ever.

I pulled my knot-filled hair into a ponytail and threw on some knee-high fuzzy socks before making my way into the land of the living. The secret to tragic moments is that you can get through almost anything in the right pair of socks.

Dad sat on a kitchen chair with his guitar, strumming the Grateful Dead's "Sugar Magnolia" while Mom was on the couch singing under her breath. Nonna stood behind Dad, one hand lightly holding his shoulder, eyes misty.

It was hard not to look at the empty spot next to Mom. Usually that was where you sat, picking at your own guitar and singing the chorus in a newly deep and rumbly bass that made me picture a bumpy ride home in an old car. Its cracking would catch my attention, but in a good and comforting way. I suppose back then you were still getting used to the changes your body had been going through, same as I was.

Wonder what you'd sound like now . . .

"Morning, sugar!"

I blinked to find Mom had stopped singing. She patted the cushion in invitation, and I made my way to the far end of the couch. I couldn't bring myself to fill the space you left. Perhaps I never would. Perhaps I'd never want to.

"Morning." I yawned and made myself comfortable, pulling one of Nonna's knitted throws over my lap.

Dad's fingers started plucking another tune and within seconds he began singing, *"Casey Jones you better watch your speed. Trouble ahead trouble behind—"* His eyebrows waggled in an attempt to get me to join in.

"How are you this morning, Nonna?" I asked, avoiding the bait.

Dad continued to play, singing the chorus along with Mom. Remember how whenever we met someone new they'd always assume I was named after Casey Jones from Teenage Mutant Ninja Turtles? And how we'd laugh and explain that our parents are eternal Deadheads. And how apparently somewhere through their smoke-hazed fog of two young people in love they thought it'd be nifty to name me after a song about a coked-out train engineer who was named after a real-life train engineer who died in a train crash.

Luckily, I wasn't the only Caruso child to receive such an honor.

But only the hard-core Deadheads guessed they'd named you after the song "Samson and Delilah."

Confession time.

To this day I'm forever grateful they didn't name me Delilah. After you were gone I asked them why they went with Casey Jones instead. They said it was because they didn't want us to ever feel like we were stuck to each other. A package deal. They wanted us to be complete individuals, judged and liked for who we were separately, not together.

Maybe our parents are undercover fortune-tellers, because honestly?

It already really sucks losing you, dude. But being the surviving *and* of a duo sucks just a little bit more, ya know?

For your entire life you were my older brother. By nine minutes and thirty-five seconds to be exact. Even without the assumed *and* that would come with Samson and Delilah, we were still an *and* for anyone who knew us as twins.

Sammy and Casey.

Samson and Casey Jones.

We'll always be an *and* for those who remember.

But now? No matter what my life brings, no matter who I become, I will always be a lost person without their *and*.

At least now, if I meet anyone who happens to know the Dead's discography as well as our parents do, I won't have to explain where the Samson to my Delilah is. No. I'll just be Casey Jones.

And they will be none the wiser.

That thought is like coming up for air after being tumbled by a rogue wave. I might finally be able to breathe again. I am so very sorry I think these kinds of things. It's awful, I know. But

I can't explain why I feel that way. Not even in a journal. Soon I'll go home and set all this bs on fire. Even though there's not enough lighter fluid in the world to burn my reality away, I sure want to try.

Over and out—

Casey Jones

DEAR SAMMY,

Bet you miss Nonna's cooking most of all. Lemme tell ya, she's been cooking up a storm since we arrived. I'm not hating it, not even a little bit. I think she could tell I was uncomfortable when we were in the living room because before Dad could start another sing-along she let go of his shoulder and said, "Amunninni Casey, today? We cóciri!" Nonna waved an arm and wandered into the kitchen without a backward glance. Dad and Mom continued their jam session while I followed Nonna, my stomach already growling in anticipation of the feast to come.

"What's on the menu?" I asked. It was nice that Nonna asked me to cook with her. Sammy, after fifty-two years of marriage, trust me when I say Nonno's passing could be felt in every corner of every room in their humble home. But especially in the kitchen. That's where they made magic. Remember?

"Ah, first we'll start with some ricotta-stuffed arancini and stuffed sardines and then you can work on the caponata while I make some ragù for your meatballs, cara." Nonna patted my cheek and passed me an apron.

While we prepped, Nonna told me (*again*) the story of how they immigrated from Sicily when Dad was only a year old. But I didn't mind. It's one of my faves. I loved hearing about how they'd been through everything together: learning a new language, making a new world for themselves and their kids.

Now she is alone, especially since the rest of us live so far apart. Nonna said maybe one day she'll move away from here to be closer to family, but she can't bring herself to leave anytime soon.

Aunt Sofia's due to arrive this evening. She can only stay until after Nonno's funeral. When we go back home, she'll return to take over companion duties for the next month. After that? Well, I guess it's up to Nonna to decide.

Today, Nonna taught me exactly how the dishes of Sicily are different from Italian dishes. Wish you could have been with us to learn too. You'd have loved it! Our cuisine leans toward the bounty of the coast and shows the influences of the people who made Sicily what it is today. Take for instance the caponata. It's an antipasto made with eggplant, pine nuts, raisins, tomatoes, celery, onions, and vinegar.

That was always one of your faves. Nonna says her favorite is sarde a beccafico aka stuffed sardines. And as far as meatballs go? Nonna wouldn't be caught dead serving them over spaghetti like Americans do, but since she knows how much *I* love them, she serves them as a stand-alone dish along with her insanely good ragù. What we call sauce is apparently what some Northerners call gravy.

Anyway, Nonna's love language has always been cooking. You feel it in every bite.

She said, "Cara, we come from the sea. It's in our blood and in our veins, so put it in your dishes and you'll never be far from home."

I didn't mind being far from home right at that moment. Not when I knew the conversations I needed to have with Frankie and Benjamin.

While Nonna grabbed ingredients from the fridge, I grabbed all the utensils and we met in the middle at her island. As she was setting up our stations like we were restaurant line cooks or something, I perched carefully on one of her barstools. But with only a pointed look and a slight *tsk* from Nonna, I jumped up to go wash my hands first.

She winked at me as I settled down again. The small talk flowed between us while our hands moved in harmony. Mine stirring together the egg-and-cheese mixture for the already cooked and cooled rice. Then I took the time to stuff each rice ball and roll it in bread crumbs while she did her magical work on the sardines.

Everything was fine until she asked, "And your love life? How is that going?"

Pinpricks of gentle heat hit my cheeks. I ducked my face down so she couldn't see and mumbled, "Well, it's complicated."

"Sometimes a little complication spices things up, eh?"

"I dunno. I think in this case it might ruin everything." My voice wavered at the end and I tried to clear my throat, but Nonna is keen for catching feelings and apparently she can sniff mine out from a mile away.

Her papery-thin hand reached across the counter to pat the back of mine. "Ah, my dear, tell me your woes."

I answered her pat with a quick squeeze and went back to forming rice balls. I was scared to tell her. Nonna wouldn't know what it's like to be in love with two people at the same time, right? She'd been with Nonno for so long I doubted she even remembered dating anyone else.

"You wouldn't understand," I managed to say in a neutral tone.

"Try me, cara."

My fingers flew as I worked up the nerve to spill the feelings I'd kept only between me and you. Paper and intentions. Feelings and the fabric that held together my emotional roller coaster of a life between lines of ink.

Could I risk it all and let someone else in? A quick peek through my window? It felt strange to voice my fears aloud. But this was Nonna. I bit my lip, holding on to the last of my reservations. And then the words poured out of me like a dam had cracked open.

"I think I'm in love with both of my best friends and I'm afraid if I tell them I'll lose them, and then I won't have anyone at all, and I don't think I can handle being alone." My lungs deflated and it took everything in me not to gasp for my next breath.

I averted my eyes, too ashamed to see what Nonna might think of my devious heart.

"Ahh."

After that one small sound of an answer, the air sat still between us. Filling the room until I couldn't take it any longer. I looked over and said, "'Ahh'? That's all you've got for me?"

Nonna's brow rose, and I waited for her to laugh and call me foolish. But she didn't. Instead she said, "I remember very well what it's like. To hold two hearts in your own at the same time is a very heavy burden to bear."

My mouth opened slightly. Did Nonna just admit she'd loved two people at once? I couldn't picture it.

She waved a sardine in the air, crumbs flying around us like miniature bread missiles. "While my heart will always live with Stefano, he wasn't the only love of my life. Just the longest." She winked and continued to prep the ingredients.

"Well, how did you know he was *the* one? I mean, did your love triangle involve Nonno? Or did he come after your other boyfriends?"

"Don't get fresh, cara. We weren't in a triangle. We aren't shapes and the love wasn't evenly matched into equal lines. But oh, it was still very powerful. You know, I knew Stefano from the time we were very, very little. However, there was another boy when I was sixteen who was so beautiful it made my heart dance every time we looked at each other. Luca Vitale. Ah, was he magnificent. And oh, what a kisser."

"Nonna! I'm impressed." I chuckled. The tension in my chest lessened as she continued her story.

"What? You think I was a maid all hidden away without passion in my heart? Oh no. Life is for living. Loving. Exploring. You should be out there now too, you're eighteen! And don't you forget it!" She waved another sardine like an exclamation point. "For a year and a half, I was torn between Luca and Stefano. We all dated, and I wasn't sure who held my favor more. Sometimes it was one, sometimes the other. Oh, the thrill of love. Keeps your heart pumping."

Can you imagine a young Nonna with two boys, all happy in love? The image warmed me. "But . . . what if the people you're crushing on are more than just a crush? Like, I mean, it's Frankie and Benjamin and I just—" I let out a frustrated sigh, not able to finish my thought. Then I decided to explain the situation. "Okay, here's the deal . . ."

The words kept flowing as I told Nonna about the spodie. The feelings for Frankie I accepted that night. And how when Benjamin kissed me, I knew he was exactly who I wanted to be with even though he's going to college in the fall. Then I told her how much my heart fell at the sight of Frankie kissing someone else.

"Even if they both like me too—and that's a big if—it's not like I can just date both of them at the same time, right?" I waved my hands in the air. "I mean what would people say? Would Frankie and Ben even consider the possibility? I can't lose them, Nonna."

Did I really want to ruin our entire friendship, the heart of the Scar Squad, on a *what-if* scenario?

My fears that she'd tell me this was a very bad, no-good idea and I should go be a hermit in the woods until my heart was purged were confirmed when her lips drew into a pucker, brow furrowing.

"I see. That is a difficult predicament." She tapped a finger against her chin.

Okay, so not quite a declaration that all hope is lost.

I tilted my head and asked, "How do I know my feelings for either of them are real if I like them both at the same time? Ben's going to Harvard in three months. Maybe if I ignore how I feel about Frankie until he leaves, none of us will get hurt."

I made up my mind then and there. It would just be easier for everyone involved if I never said anything to Frankie at all. I could push back my feelings for her and focus on Ben. The one who'd already confirmed he felt the same. Yeah. That made sense.

It makes sense, right?

You'll never guess what Nonna's advice was. You're gonna trip.

She leaned over and tapped my chest. "As if you're not hurting already by keeping your emotions all tangled up inside? No, cara. You must be brave. And if neither of them can understand what you're experiencing and give you a chance to figure it out? Then you must accept that and move on. But you owe it to yourself, and to them, to be truthful to your heart. I think you should try to date them both."

"At the same time? For real?"

"Yes. Can you google *polyamorous* for me, cara? It might be an answer to your dilemma."

My eyebrows almost touched my hairline. Can you imagine her saying that to me, Sammy? Nonna keeps it 100, for real. LOL.

I could feel my face on fire. It was so strange talking to her about this, but at the same time, maybe she had a point. I said, "Dang, Nonna. You don't think people would judge us?"

Nonna patted my cheek. "Why would you care if they did? You aren't in a relationship for the world. Stop worrying about other people's judgment and focus on your heart."

"Well, okay. Say I listen to you and go for it. What if Frankie and Ben don't want to consider a poly relationship? Worse, what if they turn away from me?" My voice cracked with the thought.

Nonna stared straight at me, so intensely I was afraid to blink. Then, with a wave of a sardine in my direction, she said the one thing that gave me hope: "Ah, my love. But what if they *do* want to give it a go?"

So now I'm in a pickle. Because I can't wuss out on the one chance I've got to explore my feelings for both of them. Can I convince them this is a good idea without them bolting?

Help.

Why there isn't a flipping rule book for falling in love is beyond me, but it sure would be nice right about now.

Over and out—

Casey Jones

TO THE WORMS, I SALUTE YOU—

Ants travel across the freshly packed lawn
their cadence carried, one hundred strong.
And the beat they cry to those above?
You'll miss me when I'm gone.
The tears that fall water the grass
that becomes my shelter, for I am cast.
And the trill of doves from way up high?
Will become my anthem, my battle cry.
Listen closely, you'll hear me in the air.
Hold tight, my Stella, do not despair.
You'll surely see me everywhere.
Just look around and you'll find that I've returned.
My body blanketed and bathed in soil.
Fear not, for I am cradled tight.
Do not lose yourself in angst and toil.
Like the stars, my memory will shine bright.
We are the earth, the earth is us,
and to the earth we remain.
Stay strong, Tesora, don't wail or fuss.

For we will meet again.
I'm never far from you, but leave I must
so please, Tesora, dry your eyes.
And if your heart's still aching, remember,
salute the worms as they pass you by.

Over and out—

Casey Jones

DEAR SAMMY,

When I hung up Nonna's coat after the funeral yesterday, a few crumpled pieces of paper fell from it to the ground. At first I thought they were tissues. I carried them with me to throw away in my room since I was headed there anyway. The hushed voices of everyone who'd come to celebrate Nonno's life were filling the hallway. And I needed some time by myself before I could face the visitors.

Funerals and I just don't get along.

I'm not saying it's all your fault, but . . .

It *is* all your fault.

Earlier that morning, Dad passed me one of my Xanax sometime between breakfast and when I needed to dress for the day. The pills were from my SUPER EMERGENCY stash. The one Mom and Dad hang on to.

They don't know about my secret stash. No one does except you and I'd like it to stay that way as long as possible. Especially since Mrs. Rodriguez told Mom and Dad I couldn't comfortably keep prescriptions like that on my person due to my erratic behavior or whatever, but *they* needed to keep them accessible at all times in case I had another panic attack.

The kind of attack where I end up in the hospital.

It happens. Usually at the worst times. It happened right before we graduated. At the beginning of the journal, when I said Ben and Frankie didn't stop by for a few days? It was because I was in the hospital and then Mom felt it best if I had some time to recover before they came over.

Sorry I didn't mention it before.

I just feel so guilty laying all this on you. I'm messed up, I know. It's not like you can even care. But I still *feel* like you can. Just picturing your reaction, knowing I broke down because I couldn't handle walking across the stage without you . . .

Don't worry. The hospital's not a bad place. I know hospitals can be but the docs at the one I've gone to really seem to care. They keep me admitted until I'm calm enough to float away. *Prrrrooobably* because of all the drugs they pump me full of. But I'm not complaining. It's a hell of a lot better than feeling like I'm having a heart attack. No lie. My hands go numb and my chest hurts so bad it's like my heart is breaking apart and then I can't breathe and I want to puke all at once.

Grief is the worst pain in the world.

To try and lessen these episodes my psychiatrist gave me a few scripts. Honestly, I think my therapy sessions are more helpful long-term than pills considering how I abuse meds, but for the big breakdowns I'm really thankful there's something I can take.

And I wish I could keep them with me for those moments, but I'm not to be trusted with any meds. Not since . . .

I don't blame *them*.

To be honest, I expected a panic attack from the moment we heard Nonno had passed on. I'd been dreading the funeral every second since. And each day I didn't freak out completely frightened me to my core. Had I become a walking statue of a human? Devoid of any true emotion or feelings? I'd been whirling through all the feels regarding Frankie and Benjamin, but those emotions and the ones from Nonno dying were like polar opposites, ya know? Same family of feelings, for sure, but completely different sensations as I absorbed them.

This was the first funeral I'd even attempted to go to since yours. While I'd been waiting for the grief to hit, it didn't really settle in until three minutes after my last bite of toast that morning. We'd only been at Nonna's for four days. Aunt Sofia was here finally. And it was time to buck up and be strong for Nonna. I just didn't know if I'd be able to.

Memories kept hitting the backs of my eyes. Teasing me to remember the past . . . Nonno stood behind Sammy and me when we were ten or so, pushing us on the swings in their backyard. Moving from one of us to the other, pressing our backs with the palms of his hands. Daring us to fly.

Remember how his voice would lift to the sky far beyond the places our feet touched as he sang tunes from his homeland? Up up up we'd travel, and then come whooshing down. Almost like he was timing his verses to our motion.

C'è la luna mezz'o mare
Mamma mia me maritari,

Figghia mia, a cu te dari
Mamma mia pensaci tu.

Si ci dugnu lu babberi
Iddu va, Iddu veni
'u rasolu manu teni.
Si ci pigghia la fantasia
Mi rasulia la figghia mia.

His voice rumbled like thunder as he belted out the first verse. We joined in the chorus, *"O Mamma, piscia fritta baccala. O Mamma piscia fritta baccala. Figghia mia, a cu te dari."*

His laughter rang out as we giggled, waiting for the second verse to continue so we could fly ever farther into space.

"C'è La Luna Mezz'o Mare" was his favorite song, I think. Not a nursery rhyme by any means, but he loved singing it to us. I couldn't help but sing it with a smile and laugh. That's what I remember most about that time.

Nonno stopped singing it once you were gone. I doubt I'll ever sing it again. It was ours and it wouldn't sound the same without y'all.

Maybe that's one of the ways we lose our history. Even the good bits. Maybe sometimes it is just too painful to keep remembering and so we choose to forget and the world forgets with us in solidarity.

When I got to my room, my fingers tightened around the scrunched-up papers as I tried and failed to think of something besides the song. Anything else. I lifted my hand to toss the bunch into the bin, but sunlight from the window hit them at just the right angle to distract my throw. Something was written on the crumpled edges surrounded by tissue paper.

When I unraveled the mess, I found a piece of printer paper between the tissues. The paper was worn, as if it had been folded and unfolded over and over again. My eyes traveled to the top. It was titled: *Cuore Mio, To My Greatest Love, My Greatest Adventure.*

Take time as your heart heals. We'll be together again, I promise. But until then? Remember to salute the worms and I'll never be far from your side.

Underneath the endearment and short note was a poem.

It was hard to keep the tears I'd bottled inside for almost a week from falling on the letter. I wiped my eyes with the back of my hand, biting my lip in an attempt to pull all the leaky bits back in. I failed miserably.

All the creases and marks that lined the paper were from Nonna's hands. She must have folded and unfolded this note a thousand times over the last week and somehow during the funeral, it got tangled up in her tissues.

How had our grandparents been strong enough to say goodbye to each other in the end? Had they known ahead of time?

To be honest? I still didn't know exactly what Nonno had died from. I hadn't asked anyone for details. I just couldn't. I'd overheard our parents talking about how he'd been sick this past year, but they tried to keep how serious it was from me. They knew how I'd respond. They were trying to protect me. It still felt awful that I couldn't in turn protect them.

I hoped I didn't seem uncaring.

As I stood there in silence looking at Nonno's poem I pictured Nonna. How strong she always seemed in front of us. This note showed her pain plain as day. A deep ache pulled at my throat at the importance of the words sitting in my hands. This was their last love letter. And I'd almost thrown it away.

At that moment, I realized I needed to stop hiding from reality. Nonna needed me more than I needed my escape. Even if I couldn't say the things she might need to hear, I could stand by her side and hold her hand. Especially while everyone around her asked how she was and gave their heartfelt condolences. People telling you how sorry they are, filling your ears with sympathy until you want to scream and tell them all to fuck off, and all the while, your smile never leaves your face. At least, that's how I felt when . . .

I gently folded the love letter back into its original shape and left my sanctuary. If Nonna could be strong for everyone out there, then I'd stay by her side until the last person left or she decided to leave them.

And I stayed until the last guest left. I don't know if it helped, but I think it did.

I hope it did.

Over and out—

Casey Jones

AND THE OCEAN SAID FLY HOME—

There's something about the way salt settles on your tongue.
Dry little crystals that you steal from your lips
as you lick them in anticipation for your next ride.
A swell forms.
The water gathers from behind, pushing toward its final crescendo
to trickle onto the sand in a gentle misleading foam.
Only to be pulled back for an encore.
And there you sit,
fiberglass and Sex Wax.
Sunlight seeping into your pores as you wait
for a perfect ride.
Nostrils and taste buds work together
as scents of coconut and the sea
relax the body into an awareness of the vastness they float upon.
The pressure builds and you lean in;
Belly tight, arms paddling
over the head through the water, again and again and again.

Legs kick out behind, perpetual motion always forward, never straight.

And as the swell grabs you, you lift yourself to standing crouch

arms flung to the side in balance with nature,

And the breeze blows in your face to remind you,

You are Alive

as the ocean, in all its glory, carries you home . . .

I think I want to be a poet like Nonno was. For the first time since you died I want to start making art. Remember when I used to draw? I used to live in daydreams. Now I live in nightmares. It would be nice if I could just wake up and start living again.

Over and out—

Casey Jones

DEAR SAMMY,

I wish life had a pause button. Like when something tragic was about to happen it'd be really sweet if a few flashing lights warned you to pull this nifty little gadget out of your pocket, or a junk drawer, or wherever you deemed an appropriate place to keep a pause button, and BAM!

Press the bubblegum-colored button (no point in it being red, as we aren't stopping life, we're just pausing it. And what better color to pause life than bubblegum pink, right? Because, like, when you're blowing a bubble there's always the pause that happens right before you pop, ya know?). Anyway, you press the button, and you get to savor that moment for as long as you need, knowing all the while that soon, nothing will ever be the same again.

If life gave me a pause button, I'd have definitely used it on April second, the day after we turned sixteen.

Remember how epic it was?

Yes, even the universe decided we were the ultimate joke, since our birthdays fell on April Fools'. But if I'd known *that* April Fools' would be the last one we ever spent together?

Well, I totally would have let you pick how we celebrated another year around the sun.

But I was selfish. I ended up choosing what we did that weekend. And it's not even that I chose poorly. Because we both had the same passion and therefore ended up with the same birthday presents. Two brand-new fish shortboards with foam tops. Brilliant and beautiful and begging to be broken in. We were aching to try them out that morning. In fact, I think you may have even beat me to the bathroom to get ready because we both knew what was in store. Like I said, it was a pause button kind of day.

Still . . .

An early-spring warmth moved through the house even before the sun was up. You kept mentioning how stoked you were because it'd be a perfect day for catching glass. All we needed to do was get dressed and dip.

We'd devised our plan of attack with Frankie and Benjamin the night before. I remember for a second you seemed undecided. I waited for you to say you wouldn't be able to make it because you were going somewhere with Scott and Kylie or something.

Then Ben elbowed you and said, "It's gonna be perfect. Scar Squad and the sea. *Annnd* look what Ronnie snuck into my bag when I wasn't looking!" Ben pulled out two perfectly rolled blunts. He held them in the air, pointing to me and you, saying, "One for you and one for you."

"Where's mine, bro?" Frankie pretended to pout.

It was a few hours past midnight. The upper half of her body was in your lap, and her legs draped over mine. I was leaning on Ben, his arm stretched out behind me on the sectional. We always felt invincible when we were connected like that. Hands down my favorite way to watch TV. A human pretzel of laughter and love.

Now I avoid that couch like the plague.

Do you remember how funny Frankie looked when she frowned? Like the audacity of us getting a present without her was too much to bear? Pure Leo energy. It's dimmed a lot since you've been gone.

I hope you knew how much you meant to both of them. Sometimes they're shadows of who they used to be. We all are. Because you took away a piece of each of us when you left.

I'd like to think that's how we'll all find each other again one day. I have no clue what happens when we die, but sometimes I imagine we go on this quest, right? We follow the light of all of our loved ones who left before us. And those pieces y'all took when you died are the ones that call us home to you. And it's at that moment, when we find each other, that we're finally whole again.

Until that time, we're walking around Earth like puzzle pieces waiting to be put back together.

You used to love getting a rise out of Frankie, but I'm almost certain you never enjoyed seeing her upset for real. I remember you laughing your ass off before saying, "Um, why are you always trying to snake my stash, greedy?"

She stuck her tongue out. "What's yours is mine, and what's mine is . . . also mine. Duh."

You tugged on Frankie's bangs. "You wish. Besides, you know it's all about the puff puff give anyway."

"Yeah, I know."

Ben leaned in close to me. His breath gently hit my neck in the most delicious way as he said, "Little does either of them realize I've got four more of these bad boys still in my bag. But *shhh*. That's for me and you to know, and them to find out later. Want to go up on the roof when they fall asleep?"

I slowly nodded and moved closer into the crook of his arm.

Best. Birthday. Ever. And we weren't even a full two hours into it.

The four of us smoked one of the blunts; then you declared we should save the other for a sunrise service. Not long after that, both you and Frankie dozed off. To be fair, so did I but the next thing I knew, Ben was shaking me awake, his finger pressed to his lips to remind me to be quiet. We tiptoed out the door without anyone waking. Oh, the butterflies, Sammy! I had so many of them fluttering around as we snuck out into the starlight that they started buzzing so hard they turned to bees.

Ben set the ladder up against the garage while I kept lookout. Once we climbed to the highest part of the roof we lay down side by side. Our bodies were so close I could feel him against me from head to toe.

The only sound was that of the lighter flicking on, then the pull and drag of our inhales as we burned the blunt down. The stars were magnificent. Ben pointed out some of the constellations he knew by heart: Andromeda, Cassiopeia, and his favorite stars, the star-crossed lovers Vega, Deneb, and Altair. Which apparently make up the Summer Triangle, which consists of like three other constellations. Sorta fitting, all things considered, lol.

And you're out there with them in that infinite galaxy being your brightest self, I'd swear on it.

It'd been a long time since we'd gone stargazing, but I managed to find the Big and Little Dippers with his help. One of the things about Ben I love the most? He doesn't make you feel stupid when he's talking. It's like you can feel his excitement about sharing knowledge and that is invigorating because he does it in a way that's inclusive, not gloating.

Did you know we once spent an entire afternoon in fifth grade reading a book in the library about all the different stars in our solar system while you and Frankie had basketball practice? It became a weekly thing for us. Something private that we shared. I never told you or Frankie. Not sure if he did either.

Did you and Frankie have your own secrets you kept from us? How about you and Ben? You must have, because definitely I do.

We stayed up until about four-thirty and then, as the night faded from its shadows, he leaned over and kissed my cheek.

"Happy birthday, Case."

Even when his lips left my skin I could still feel them. I think my smile was so massive it almost cracked my face in half. We snuck into the house, trying to contain our giggles, and crawled back onto the couch, where you and Frankie were already tangled up in the deep throes of slumber. The alarm went off at five-thirty. Didn't matter. We were so pumped it was like we'd gotten a full night's sleep anyway.

Mom was already awake when we walked into the kitchen. At first, I was certain she knew Ben and I had spent most of the night on the roof. I avoided her gaze, waiting for her to call us out.

The bitter scent of brewed coffee lingered in the air. She tossed us each an orange to offset the leftover cake we'd pulled out of the fridge and were gouging forks into. Savage. When we finished the cake and fruit, she passed me a bag full of sunscreen and snacks for later.

"Happy birthday, my loves." Then she gave the four of us a kiss and a hug. God, Sammy. She was so full of light as she said, "Have fun, kiddos."

She's not like that anymore. Not at all. Now she looks at me with haunted eyes when I leave the house. Especially at night. Like she wants to call me back. I can see her biting down on her lips just so she won't.

She pretends it's all good. Probably so I won't feel bad. But it's not enough. She isn't a very good actor. Sometimes I wonder if it will be easier for them once I move out. Will they be relieved they can stop pretending? Stop spending their entire days making sure I'm okay? Stop acting like everything is fine just so I won't break down at seeing them sad?

You did that to her. To them. It makes me want to rage.

Fuck. I'm sorry. It's not fair of me to lay the blame on you.

Outside the air was balmy but the tallest of the palms swayed with a hint of wind to come. Surf report showed three-foot waves were rolling in, so we strapped our boards to the rack of our beach cruisers and took off for A Street. That was our favorite place to rip. Still is. There's a lot of things and places I can't handle now, but I feel your presence in the water, especially at that beach. I'll always feel you there.

The coolest thing about that particular spot in my opinion is how the sandbar always changes with the tides. That day we ended up riding a little north of Fourth Street where perfect swells were coming in like they were on a conveyor belt. Glassy and calling our names. We paddled toward the sun, which was barely peeking over the horizon.

I loved how freely you sang under your breath, setting the mood. The rest of us joined in until our voices filled the dawn air in an awkward harmony. But we didn't care.

Frankie lifted her head to the clouds, belting out the wrong words on purpose, while you slid the edge of your palm along the surface of the ocean with devious intent, sending a perfect arcing stream of water in her direction. Immediately, we all forgot about our destination and an epic water fight erupted. Benjamin jumped up on his board in a crouch and then dove sideways, creating the mother of all belly flops, which sent spray flying well above our heads. After that it was an all-out war.

When we were finally tired of splashing each other we climbed back on our boards and continued to paddle out.

"Case, see that spot?" You pointed a little to the left to a space far in front of us.

"Yeah."

"Let's head that way. Less people."

"Sure thing."

"Bet you five bucks I can catch the first ride into shore."

"Bet."

I started to paddle. No way was I going to let you beat me. Soon, Frankie and Benjamin fanned out behind us. This was our race and ours alone. You and I were neck and neck, reaching for a spot that only we knew. Well, one that only *you* knew and had invited me to tag along to find.

In the end, I don't know what made me stop chasing you. All of a sudden it just felt right, you know? Like that exact spot in the vastness around us was where we *needed* to be. You ran a hand through your cheek-length brown hair to push it out of your even browner eyes and said, "Don't take your eyes off that swell there."

I leaned down onto my board and got ready to kick.

That moment felt so special when you held out a hand and said, "No, not yet. That one isn't for us."

The ocean rolled in and lifted us as if we were being rocked to sleep. We watched the wave continue to pass. Frankie and Ben were duck-diving in harmony to catch up to us.

We looked over our shoulders, in search of the perfect ride.

"There, that's the one we're waiting for." The sun caught your eyes just right and they glinted with joy. You turned and began to paddle back the way we'd just come.

For a second, I readied myself, bent on following and outriding you. The wave was mine. At the last second, something pulled at me to stay put. So I stopped moving my arms, sat up, and watched as the swell lifted me and followed through to carry you home.

And as the sun rose in all its glory, you caught the first wave in.

It was the perfect ride. The perfect morning. I wish with all my heart I could have paused that moment and watched you fly home a few more times.

I can't believe you bet me you'd win, while knowing the entire time the wave was yours from the beginning.

I'd give anything to see you ride again.

Over and out—

Casey Jones

THERE'S A HOLE, LOT YOU'LL MISS, IN MY HEART—

I hate you.

And I'm sorry, but I do.

Not just because you left.

But because you didn't choose to stay.

Here.

With us.

I don't think you took the easy way out.

But you did leave.

And it hurts.

I'm dying because you're dead.

And I don't really hate you.

Maybe only a little bit.

There's a hole in my heart filled

with a million memories.

Each one sharp and stinging.

Why didn't you ever say how lonely you were?

Was it an accident?

Over dose, under panic, around the problem, through the manic.

I know you didn't mean it.

Come back.

I wish you could just come back.

DEAR SAMMY,

There's a stillness to death that the world doesn't tell you about. You don't learn the truth until you experience a loss. Not just in the finality itself. Although I suppose you can't get any more still than that. But there's more. It lives in the air the rest of us—the ones still left on this dumb planet—have to move through. It's in the way people you've known your whole life approach you.

The concerned and well-intentioned creep toward you in a soft-yet-determined motion; always taking care that their movements are slow and steady. They treat you like a wild animal. If they move too fast, you'll surely escape.

It's in the meals spent around silences that have filled you up so there's no more room left for food. You just push the nourishment on your plate around aimlessly until someone says you're excused.

It's in the emptiness of my texts to you. The absolute futile mission. I keep sending them out knowing they will never be returned, but I just can't stop because to quit means to admit *you're* gone. So I keep writing. And calling. Just to hear your voice again even if it's five seconds of *Leave a message, sucker, and you might get lucky.*

A lie.

But a needed lie since those words were your last. And we're all aching. Mom and Dad keep paying your phone bill because they can't bring themselves to let that piece of you go too. Even though we've all recorded it on multiple platforms and even though we have hours of videos with you saying much, much more.

So I call. And call. And call. Sometimes, I even leave a message.

But for all the emptiness, I was never completely alone when you left me because I had the Scar Squad and they had me. They're the only people in the world who let me simmer in the silence until I was ready to be heard again. Holding hands. Heads cradled against each other while the TV droned on in the background. Bursting into tears at the stupidest commercials, screaming like wounded animals . . . because we were. We still are.

We'll never be fully put together again.

It was on one of those days it occurred to me that the three of us would be lifers no matter what the future brings.

Even when Ben leaves for Harvard. When Frankie takes off to NY. When I'm still here trying to give myself permission to do something. Anything. Without you.

We were all piled up on my bed and Mom had just brought in some sandwiches, knowing they'd go uneaten but still trying to do something to take away her own pain. I was lying in the crook of Frankie's arm and Benjamin was draped over our legs as we listened to the most melancholic playlist that Spotify ever created.

Frankie was messing with her braces, sticking her fingers in her mouth to try and rearrange a disconnected rubber band, and there was something so simple and sweet about the moment that for the briefest of seconds everything almost felt normal again.

I remember sitting up and sighing. The feeling washed over me in a way that was similar to the perfect shower after an epic surf sesh. I soaked it up. Letting the stillness evaporate. Knowing it would be back sooner than I wanted.

"I swear I'm going to find Tita's pliers and rip these fuckers off. I will. Just say the word," Frankie grumbled, the rest of her thoughts getting lost between her forefinger and thumb.

"You don't want to do that. If you do, you'll end up with perfect teeth like me." Benjamin sat up and grinned. The bottom row of his teeth was crooked but that only made him cuter.

Frankie, however, pulled her fingers out of her mouth immediately and said, "Okay, you convinced me. 'Sides, if I damaged my grill, Grams would find a way to make me pay her back."

I leaned uncomfortably on my elbows. The back of my head was damp with sweat from all my hair suffocating me as I'd lain in Frankie's arms. I guess I'd forgotten to turn my bedroom fan on to cool it down. I shook my head, trying to get the air moving through my hair, and said, "Just think. One day you'll have a grin to rival any movie star. That kind of smile isn't cheap." I laughed hollowly as memories of you and me trickled in. I couldn't escape them.

Mom and Dad discussing which of us would be able to get our braces first since they could only afford to pay for one set at a time. You volunteered to be second, so of course I did too, because I totally didn't want to seem greedy. This debate went on for weeks on end because we're both stubborn and refused to lose.

And in the end, it was all for nothing. Neither of us got them because, well . . .

Life, or maybe I should say death, got in the way. I suppose the lane's wide open for me to get braces now. Except I don't want them. Not if you can't have them too. It wouldn't be fair.

Is this how it's going to be for the rest of my life? This guilt? I hate it.

"Braces are dumb anyway." I jumped off the bed and slid my shoes on.

Both Frankie and Benjamin sat up. Frankie's face fell.

I couldn't stand to see her hurt so I said, "I didn't mean it. I'm just—" I shrugged.

"'S'all good. What's up?" Frankie looked pointedly at my shoes.

"Want to go for a walk? It's too hot in here."

"I'm in."

"Me too."

They threw on their shoes and we left the house and walked and walked and walked. The entire time we didn't say a word. And it was so comfortable in that silence I could have cried. That's when I knew. No matter how shit life would get, we would always be there for each other.

MEMORIES ON THE CORNERS OF MY MIND BECAUSE THE MIDDLE SURE IS BLANK—

Hap*pi*ness: an illusion.

Also, a feeling that everything is much better than okay.

A gurgle in your stomach.

A smile through tears.

A promise kept.

Un*hap*pi*ness: a reality.

Also, a feeling that everything is much worse than okay.

A gurgle in your stomach.

Tears through a smile.

A promise broken.

Is there an emotion that sits somewhere in the middle of happiness and unhappiness? Can I live at that intersection? That's the road I'd be most comfortable on right now. Because trying to exist on only one or the other?

Exhausting is an understatement.

If we could live through that day, that year, *this year,* then I doubt they'd leave me now just because I'm crushing on them both.

Then again, I never thought you'd leave me and here we are . . .

I think I need to text Frankie. Or call. It's time. Or maybe I can wait until tomorrow?

No. You're right. You're right. I can feel your judgment in the air. Fine.

Frankie deserves more than silence. If I keep ignoring her, it won't be my feelings that push her away. She'll dip because I've been a shitty-ass friend since Nonno died.

Ugh. Okay, okay. I'll accept blame. I've been a shitty-ass friend since Ben kissed me.

See, if you were here I wouldn't even need this dumb journal. You woulda helped me figure this out from day one. But you're not. Because you suck.

Still, I'll tell you what I do in the end. Just in case the slivers of ash from when I burn this paper confessional make it up to wherever you are in the sky.

It's time to pull up my big-girl britches. I don't have enough guts to call but at least I can text.

Wish me luck. BBIAB—

—Okay I'm back.

Insert the biggest sigh ever. Why am I such a pussy?

Here's the gist of my convo with Frankie. Don't laugh. I know you're laughing, but let's just pretend you aren't for my ego's sake . . .

Me:

Sup stinky. I know. I know. Before you lay into me I swear there's a good reason.

Frankie:

Sup duder. Been a hot minute.
Everything ok?

Me:

Yup yup. Just having to go through all of this again is

Frankie:

a lot?

Me:

So much

Frankie:

I wish I was there with you.

Me:

Me too. You don't know how much I wish you were here.

Frankie:

I could hop on the next flight if you want. I've got 3 days off in a row and I could always call in if you need me longer.

Me:

And this is one of the reasons I love you but don't waste your money. I'll be home in a few weeks and I think I'm going to get through this. It's just hard, ya know?

Frankie:

Yeah. I get it. For real though, you
can't leave me on read all the time.
I miss you. :(

Me:

I'm sorry. What are you up to today? I really want
to talk to you about something important but
it's like phone call serious, not text.

Frankie:

Think I might catch an afternoon set
with Ben if he ever gets out of work. If not,
might take Raine on a date. 😬 You could
always call me now before I dip?

I shit you not, Sammy, when I read her plans a fist closed around my heart and squeezed. She wanted to spend her afternoon with Raine? On a date. "No" escaped my lips as my fingers pounded out a reply. How should I respond? I doubted typing *the fuck you aren't* would work. So what options did that leave me with? Shit.

Me:

Uhhhh. Nah. We can catch up later.
You go enjoy that date

Frankie:

What the heck? You said it's important.
Plus you NEED to tell me what happened
with Ben because he's freakin fort knox. Spill.

Frankie could see I'd already read her last message. I couldn't just ghost. The longer I waited to respond, the more awkward this would be. Was my reaction even fair? Of course not. I'd kissed Benjamin ffs. Well, *technically* he kissed me, but I totally kissed him back. More than once. So why did I feel it wasn't okay for her to date Raine? Especially when the main reason I wanted to talk to her was to bring up the idea of trying to date her *and* Ben. *Aaand* to even bring that up I needed to actually tell her I was crushing on her.

Fuuuuuuuck me running. Why are feelings so difficult? Why can't you just, like, nod and the person you're interested in nods back and then y'all go skipping off into the sunset for a night surf sesh and make-out extravaganza? That would be epic.

Instead you actually have to talk about feelings and open yourself up to rejection and and and . . .

The world started closing in and I was finding it difficult to breathe.

I wussed out and turned my phone off and now I'm writing to you about it because apparently I'd rather avoid life than live.

As if you weren't well aware of this complication already.

Sammy? I think deep down I'm terrified she's going to say she doesn't see me in *that* way. And if she chooses Raine over me, I don't know how I could be okay with that. Honestly. I really do think I wouldn't be jealous if she wanted to date us both, especially because I want to date her and Ben. But the idea of Raine being the *only* one? Envy doesn't even begin to describe how I'd feel inside.

Raine is a flipping skaggy poser bitch. She's a sloppy drunk who can barely stand on a ripple much less a decent swell, and the amount of shit she talks? Especially to me? Bro, it amazes me every time I see her eyes are still blue 'cause they should be doodoo brown. That's how much she runs her mouth, my dude. She is total shit.

I mean. She really, really is. And not because she's hitting on Frankie, I swear. The girl is as interesting as drying cement and as mean as a horsefly.

. . . Okay. Okay. I won't leave Frankie hanging. I know you wouldn't. Neither will I.

I'm turning on my phone and typing out the first thought that comes to mind.

Here's what it is—

Me:
**Hope the swells come rolling in
for you, Frankie. Gtg.**

There. Happy now, Sammy? Seriously, though, I do gtg, this is all too much right now. Talk to you later, ass.

Over and out—

Casey Jones

DEAR SAMMY,

Nonna's front hallway is lined with photos, and we are in SO
MANY of them. Did you check them out last time we were here?
I've never really paid attention to them until earlier today. So
many. From the day we were born to only a few weeks before *we*
became *me*. There's even a section dedicated to the Scar Squad in
all our glory.

I spent about an hour moving down the hall, inch by inch,
staring at each pic and trying to relive those moments in my head.

There's one of me, you, Mom, and Dad at the beach. We're all
sitting in a semicircle in the sand around Nonno, who is buried
neck-deep. There are half-assed sand castles all around the mound
of his body, and we look so PROUD of what we've done. He has
the biggest smile on his face, like instead of just tolerating us he's
proud of us too.

Nonna must have been the one taking the photo.

I swear, all the best moments of my life have been spent in
the water or on the beach with you.

Remember the day we went to the beach with Mom and a
rogue wave almost brought us out to the unreturnable part of the

sea? We couldn't have been more than five. Six tops. Seven on a good day.

As usual, we left our flip-flops in the car. And as usual, we regretted it immediately. Mom ran with us toward the shoreline, our bare feet barely touching the ground as we booked it. It was one of those days where you could fry an egg on the sizzling sand. But even though the thought of frying an egg on the sand was cool, no one wanted burned feet, so we ran like the world was on fire straight to our only source of relief.

The ocean.

And when our burning toes reached the safety of wet sand? Total bliss. That first rush of water zooming in to play around our ankles was as satisfying as Mom slathering aloe on our sunburns. Those kinds of moments made me understand the phrase *hurts so good.*

I remember laughing. Giggling. Chasing each other around Mom's legs as her feet disappeared into the sand with each oncoming wave. She was our pillar. Her shadow, our protection.

Once we tired of that game, we made our way onto the dry bits of the beach so Mom could put down our treasures. A bagged lunch, an old beach blanket, and a sun-bleached umbrella. We helped her set up shop, then we built sand castles while she unpacked our turkey-and-cheddar sandwiches and juice boxes.

Remember when you asked Mom, "Can we fill up our bucket at the edge? We'll be careful."

She nodded without concern. We were beach babies born and bred. The ocean was in our blood. We were at home there. Why worry about what-ifs in your place of comfort?

So you grabbed my hand and we ran to the edge, watching the tide roll in. It came to us in spurts and starts. Sneaking up to grab at our feet and entice us back into the depths. We dug excitedly for our prize, the soft wet sand that made the best castles, the kind that dribbled out of our hands to create melting coral-like structures straight out of a Dalí painting.

"Come back," I warned when you went farther than the shoreline. I watched in awe as the water crawled up from your ankles to your calves. Little droplets of salt water dripped off your bushy bangs when the waves splashed against your legs, rising into the air to soak you.

"Come on, don't be a wuss," you replied.

So I put my bucket in the dry sand where it was safe and left to follow you.

Because that's what I did. I always followed you. Even when I knew it was a bad idea. We ran into the ocean as the water reached our knees and then our thighs, splashing and laughing and screaming.

But the ocean had different plans that day. A wave stronger and more powerful than the rest came rumbling in, towering over our heads. We were too far out to run to safety. So you grabbed my hand and pulled me under so we could kick, kick, kick with all our might to reach the other side. Our cheeks bulged with stale air. With each push we were one inch closer to breathing again.

When we surfaced, we continued to kick, remembering every trick we'd been taught since we were little. We'd been dragged into a rip current and no matter how hard we tried to swim back to shore, the water kept pulling us farther and farther out. But you never let go of my hand.

In retrospect, it probably wasn't the smartest move since it limited our swimming, but at the time, your contact kept me from freaking out.

Then when our initial panic eased, we remembered what to do. You don't swim against the rip current, you flow with it. *Remember, Casey, swim in line with the shore until it isn't pulling at us anymore.* Your features were set in determination. We were going to live.

"*M-o-o-o-om!*" we yelled together.

From her place in the sand, Mom jumped, our lunch and her paperback book tumbling to the ground. She started running at an angle, predicting where the current would deposit us and guessing correctly. She dove into the water, gaining ground like she was swimming through molten glass instead of an outgoing tide.

When she reached us, she didn't scold. She didn't yell. She swept us into her arms, planting kisses on the tops of our salty heads and saying, "My, what brave fish you are!"

Because we were. Because we were together.

How am I supposed to be brave without you? Why did you let go, Sammy? It isn't fair. I hate it here without you. Sometimes I can still imagine your hand holding mine, giving me strength when I need it.

I hope it's enough but what if it's not?

What will I do then?

OVERHEARD CONFESSIONS FROM THE TWO-FOR-ONE SECTION—

I run past your bedroom, on tiptoe
because you can't feel my presence anymore
the way I still feel yours.
Everywhere.
Except there.
There your childhood, *our* childhood, is
trapped forever
in an unrecognizable room
where all of your most cherished belongings now reside
in 16x12x12 inches of space.
Lined up in neat rows, shoved to the back of the closet
for convenience.
But don't ask me whose
because since you've been gone
it's never been convenient.
Twins were never meant to be singular
and yet,
here I am. Alone.
You have been compartmentalized into bits of cardboard and
packing tape;
and if I open the door,
if my fingers manage to find a way to twist that knob,
I know you will truly vanish.
I am not ready.

While the door remains shut

there's still a whisper of a chance for you to exist.

Even if only in my imagination.

I need to hold on to you a little bit longer

so I tiptoe,

just in case you're listening,

and want me

to let you go.

Over and out—

Casey Jones

DEAR SAMMY,

Nonna and I went to an art fair today. Two monochrome characters surrounded by swirls of color: vibrant, loud, soft, subtle. We strolled through dances told in canvas and wood and glass, all the steps to be studied and practiced, if only you could find the nerve to take the first stroke.

There was an air of merriment, painted faces. Fresh lemonade. The kind that promises to quench your thirst but makes you even more desperate. How does that happen anyway? It looks so refreshing, but it's deceiving. There you are at a festival or fair, dripping sweat, craving something to cool you down and ease your dry tongue. And from the depths of your despair, a beacon calls out, made of wood and yellow paint, beckoning you over.

So you pay for a cup, knowing soon your worries will be over. Your mouth pulls at the straw like this is your last drink you'll ever have.

And BAM!

There you are, empty cup in hand, more parched than when you first stepped in line. I suppose there's a valid reason they call it a beve-RAGE after all.

I don't exactly know how it works. The science between lemonade stands and their siren call. How they manage to draw you into their world of derelict beverage disappointment. All I know is that I feel this desperate thirst each and every time I drink lemonade. Afterward, I'm always more parched than before I began. And yet. Somehow. Some way. I still gravitate to the lemonade stand first.

Such is my life.

Nonna pointed us toward a booth covered in silk scarves and floral parasols and filled with sepia paintings. "Come, cara, we'll find magic here." She grabbed my hand and pulled me toward the little square booth. "Remember when you used to paint? I've saved every piece of art you've sent me. It's been quite a while since that's happened." She looked down her nose at me. Not an accusation, exactly. Not from her.

"Yeah, I remember. My head used to be full of daydreams. Not so much anymore."

"Oh, my dear. I promise you'll dream again. Come, let's find some inspiration."

Inside we found the most delicate architectural designs painted on canvases in soft burnt reddish-brown hues, accented by pops of white and cream and black. If you let your fingers run over their surfaces you'd feel the stone, brick, and wood that was used to build the structures. I closed my eyes and imagined that Nonna and I were transported to an old crumbling castle in a meadow filled with wildflowers. We stopped to gather the flowers on our walk, fairy crowns surely in the making, as she told me stories of Nonno. Her face creased with the happiness that comes from reliving memories that belonged to only them.

A sharp *tsk* brought me out of my daydream. I blinked myself back to reality and turned to see the artist opening her mouth to condemn me.

I didn't blame her. The price tag on the piece I'd been touching was more than three of my paychecks put together. I dropped my hand and continued on with a sheepish grin, making sure to keep my arms at my sides. I suppose it was enough of an apology because she settled back into her chair, reached into the folds of a fabulous zebra-striped shawl, and passed Nonna a business card.

With a reserved smile, the lady said, "If you're in the market to buy one day and my booth isn't here I've got a studio downtown."

Nonna examined the card with a sharp eye and clucked her tongue. "No point in waiting for one day. I'll take that one there. Eh, cara?"

I followed her gaze to the crumbling castle in a flower field. "But Nonna, the price—"

"When you're my age, money is for spending. Nothing goes with you when you're gone so why hang on to it for later?" She gently chucked me under the chin.

The artist smiled a genuine smile this time. "Shall I get someone to help you carry it to your car?"

"Oh no, my Casey here is strong. We'll make do. But first, we're going to wander." Before the artist could question our true intentions Nonna continued, "I shall pay now and when we're done, we'll be back." She handed over her credit card.

The painting really was beautiful. I wonder where she'll hang it? I promise to let you know since you'll never see for yourself.

This time when I let my finger trail over the meadow there was no *tsk*ing to be heard. I needed to ask Nonna to tell me more stories about her trysts with Nonno and Luca. What made her choose Nonno in the end? How did she know he was *the one* for sure? Why didn't she stay with both of them?

Honestly, I'm not even looking for *the one.* Or even *the two.* I'm seventeen. I just want to know who my *right now* should be.

My phone buzzed in my pocket. I pulled it out and my heart beat a little faster at the name flashing on the screen.

Frankie:

Yo, you forgot about me out there or what?

Me:

I didn't. Swear. Just wandering an art market with Nonna. You'd love it here. Some wild freaks in the area. The good kind. You'd fit right in.

Frankie:

Nobody is as freaky as me.
Nobody.

Me:

Maaaaybe

Frankie:

No. Bod. E.

Me:

Fair. What are you up to?
Fun time with Raine the other day???

Frankie:

Seriously? What is your major malfunction with her?

"Shit."

"What's that, cara?" Nonna asked.

"Nothing. Just texting Frankie. I'll meet you outside?"

Nonna waved me off as she finished her transaction.

Me:

(How long do you have? Um, she
doesn't deserve you. I'm jealous, okay.
You know how she feels.)

Me:

Sorry. I'm just in a mood.

My fingers traveled over the face of my cell where her profile pic was blowing me a kiss.

Frankie:

I can tell. Wanna talk about it?

Me:

**Maybe tonight? I'll hit you up
when we get back to Nonna's.**

Before she could respond I pocketed my phone. I know, Sammy, it was a wuss move. I'd planned to text again. Just not there. Not then.

By the time Nonna reappeared I'd regained my composure somewhat. "What's next?" I asked with what I hoped was enthusiasm.

But you know Nonna's radar is on point. She totally wasn't buying it. "Trouble?"

My hand floated up into the air between us, rocking side to side. "Meh."

"Ah. I see. Well, I suppose a quick lunch might fix things up a bit."

"Doubtful," I mumbled. Louder I said, "Maybe."

A few blocks away there was an old diner with a big blue awning and welcoming paint swirled on the window with hand-drawn pictures of pies and milkshakes. Nonna took the lead and we sat in a booth by the window where we could people-watch as we ate.

"Let me guess. You're still struggling with l'angoscia? Heartache?"

"You could say that." My fingers were folding the paper I'd ripped from the straw into tiny triangles, over and over, as I avoided her gaze. Sometimes it's the only way I can keep my mind steady. It's like if my fingers are moving then my brain can slow down. I don't know if that makes sense, but regardless, it calms me. Same when I jig my leg up and down or tap my thigh. I swear most of the time I don't even notice I'm doing it. Wonder if you ever noticed? You never talked to me about it, so probably not.

Grabbing a meal with Nonna is always a good time, right? Well, I tried to pay attention to the moment and not get lost in my thoughts.

"Hi, what will you be having this afternoon?" A middle-aged lady with washed-out blond hair and a pencil stuck behind an ear.

I quickly looked over the menu and said, "Cheeseburger and fries."

Nonna said, "I'll have the same. And two of your Rainy Day milkshakes, please."

The waitress winked. "Sure thing. Would you like a couple waters while you wait?"

I nodded. As the server laid down silverware and our waters, Nonna steepled her fingers and sat quietly. Taking advantage of the pause, I used the time to study the people walking by. A mom surrounded by a bunch of little kids with ice cream cones was pushing a stroller. She looked exhausted.

Wonder if Mom ever wished she'd had more children? Wonder if she likes that there aren't more of us running around in the world or if she regrets that she only had us, now that I'm an only child?

It feels so strange. So surreal. And these thoughts happen when I least expect them. As you can see, they were turning sour, so I focused my attention back on Nonna. Even talking about Frankie and Benjamin would be less stressful than thinking about you.

"Rainy Day milkshake, huh? What's that made out of?"

"Well, let's see." Nonna pulled the menu close to her face, squinting. "Says here it's made out of orange juice and vanilla ice cream."

"Like a Creamsicle." I nodded. Made sense. Vitamin C on a cloudy day. "Wonder if it's good?"

"Guess we'll find out soon enough. Now. I've been thinking about your problem and I believe I have an idea."

I laid my head down on the cool table. I didn't know if I was ready for any ideas, but I couldn't exactly say that to her, so instead I said, "Shoot."

Nonna rubbed her hands together. "It's quite simple. If you're up to the idea of dating both of them, the first step is to ask each of them out on a date."

"Super simple. Sure. I can see it now." I let the balled-up paper twirl out of my fingers and watched it zigzag to the tabletop. Much like my heart, the paper fell, landing on the surface of the table unceremoniously. Trash.

"Or you could bottle up your feelings forever and say nothing. Maybe one day even explode." Nonna nodded solemnly.

"That actually doesn't sound like a bad idea."

"*Pfft*, cara. You are not a weakling. That is not what you want."

I shrugged. "That's the problem. I don't know what I want."

Nonna turned and smiled as the server handed her a Rainy Day milkshake. "No time like today to find out then, eh?"

Admittedly, I was a little curious to see what she had in mind. "Well, how should I approach Frankie? With Benjamin it's a bit easier. We already know we like each other. But Frankie has no clue. I wish Sammy were here. He'd know what to do. Probably tell me to run." For half a heartbeat I could feel my mouth turn up in the lightest of smiles.

FYI, it's not often I can talk about you without feeling devastating heartache. So those ephemeral moments are absolutely priceless.

Nonna's eyes glistened. "Me too, cara. Me too." Her wrinkled hand reached across the table.

I met it halfway with my own and there we sat holding hands, drinking milkshakes, and wishing for a future that could never be.

If you'd been there at that moment I know you'd be telling me to go for it too. That you only live once, and you've got to put yourself out there even when it's scary. Even when you might get hurt. I could feel it deep in my bones at that diner. I can feel it now as I write. And I can't go against yours and Nonna's advice. Who knows, you could haunt me or something if I do.

In that moment, though, a small giggle escaped, and instead of covering it up I let it out with a sigh. Was this what healing was like?

Before I could truly feel good about it, fear washed over me. I shut down, pulled back my hand, and pushed the milkshake away.

What if I wasn't ready to heal? What if healing meant letting go? The pain keeps me alive. If I lost it would I then want to disappear? Like you?

"Sorry, Nonna. I need some air. Meet you by the car, k?" I rushed out of the diner. I knew I was being rude, but I wasn't ready to face the truth. Not ready for any of this. Not by a long shot. So I did what I did best. I ran.

Will I spend my entire life running from the truth, Sammy? I'm so tired. I don't think there's a destination far enough away for me to ever escape. Not even if I followed you. Not even then.

Over and out—

Casey Jones

APOLOGY—

A pact made between the heart and mouth
In an attempt to repair the hurt you've caused in another
Also,
to lessen the burden of guilt for your wrongdoing
Even if you deserve the guilt

FORGIVENESS—

The act of letting go
removing that which pains you
Setting yourself free from their guilt

UNDERSTANDING—

never.

Over and out—

Casey Jones

DEAR SAMMY,

Did it hurt?

I worry about that all the time. Like, were you in agony until you left the world or were you blissed out and unconscious? I really hope it was the latter because I struggle constantly thinking about you being in pain in your last moments of life.

Were you alone?

That's my other fear. That you died all alone. And I know that's silly because when we die we are by ourselves in the greatest sense of being alone, but still. I want to know if anybody was there to hold your hand.

When they found you on the curb of the hospital, blue lips, white skin, halfway dead and no hope, they said you were all alone. But someone—maybe many someones—dropped you off. A part of me hopes I never find out who you were with, because I swear I feel like I could kill them for being a part of what killed you.

Would you still be alive if they'd noticed sooner?

Did you do it on purpose or was it an accident?

I hate these questions most of all. For a lot of reasons. Especially the last one. Because of how both options make me feel. No matter what, there will never be a satisfactory answer for either scenario. I'm sorry to admit that. It's facts. I know that makes me an asshole because I can't put myself in your shoes and empathize with whatever was happening in your life. I hope one day I can.

I love you no matter what. I'm so angry, though. I feel it in my teeth and the soreness in my jaw is constant because ever since you died I cannot stop clenching and grinding, and that's just the tip of the iceberg of new issues I have developed.

Not blaming you. This time my body's at fault. *Buuut*, well. I don't even need to say it, do I?

Another thing that bugs the heck out of me: I can't ask anyone if you died on purpose or not and expect to hear the truth because no one but *you* knows anyway, asshole.

I'd like to think we were closest of all, so if *I* still don't know the truth how could anyone else?

I don't even know if I *want* the answers.

Even when the alternative is that my brain refuses to let the questions go. They tumble around my head all the time. I could be in the middle of the most mundane moment ever and BAM.

Did it hurt?

Were you alone?

Was it on purpose?

Over and over until the words blend into each other and become one fucking giant scream in my head. Even my memory of you. I don't want to forget what you look like. What you sound like. Who you were. But how am I supposed to hang on when to remember you is to drown in constant agony?

I hate the word *overdose*. It's such a minuscule word for such a massive event. *Overdose* is not enough of a word to fill the void. It's too weak.

If you'd only stayed with the Scar Squad instead of Scott and Kiley that weekend you'd still be here. I know it!

I know I'm lying.

I noticed you drifting away after our sixteenth birthday. Something was calling you in a way none of us could compete with. You traveled the fork in the road with a smile. Maybe escaping was the only way for you to be free from whatever was holding you down.

I hope I wasn't the problem. From the outside, everything looked so perfect for you. You were, like, the best athlete I knew. All you had to do was smile and a person would fall in love with you. You even convinced your teachers to give you As when you were clearly a B student at best (and that's being generous :P). And I'm almost positive you're Mom and Dad's favorite. Especially now.

What I'm trying to say is, you never failed at anything. Except staying alive. The one thing that mattered most. You were pretty much perfect and it still wasn't enough.

And here I was your shadow all this time and now you're mine. One I can't get rid of. I swear I tried not to be jealous while you were alive. I promise. But the hard truth is, I was. I *still* am. And as hard as I try (and I try all the time) I cannot forget a single millisecond of *that* morning.

Not the smell. The taste. The sound. The sight. It was an all-senses-on-deck kind of experience and my body will never ever let it go . . .

Rain poured. Not the usual late-fall sun-showers that drift in like a breeze, the ones that tickle your skin with promises of a clear afternoon ahead. No. This was a torrential downpour. The kind that shakes the palms and floods the streets and entices surfers to the best beaches, knowing the swells will be stellar. Even Mother Nature prepared for your departure by banging on the Earth until it felt like we'd all shatter.

Is that how she calls everyone home?

I should have paid attention. Maybe I would've picked up on how strange things were turning. I knew something was wrong. I just didn't know how *much*. I should have.

Maybe I could have sav—

No. I can't even write *that* maybe down.

When I woke up, I thought you were out catching a set. I was so pissed you'd let me sleep in and went surfing without me, so I went back to bed angry. I planned to let you have it when you got home for being a selfish dick.

Then there was a knock on the front door, and I heard Mom say, "Morning, sunshine. She's still passed out but feel free to wake her up."

Frankie burst into my room, peeling her soaking-wet jacket off and throwing it on my desk chair. Then she jumped on my bed to shake her sopping hair in my face. Little droplets pinged my nose and I closed my eyes. "Go away, I'm still asleep."

"No you're not."

"Yes, I am."

"Nope."

"Uh-huh."

"It's ridiculously obvious you're blatantly awake. Now come on. We've got shit to do." Frankie emphasized the immediacy by tugging my blanket off me.

"Can't you see I'm pouting? Sammy took off without us. *Again.* I bet it's ripping off A Street." I yawned and sat up.

"Well, why don't you get dressed and we'll meet up with him?" Frankie jumped off the bed and raced to my closet, digging for a clean suit. "Here, catch."

I snatched my favorite bikini out of the air with one hand and my purple rash guard with the other.

"That'll do, Donkey, that'll do," I said as I got dressed.

"If you think I'm making your ass waffles, you're certifiable." Frankie adjusted her board shorts and turned to look at her butt in the mirror. "Damn, I look good." She did a little dance, which made us crack up.

Everything was so carefree in that moment. So perfectly simple. Soon we were dancing around my room and my grumpiness started to fade away. It was a bubblegum pause kind of moment. I wish with all my heart I could have made it last just a little bit longer.

"Should we text Ben and see if he's up?" Frankie reached into her pocket for her cell.

"Already did." I waved mine in the air. Before I checked to see if he'd responded, I gathered my hair into a bun and threw on a raggedy pair of jean shorts over my suit.

"Casey, have you heard from Sammy this morning?" Mom's grumble traveled under my door. At the time she and Dad only talked about you with irritation. Ever since we'd started our junior year, it seemed you (their golden child) were getting dull all of a sudden. Not that I was keeping tabs. I did enjoy finally being on an equal playing field, though.

What I wouldn't give to go back to being second best.

The kitchen gleamed, sparkling in the early-morning light. Mom only cleaned on the weekends when she was worried. From the look of the house I swear she was terrified.

"Seriously, Case. Has he texted? Anything?"

I grabbed an everything bagel—the pleasant scent of garlic filling my nose—and tossed one to Frankie before saying, "Nope. Haven't talked to him since *yesterday*. Figured he was already out riding, considering." I pointed to the window.

Mom bit her lip, wringing an old dish towel between her hands. Before she could say anything, Dad called from the living room, "His board is in the garage. And his bed looks like he hasn't been in it." The sound of a newspaper rustling followed his words.

I was livid because if you had snuck out again, then the whole weekend would be a complete loss. Frankie and Benjamin were supposed to sleep over that night, and when you finally came home you'd be grounded for sure, which meant no one would be allowed over. I totally thought that was unfair. A double punishment for a single mistake. But those were House Rules. And if you wanted to keep a room in the Caruso house then you abided by them.

To think about how silly it was to be that angry over such a trivial problem. Getting pissed because you were out all night and we'd all be grounded when you returned. Not aware that in only a few more minutes I'd give anything to have that be the actual truth.

I really, really wish I could go back to a life where the small stuff mattered because I hadn't experienced the big stuff yet. It was so much easier then.

I still feel guilty for being angry with you. Like those were my last thoughts toward you while I thought you were still alive. And here I am, furious because:

1. You left me behind and

2. You didn't care that we'd both be paying the price for you getting in trouble.

It's so basic. So unimportant. And yet, right then, it was everything . . .

Frankie frowned. Because of course she knew what it meant when one of us was in trouble too. I could see the wheels spinning in her head and couldn't wait to hear her cuss you out when you got home.

I felt bad for her that you'd put us in this predicament in the first place. Especially since her abuela had a closed-minded friend in town who loved to poke her nose into Frankie's business, and this sleepover meant Frankie could avoid all the pestering questions of a generation that didn't quite understand why anyone would be interested in the same sex when there were "babies to be made and families to be built."

Like, even if Frankie was straight that stuff wouldn't be on her radar. We weren't sitting here spending our time planning families at sixteen years old. And how backward was it to think a gay couple couldn't have kids or a family if that was what they wanted in life anyway?

Frankie needed to be with us and *you* were fucking it up.

Does that make sense? Can you forgive us for being mad? We didn't know. If we'd known what happened to you we would have never . . .

I tried to make my voice sugar-sweet and said, "Ma, I know you're stressed, but can we preemptively get a pass if Sammy is about to be grounded? Mrs. Romero has company and she was expecting Frankie to sleep here tonight. . . ."

The pause hung in the air. Pulling my best puppy-dog stare, I let my lower lip pout out in a plea that she couldn't possibly deny.

Mom turned to study us.

Frankie plastered on the sweetest smile I've ever seen her conjure. "It would be a big help, Mrs. Caruso. Mrs. Destefanis is nice enough in her own way, but the woman cannot wrap her head around the idea of lesbians. No matter how many times Tita explains I'm just not wired to be heterosexual, the lady refuses to understand. You'd be saving me at least a month's worth of therapy by letting me crash here tonight."

Playing the therapy card. Nice. I bit my lip to keep from smiling. Frankie was a pro. She batted her lashes. No way would Mom be able to deny us this.

"Well, I suppose I can't in good conscience send you to a night of needless torture, can I?"

Frankie and I shook our heads. "Wouldn't be a good ally if you did," I said.

Mom grabbed Frankie's hand. "Fine, fine. You can stay. But *only* you, Frankie. One of you will need to tell Benjamin no. Got it? No mistake, Sammy is in for it. Once I find him." The smile drifted away and a worried look settled back in her stare.

Well, at least I got one out of two for the sleepover. *Not bad.* I said, "Rock on. I think Frankie and I are heading out. If I see Sammy, I'll try to send him your way."

Mom started cleaning the counters again. Dish towel twisted between her hands as she vigorously scrubbed an already spotless area. "Good luck with that."

She was trying to joke but the worry lines crinkling around her eyes and the downturned pull of her mouth made me feel like there was more to this moment than she was letting on. Before this morning, neither of us had ever snuck out for an all-nighter without showing back up by breakfast. Usually when we did sneak out, we made sure to be back in bed before sunrise, and always took the time to at least tell each other where we were at.

The entire thing stunk. I tried to level my shoulders down to their usual position. They'd crept up to my ears as my anger grew.

Sometimes you were so selfish. You had this way of ruining everything.

No way was I going to let you ruin that morning, though. Frankie and I had other plans. I scooped my backpack up and kissed Dad on the top of his head as we passed by the sofa on our way to the front door. "See ya, Pops."

He held a hand up in a lazy wave. "Bye, Bean."

I started talking to Frankie as my hand clasped the doorknob. "I hope there aren't too many tourists out. They always get in the way of a good wa—"

I never had a chance to finish my sentence because when I opened the door, the sight before me made all the words fade from my brain. I jumped back with a short "Oh!"

Standing in the doorframe were two St. Augustine police officers. One's hand was raised in the air, like he'd almost attempted to knock before I beat him to the punch. He stepped back quickly and dropped his arm, cheeks blazing as if he'd been burned.

The other officer ran a shaky hand through rain-soaked hair and said, "Excuse me, is this the Caruso residence?"

I should have known from the way they avoided eye contact something was wrong. It should have been obvious from the tone of his voice. The way the one fidgeted, moving his weight from one foot to the other, that this was not a social call.

But in what universe would it ever occur to me that the next sentences out of their mouths would destroy my life forever?

That at 9:42 a.m. on a nondescript October morning, I was about to lose the person I loved (and sometimes even hated) most in this world.

That once they opened their mouths and began their *sorry*s, life would NEVER. EVER. Be the same again.

Overdose . . .

It's such a small word for such a horribly massive event.

Fuck. I miss you so much, Sammy. And I still don't understand. How. Why. Not even a little bit. Not even.

COLD BONES BREAK HEARTS—

Brittle as skin
That's lingered too long beneath the sun
Burned and baked and paper thin
My heart aches for your return
But the bones are cold
Deep underground
And will never see the sun again.
Choices are made
Without a choice
Given up and taken
The body fades, the memories last
But the bones are cold
Deep underground
And will never see the sun again.
Your voice remains
To fill the dulled shadows
No matter how I try to forget
Amplifying emotions, stripping my sanity
But the bones are cold
Deep underground
And will never see the sun again.
I'll run away
To a place that you can't reach me
Until I can learn to let you go
And I'm sorry that I'm not stronger

But the bones are cold

Deep underground

And will never see the sun again.

I want to hold on longer

Yet I can't

So I'll set fire to it all

And try to find you in the ashes

But the bones are cold

Deep underground

And will never see the sun again.

Over and out—

Casey Jones

DEAR SAMMY,

Nonna's been . . . Hmm. How do I explain?

Okay, I know her intentions are good, right? And the thing is, it's actually nice getting all of her attention—for once. And less selfishly, I hope it helps her by helping me. Maybe it takes her mind off missing Nonno or something. Whenever she brings up my love life (or lack thereof), her eyes light up and the sadness that sits in the lines around her cheeks softens.

That's a good thing. Even when I'd rather be talking about pretty much anything else.

The bad thing is, I'm not so sure her advice is solid. Since the moment I confessed my heart's deepest desires, Nonna's been telling me to go for it, right? To put my heart on the line and try it out with both Frankie and Benjamin and see where the cards fall.

Well, Aunt Sofia heard us gabbing about my next move tonight and let me just say here and now, she vehemently opposes Nonna's advice.

You know how Dad and Sofia are always *yes, ma'am, no, ma'am* to Nonna about everything? Even if it doesn't make sense, they'll still agree with her because she's *Mamma* and therefore everything she says is law—even if they dispute it later behind her back. As long as they agree with her to her face life is good.

Well, when it comes to my love life, apparently that's where Aunt Sofia draws the line. Like, picture a spitting cat. Maybe one who's been run up a tree by the neighborhood dog pack and decides they don't want to take it anymore so today's the day they fight back. They climb down the trunk, land on the grass, eyes blazing, fur all wacky and standing on end, spitting and ready to swing those claws at the first mutt that tries them.

Okay, you've got that in your head? Now picture Aunt Sofia, all five feet three inches and 280 pounds of her, full of the same angry energy, bearing down on Nonna like she'd just told me to run away to Antarctica and take up underwater basket weaving.

She was unstoppable!

"Momma, I'm going to need you to stop before you ruin Casey's life. Do you hate her? Is that the problem? Hey, Alessandro, do you hear what fluff Momma's been stuffing into the head of your little girl? Did you guys piss her off or something?"

Dad yelled from the living room, "I'm staying out of this one, Sofia!"

Nonna gasped, "Excuse me?" Her hands fluttered around her body as she left my side and strode over to where Aunt Sofia stood by the fridge.

Sofia winked at me before saying, "You must despise Casey. Honestly. It's the only thing that makes sense. Otherwise, why are you filling the girl's head with awful advice? Do you want her to be alone forever? Is this your plan?"

"*Pfft,* you know nothing of the heart, Sofie." Nonna waved her away.

I pointed to both of them. "Um, okay, that was super harsh, Nonna. And Sofia, there is nothing wrong with being alone, as you already know so well."

Aunt Sofia's eyebrow arched as the word vomit poured out of my mouth.

You would've doubled over with laughter if you'd been there. I am sure of it.

I tried to recover, saying, "You *know* what I mean. Because you're good at it. I mean, because you're a badass. I mean—"

"Yes, yes, we all know I'm a boss bitch, now get to the point?"

I gulped. "Maybe *that's* my destiny. Not to be with anyone. To be forever alone and be perfectly okay with it, like you. It sure seems less stressful."

I turned to Nonna. "Besides, I never said I was looking for a *forever.* I'm just interested in exploring a *right now* with Frankie and Ben. And to be honest, even my *right now* could seriously last all of five minutes and maybe I'll just change my mind again."

"No, no, cara. U sceccu unni cari si susi." She nodded solemnly.

Sofia exploded into a laugh. "Seriously, Momma?"

I looked between them. Sometimes it really sucked that I hadn't spent more time learning the language of our people. Like right then. "I don't know what that means," I admitted as my cheeks heated.

Sofia coughed. "The translation more or less is 'Where the donkey falls, it gets up.'"

"You're calling me an ass then?" I ducked preemptively as Nonna turned and swatted at me.

My answer sent Sofia into another peal of laughter. "Not quite."

"Perseverance. You may fall. Many times, in fact. But you will always get up where you left off and keep trying."

Sofia rolled her eyes. "I don't understand wanting to be with two people at once. It's hard enough trying to keep one happy."

"You're saying you've never ever considered it?" Nonna gave Sofia a look I couldn't read.

"*Nooo*. I'm just saying it wasn't the right choice. For me."

"Well, it's a good thing you're you, and I'm me, and Casey is Casey. That way we don't try to start living each other's lives instead of our own, right?"

"I guess, Momma. But the same could be said for you telling Casey what to do. It's up to her to decide. Not us."

"I've never told her what to do. I only want her to not be afraid of the choices she's about to make. There's a difference, you know." Nonna leaned in and gave my cheek a pat. "Don't give up on your heart. Go for it, cara, whatever *it* may be. Choose happiness and the rest will always fall in line."

My thoughts immediately turned to you. *You* didn't get back up. *You* didn't choose happiness. *You* chose destruction.

I am not *you*.

Before the panic could set in, I blinked you out of my head and focused on Nonna. "Sure, maybe I *should* choose happiness, but it's not exactly an easy choice."

"The answer is simple, really," Sofia said.

"Nothing is simple but a good meal," Nonna replied.

Sofia continued as if Nonna hadn't interrupted. "All you need to do is figure out who you care for *more*. And if you can't, then ask yourself, out of the two, which one would break your heart more to be without?"

Nonna elbowed Sofia gently. "Or ask yourself how each of them makes your heart whole and then tell them. . . ."

I chewed on my thumb, remembering the spodie where Benjamin kissed me. It was a perfect moment. A soft, reassuring sensation settled in my belly, like being comfortably full after dinner.

Then I remembered how I felt seeing Frankie and Raine together. The fire that burned inside me. How the world lights up whenever she walks into a room.

I didn't want to choose one or the other. But Sofia's answer seemed so much easier than Nonna's.

My back pocket vibrated, and Frankie's ringtone blared into the silence. Not even three seconds after it stopped, it started vibrating again. But this time it was with Ben's signature beep.

That was how the Scar Squad rolled. Even that far away. It's like we had this invisible connection that alerted all of our senses when any of us suffered.

And there was my answer.

Staring me straight in the face.

It'd been there all along.

"Thanks for the advice. Both of you. I appreciate it, but I think I'm going to do this my own way." I grabbed my phone and walked out of the kitchen, saying over my shoulder, "I'll see ya in a bit. There's some very important people I need to call."

I caught a glimpse of Nonna and Aunt Sofia standing together as the door shut behind me. For some reason I expected the bickering to continue.

Weirdly, though, Nonna and Sofia only smiled.

Over and out—

Casey Jones

DEAR SAMMY,

Last night when I made the decision to call them I knew there was no turning back. The cell felt heavy in my hands. Almost as if the whole Squad was tucked into my palm. I needed to call Frankie first. There was no point in disrupting what was happening between me and Ben if Frankie didn't even want to take a chance, ya know?

Ages passed before I could lift the phone to my ear and when it rang I wanted to hang up and run. Remember earlier when I wrote to you about breathing? How it's underrated? Well, let me just say, I wasn't lying.

Inhale, exhale. Don't. Forget. To. Breathe.

Easier said than done in this case. Which, to be honest, is totally strange. Usually breathing's all I can concentrate on. This time, it was like my body bailed on all functions and said, *You're on your own, kid, for the foreseeable future.*

Somehow, I still managed to hit call.

Frankie picked up on the second ring.

"Case! Don't think I'm weird, but I swear I just got this feeling like you needed me."

Understatement. Biggest understatement of the year.

"Yeah, heh. Funny you should say that." I hoped my gulp as I tried to swallow my spit without swallowing my tongue wasn't as loud to her as it was to me.

"You sound strange. Everything okay?"

"In a way? I suppose it depends on how the next five minutes goes." I could feel my pits working overtime. I pulled at my shirt to try and get some semblance of air flow going.

"That super sounds like everything is not okay." Frankie's voice lowered with concern.

"I'm fine. Swear. There's just something important I need to say and I'm not sure where to start."

I was an entire mess last night. My mind kept running. You know how I get. I almost hung up on her . . .

But then she said, "You can tell me anything. Duh."

Normally, I'd agree. This time? Ugh. Why did this have to be so hard? "I know. I know. I'm just not sure how you're going to react."

Silenced seconds ticked by. At that moment I wished there was a way to beam myself right into her room, where we could just stare each other down and let the truth fly. My fears and worries would turn to dust as I laid my heart bare to one of the people I loved most in the world.

Then Frankie's voice lifted as she said, "Should I be scared? I think maybe I should be scared."

"Ha ha. I'm trying to be serious here." Her joking did settle me down a bit. I leaned off my careful perch on the bed to maneuver the window with my free hand. The slightest bit of breeze drifted in, cooling my sweat on contact.

"Oh, this is a serious conversation? Well, that's good! Because I've got some pretty important news too!"

Different scenarios traveled through my head. *Are her parents coming in for a visit? Has she quit her job like she's been threatening to do forever? Did Tita finally find out about the bottle of brandy we stole? Oh. She will be super pissed. I'm sure we can make it up to her somehow.*

Frankie cleared her throat. She clearly thought I was taking too long and suggested, "Why don't we both say what's on our mind at the same time. Then we can actually talk about it instead of whatever it is we're doing right now."

Always the pragmatist.

I started to say, "I think we should go on a—"

As Frankie said, "I asked Raine to be my girlfriend."

And this, my dear Sammy, is why you should never ever listen to your relatives about relationship advice. They will destroy you with hope and wishful thinking and pretend it's for your own good.

I pulled the cell from my ear as if it'd just electrocuted me. Maybe there was a bad connection. Perhaps I'd imagined she'd just said she asked Raine to be her . . .

I couldn't even think of the words *girlfriend* and *Raine* together without cringing, much less imagine Frankie and Raine as a couple. I was too late. My mind felt like a million cotton balls had all been shoved between my ears and then doused in gasoline.

"Fucking Raine?!" The words flew out of my mouth before I could stop them.

Frankie exhaled so hard I was surprised my eardrum stayed intact. "Hold up. First of all, what's wrong with Raine? Second of all, what's with the hostility? And third of all, you never finished what you wanted to say."

The dam I'd built up over the last few weeks broke. Suddenly, I found it wasn't hard to talk. At all. From one heartbeat to the next it sank in that this could be my last chance to tell her everything, and if I didn't try, then she'd be with Raine for the foreseeable future. And yeah, I'd be with Benjamin. (Which would be AWESOME, but I'd always have that what-if rolling around in my head too, which would probably destroy the three of us in the end.)

And there Frankie would be, all cuddled up with Raine, and eventually I'd hate her for it because deep down inside I'd hate myself for being a pussy and giving up before anything even had a chance to begin. And, and, and, and.

And.

I blurted out, "I'm in love with you, and I think I have been for a really, really long time, and it kills me that you and Raine are going out. Like I'm dead. *D.E.A.D.* I hate that she's your girl-l-l-l-friend. Ugh."

The word *girlfriend* couldn't even get out of my mouth without tripping me up. That's how much Raine sucks. Did I stop there, after I'd just basically slammed her new girlfriend and declared my love, dear brother of mine?

Of course not.

When I go in, I go all the way in.

I took a quick breath before she could answer and said, "But what I just said about your girlfriend's not even fair because I do love you but I'm also in love with Ben, which I don't even have to say because, well, you already know. But I need you *both* in my life, like, in a way that's *more* than you already are. I want to see if maybe you'd both be open to dating me? Because, well. Like I said. I love . . . you. Both of you."

My entire body deflated as I realized what I'd just said out loud. I clamped a hand over my mouth and quieted a squeal I'm almost positive Frankie heard anyway.

"Duh."

Did she just say Duh? I blinked. Maybe this was all a daydream. I mumbled, "I didn't lose you, right? You understood all the stupid stuff that fell out of my mouth just now?"

"And right into my ears? Yeah. I heard, alright."

"And all you have to say is *Duh*?"

"We've known each other for how long, Casey? I mean, I didn't know one hundo, but there was like a ninety-five percent chance you were crushing on me. I bet Tita last month you were catching feelings. I mean, remember when you tripped out about putting your bathing suit on in front of me? Like, come *ooooooonnn*."

"You told your ABUELA?! I can't believe you two were betting on my heart. What the actual—"

"Chill. I didn't *actually* make a bet. Well. Not a big one anyway. You know Tita, she's the perpetual gambler. And to be fair, she bet Ben would win you over before you could admit your feelings to yourself, much less to me. 'Sides, she's the one who noticed maybe things were starting to be a little different between us in the first place. Regardless, I knew you were crushing."

"Uh . . ."

Frankie's voice softened. "I also didn't want to push the conversation so you could come to terms with whatever it was that was brewing between you and Ben finally, or, ya know, I didn't want to make things even more awkward, in case I was wrong. Which, apparently, I'm not. Because as we already know, I'm always right."

"I'm not catching feelings. They caught me. I didn't know how to act. I still don't know how to act."

"I could tell then. I can tell now." The snark returned with a vengeance.

It was easy to picture her with a big satisfied smirk plastered all over her smug mug. I know you can picture it too. A true Frankie special. Usually she reserved them for you, but this time, I honestly deserved it.

I huffed. "I think you like to see me suffer." A little part of me hurt over the fact she'd let me carry on this way for weeks without keying me in that she knew. I'd been *suffering* for fuck's sake. All for nothing. So booty. See, this is why it would be so much easier if you were still here. You could've helped prevent all this.

At least I told her. At least there was that. Not that it felt any better. To be honest? It sort of felt worse.

So much for those who say unpacking your feelings sets you free or whatever. I think Nonna got her proverb messed up after all. Maybe I was just the donkey perpetually falling. Maybe it would never be my time to get back up.

The morbid side of me wondered if Carusos weren't destined to persevere, only to fail. Perhaps our DNA wasn't cut out for survival.

Frankie said, "I think you like to see yourself suffer."

"Ouch." That stung. She wasn't wrong, though. I sighed. This part of our conversation was going to be the most painful. I could feel it. "It doesn't matter anyway. You and Raine are together. I guess I'll just try and make myself go back to the way I used to be. It will be hard. But I think eventually I'll be able to pretend like I'm okay with everything."

"Dude, drama much?" The lightness in her words made up for the sting of them.

"I mean, would I be me if there wasn't some kind of drama involved?" I weakly joked back. My hands were shaking at this point. I took turns rubbing them along the edges of my shorts, trying to calm myself in any way possible.

The only bright side of this entire conversation—if it could even be considered a bright side—was that Frankie and I could still joke together as my heart shattered into a million pieces.

"No, Case, I can't imagine a drama-free you. Which should make what I'm about to say that much more interesting."

"Now I'm the one who's afraid." My heart began to tap against my ribs. Speeding up and fluttering like it was a windup toy with somewhere to go.

"Don't worry, I don't bite. Hard."

My knee started bouncing. This didn't sound like the beginning of a friendship breakup. So what was it?

"Look. No matter what, I love you, Casey Jones. Always have, always will. But you have to stop being scared of the what-ifs, you know? I get it. I do. Sammy's death really fucked you up. The thing is, you're still alive. Don't let that go to waste. Understand?"

"So you don't hate me?"

"Hate that you love me? Not even close."

"Not even that I love you *and* Ben?"

"I mean, there's no accounting for taste . . . but no. Not even then."

I chewed my lip. Okay. She could understand my feelings even if they weren't reciprocated. Now all I needed to do was figure out how to get rid of my crush on her before I went home so we could go back to being best friends and I wouldn't have the urge to throw Raine to the sharks.

Which, of course I wouldn't *actually* toss her. Because I doubt she could even swim properly.

And also, because I have a moral compass and I care about Frankie, even when she's dating someone totally beneath her league who doesn't even surf, and we both know Frankie could do a hell of a lot better. Like me for instance.

But I digress.

"I'm glad you don't hate me. What's that?" I needed a break from this convo. It was too much too fast so I let a pause linger before I said, "Oh, I gotta go. Nonna's yelling for me to help her cook. Call you later?"

Yeah, I lied. Sue me.

Frankie let out a little laugh. "Sure. By the way, you were so caught up in *you* and all *your* feelings you never let me finish what I was trying to say in the first place."

Great. Now we had to talk about her new relationship? *Ugh.* I squared my shoulders. Being a best friend sure had its moments. "Well, I've got about thirty seconds before Nonna sends in reinforcements, so make it quick."

"She said no."

"*Wha—aat?!*"

"Casey. Raine said no. Apparently she isn't down for relationships."

"Sooo you're still single?"

"Uh-huh."

"And now you know how I feel about you?"

"Yup."

"And?"

"And I think I can hear your nonna calling you. Don't worry. But I feel like this is a conversation we need to have in person. K?"

"Oh. Okay. Yeah. You're right. Okay. Talk soon then?"

"Talk soon. Love ya, Case."

"Love ya." I hung up, holding the cell in my hands like it was a newly discovered treasure.

We were going to have a conversation in person. And she didn't tell me to fuck off. And she said she loved me. Of course, she always says she loves me. But what if this time she meant she *loooooves me* loves me?

I started sweating again. I had a chance with Frankie too. All I needed to do before going to bed was call Ben and try to explain things and then get through the next four days without falling apart.

Piece of cake.

Except . . .

That was yesterday, and I haven't called him yet. But I swear on all that is holy I will before I go to sleep tonight. Promise.

Over and out—

Casey Jones

DEAR SAMMY,

Another reason why I hate that you're gone? I have to suffer by myself. Do you see now how much crap seventeen-year-olds go through? You're missing out.

I sense your presence sometimes, though. Especially today. This morning I went to the graveyard to visit Nonno with Pops. I don't think you understand how hard visiting a grave is for me.

It's like my skin is covered in spiders—big ones—the kind with hairy legs that drip venom and leave rows of fiery welts I can't get rid of.

It's like my throat is filled with rocks. Chunky ones, jagged ones, the kind that scrape and poke at the soft skin inside and make it impossible to talk, much less breathe.

It's like my hands are caught in a fall windstorm, a late-season hurricane, the kind that destroys entire neighborhoods and rips the leaves off the trees and turns them into dust, and my hands won't stop shaking and trembling no matter how hard I shove them in my pockets to make them quit.

And my eyes?

My eyes fill with salt water, which immediately reminds me of you and the ocean, which makes me cry even more, stinging and burning, and it's so hard to see things clearly, and I swear I must blink a million times just to be able to make out the gravestone that reminds me of you.

Because anything and everything about death reminds me of you.

Which super sucks. I'd give anything for *life* to remind me of you again.

And all that is just the tip of the iceberg. This entry right here? Well, let me tell you, I've barely scratched the surface of what I experience when I'm faced with the thing I hate most. The thing I fear most.

I have no control over my reaction and it's terrifying.

But Pops needed me. So I went.

I've got to say watching Pops is the absolute most awful heart-wrenching thing. Especially when he tries to hold his tears back because he's *a man*, whatever that's supposed to mean.

I wish y'all weren't taught to suppress your emotions. Maybe then you could work through them in a healthier way. Not to say my methods are healthier, but at least no one judges me for crying. Except, maybe they do. Maybe that's exactly what they're doing when no one notices my tears because they expect it from me. Because I'm *a girl*.

Okay, I think it's safe to say gender presumptions can go kick rocks.

I digress.

So, Pops. He stood over Nonno, the newly planted grass mound sending this rich scent of freshly turned earth, a promise of life to come (which is quite ironic all things considered), straight into our nostrils. I inhaled it like it was the first hit of a rolled joint, like it was the first breath after being pummeled underwater, like I'd just been born. I held on to that promise of life. That lie. Because to consider anything else would be to admit Nonno was gone.

Just. Like. You.

My brain can't handle death in large amounts. Everything has to be compartmentalized. It was all I could do to make my body stay still and not go into flight mode. And it was working as long as I kept my mind blank.

I was doing a pretty good job of it until Pops grabbed my hand and said, "Think they're together? I hope that if nothing else is true about Heaven and Hell at least they're together out there among the stars, waiting for us."

"No. I mean, I don't know. Maybe? I doubt it." I twisted my shoe until my toe edge was digging a hole. Back and forth. Back and forth. Dad's fingers squeezed tighter around my own but he didn't challenge my beliefs. Or lack thereof.

It's not that I don't believe in Heaven and Hell and God and stuff, it's just that I don't quite believe in them either.

It's a nice thought at least. You two together. Taking care of each other, or whatever happens to people when they die. Do souls even need looking after? Or do they just float along, returning to stardust and dreams until they're called back to the mortal coil?

And if that's the case, who's to say that's not the true Hell— you think you've escaped and then learn you have to do this all over again?

Yeah, I just don't know.

"I'd like to think of them together in some way." Dad ran the back of his hand across his face. With that subtle motion of pushing tears away, it was like you could see his back straighten. Like the burden of sadness wasn't his to bear publicly as long as he kept on his *I'm a man's man* disguise. Everything would be fine, as long as he corralled all his emotions and shoved them deep inside for no one to see.

Men don't cry. Girls cry too much.

Bullshit.

The world is full of undeniable bullshit and it just keeps getting regurgitated generation after generation. But maybe we'll be the ones who change it all.

I mean me.

You don't get a chance to have a voice anymore. Why did you give up your voice? Was it because no one ever listened?

I swear, I tried.

Since I don't honestly know if I believe in a Heaven or Hell or reincarnation, I pretended along with Pops that Nonno and you were out there bro'ing it up. Maybe as I write, you're even taking him to the galactic equivalent of a spodie. Bet that's one killer light show.

Nonna had given us a beautiful bouquet of flowers to bring along. Dad let go of my hand long enough to stick them in this little hole by the headstone.

I tried not to read the inscription but it was hard to ignore the empty spot where Nonna's tribute would go, once she . . .

All of a sudden, the world began to swallow me whole. Dark spots pulsed at the corners of my eyes and little bright stars traveled beyond my vision. Without warning, I ended up facedown on the gravesite with my feet fanned out behind me.

It occurred to me then, I was giving Nonno's grave a much more personal greeting than I ever intended to. As I finally looked at the words that dug into the marble—the true finality of life come to an end—the only reaction I could manage was a sound somewhere between a cry and a scream. The grief that has lived inside me since you died left my lips with fury. Dad kneeled, wrapping me in his arms, rocking us back and forth as we allowed ourselves to finally mourn.

No idea how long we stayed there. By the time I could pull myself together it felt like I'd melted. Every body part weighed a million pounds. Eyelids. Legs. My brain was full of cotton, as was my tongue. And my eyes were as puffy as the first spring day the cottonwoods send their fluff across the town. Dad didn't look any better.

When he stood, he brought me along with him. We didn't talk. Didn't need to. This was the first time we had grieved together. There was no mistake, today was as much for you as it was for Nonno.

Let me just say, holding in a good cry for that long is absolutely exhausting. We went back to Nonna's and I crashed hard. But when I woke up a little while ago? Well, I can't say for certain yet, but it seems like the pain, the rage I've carried with me everywhere weighs a little bit less.

And the new emptiness that's taken its place? I'm not sure how I feel about it. Rage has kept me moving forward. Without it, will I fall apart?

I don't want to lose you, and this anger sometimes feels like it's the only thing I have left to hold on to. The last of you.

Help.

WASH AWAY MY FEELINGS SO I CAN FEEL AGAIN—

They say tears clean but

for some, it's an act of shame

So how can I be clean when it feels so dirty?

They say tears wash away the pain but

for some, it's a release of burden

So how can I be painless when it hurts more to cry?

Wash away my feelings so I can feel

Numb me with normality in a world that doesn't predict

What I can and cannot do just because of what's between my legs

Let us all wash away the pain and breathe the fresh air of grief, unloaded.

Unjudged.

Everything hurts

Please, let us cry.

Over and out—

Casey Jones

DEAR SAMMY,

Sooo obviously I haven't called Ben like I promised I would, however, there's a valid reason coming . . . Honestly? The last thing on my mind yesterday while I was facedown on Nonno's grave having an existential crisis was Ben. See, even you can't argue with that one. Solid 10 when it comes to excuses, in my (Not So Humble) opinion.

Now that I've recentered, since I've already chatted to Frankie I really need to see where Ben's head is at. I think this could actually work. Nonna is one smart cookie. Just think if I'd listened to Sofia? I might've lost out. Now there's a chance to explore all my feelings. To be honest, I'm getting excited.

I like that.

I miss the rush of looking forward to something. It doesn't happen much anymore. How mind-boggling is it that I could be dating the Scar Squad? Lol. Bet you'd feel like a fourth wheel. You'd sorta know how I felt whenever I spent time with you and Scott and Kiley. But not really. I suppose it's different.

This was meant to be. Like, no matter what, Scar Squad for life, always has been and always will be. But now it's amplified. In the back of my mind I'm aware of the fact that Ben will be leaving for Massachusetts in a few months, but that's only a plane ride away, right?

Long-distance relationships don't scare me. Much.

What's that? You think I'm getting ahead of myself? Okay. Okay. You're right. None of us have even been on an official date, much less called a ship. But we're on our way. Baby steps. Tiny. Itsy-bitsy baby steps.

Remember that seventh-grade field trip to the Jacksonville Zoo where I ended up in the trash can? For some reason the PTA decided busing half the middle school to a zoo an hour away in the last week of May during a record-breaking heat wave to celebrate us becoming eighth graders was a brilliant idea.

Ha.

From the second we stepped off the bus—sticky, cranky, and hangry—we knew how painfully this end-of-the-year trip paled in comparison to the epicness of the eighth graders' chartered party boat with catering, a DJ, snorkeling, and a twilight dance.

At least we got melted soft serve and Randolf the perturbed peacock, who loved nothing more than chasing us around until half-eaten ice cream cones were being used as ammo to block the bird's and his minions' advances. Missiles of liquid sugar flew through the air as Randolf kept coming—an evil glint in his eye—warning us we'd be going down next.

We ran in packs, shirts sticking to our backs, shorts riding up our thighs, hair plastered to our heads as the burning Florida sun beat down on us all. Of course, the Scar Squad stuck together and made the most of it, because that's how we rolled.

You and Frankie barreled through the crowd, parting the seas of stay-at-home moms with their double-stacked strollers, college kids on first dates, senior citizens with pity and whimsy radiating from their eyes as they tried to remember their past and forget their futures.

Ben and I followed in your wake, occasionally stopping to check out the habitat of whichever sleeping animal we happened to be passing. Because of course the majority of the animals were trying to beat the heat with midmorning naps.

"I think I'm actually melting." I pulled at the front of my shirt. It peeled away like it was an extra layer of skin.

"Could be worse."

"How?"

"We could be on the sixth-grade trip. They're at the park. Field day and lukewarm hot dogs." Ben pretended to shudder.

"I dunno, I wouldn't mind the slip-and-slide they always set up right about now. Just picture it." I waved my arms in the air and mimed belly-flopping onto one.

"You mean the extra-wide garbage bags they pretend are the real deal? My knees still have scars."

"Aww, Ben, don't be such a wuss. Scars give us mystery." I waved my right elbow with the puckered scar from surgery all those years ago when we collided on the playground.

"Is that what you call it? Mystery? Look, something's finally awake."

I followed his outstretched arm with my eyes. Beyond the short but five-inch-thick plexiglass wall, a family of river otters were chasing each other around the enclosure, diving in and out of the pond and having more fun than probably anything else in the zoo.

Which, let's face it, wasn't an impossible task. Still. Otters!

Peals of laughter escaped us as one of the babies jumped on its sibling's head, making them tumble from the sunning rock right into the water below.

I stole a glance at Ben from the corner of my eye. I had never really paid attention to how his cheeks dimpled when he laughed, but it was all I could look at now, and when he pushed the middle of his glasses up the bridge of his nose, a weird twist of my stomach made me grip the plexiglass harder than I intended. The rough edges dug into my palms. I welcomed the distraction. "Maybe this isn't so bad after all."

"I could think of worse." His nose crinkled along with the edges of his eyes.

At the time I wondered what he was picturing. I never did find out in the end because right then you and Frankie elbowed between us. I suppose you'd finally noticed we'd stopped following.

"Check it out. So cute!" Frankie clapped her hands, her pigtails bouncing around her shoulders as she balanced on the balls of her feet to get a better view.

You turned so your back was against the wall, occasionally looking at the otters over your shoulder. Your voice held a note of boredom when you muttered, "They're alright."

Ben rolled his eyes. "Better than anything I've seen so far."

"That isn't saying much."

"True." I shrugged. It wasn't like we really had any other options. Everything else was hiding away or passed out.

"Anyone want to have some fun?"

We all looked at you. Frankie said, "Let's."

"Okay, follow me."

So we did. Because we always did. We raced along the sidewalk to the primate habitat to swing from the monkey bars placed along the edged pathways, calling out to the gorillas to wake up and swing with us.

A large silverback sat in a corner, sniffing a finger, looking terribly unimpressed with our behavior. You dropped from the bars and stared unblinking at him. Benjamin took advantage of the distraction and swung to the ground, tackle-diving for you. You began to wrestle, pulling out of each other's locks, each determined to bring the other down.

Frankie and I traded bets on who'd win. She called out for you as I cheered Ben on.

Your head shot up, eyes narrowing.

I gulped. Apparently you didn't appreciate the lack of sisterly support.

An evil smile grew on your face. "Come here, Case. Join in."

"Uh, nope." I held up my hands, backing away slowly.

"Scared?"

"Nope."

"Aw, come *onnn*, Case. We can get him. Me and you." Ben shifted to the left and lowered down with his arms spread open wide like he was trying to corral the both of us.

"I think it's a trap." I took another step back.

On the other side of the path, Frankie called out, "Oh, don't mind me. I'll just be over here, blending in with the pavement or something." Frankie climbed a bench and sat on the back of it. Feet tapping impatiently as she waited for us to declare a winner so we could get to more interesting things.

None of us took the bait or tried to pull her into the match. Not after last time. You still had two fading indentations on your arm where her teeth had dug in. In general, Frankie was a pretty tough chick. But that year she drew the line when it came to wrestling or made sure we paid the price for it. So we stopped including her, which was fine by me. I remember I was more than happy for her to sit this one out. One less person to take down.

Even then, the odds were not in my favor. Not unless I could turn one of ya. "Come on, Benny, come to the dark side."

You paused. "Uh, we're the dark side, dork."

"*Pfft*. Okay, Han Slowmo and Luke Suckwalker."

The moment you shared a look and moved forward as one I knew I was going to be toast. So I did the only thing anyone with a brain would do. I ran. Backward. And when I turned to make a better escape, remember what happened?

I fell.

Right. Into. The. Trash. Can.

One second, I'm ready to take on the world. Next, I'm flying tip over tail toward epic proportions of humiliation.

And then it got worse.

When I tried to pull myself out, I realized I'd become stuck. The smell was awful. The fact that it was, like, the hottest day ever did me NO favors. Scents of rotting bananas and unidentifiable baby foods hid a faint layer of what I prayed was not a dirty diaper. My fingers grasped a used Popsicle stick and something gross and slimy.

"Help. Get me out of here!"

Pressure on my calves as hands wrapped around them calmed me slightly, but the full belly laughter that was amplified within my tin dome made me almost puke. I decided perhaps I was better right where I was.

"We're trying, Case! Brace yourself in three, two, one, heave—"

Just like that, I sprang out of the bin like a Pop-Tart.

"Oh, oh no!" Frankie covered her mouth, trying her hardest not to laugh.

You on the other hand waved your cell in my face. "Smile."

"You dick!" I reached for your phone and missed. "Why would you take a pic of me? Like this?"

"Oh, don't worry, I didn't take a pic."

Relief flooded through me. "Whew, for a second there I thought—"

"Ha. I filmed the entire thing." You danced around me, holding the cell high. "Oh, I can't wait to post this. It's going to be great. You'll die when you see."

I pictured every seventh-grade face on the bus watching the clip on repeat as we rode home. "Not if I'm already dead."

You laughed.

It was more than I could handle. "Changed my mind. I'll stay alive for now, but I wouldn't be so sure about your own life-span, bro, because if you even think of posting that video anywhere? I swear on the Squad I *will* kill you." I attempted to pull a stray banana peel off my shoulder and cringed.

"Don't worry, I've got your back." Frankie winked at me and then turned. "Oh, Sammy? Come here for a minute."

"Heck no. This is pure gold right here." You ran without a backward glance.

"I'm so screwed," I mumbled to no one in particular.

"Not yet." Frankie took off on the chase and you disappeared around the corner.

She always came to my defense. Still does, ya know. No matter what. Even against you. I love her so much for that. I'd give anything to hear you two argue again. Anything.

I stopped paying attention to you two when I heard someone walking toward me.

"Don't even." I flicked some nachos off the front of my shirt and glared at Ben.

He paused, less than a foot away. "Easy there, killer. I just want to help." His voice lifted with laughter but his eyes were sincere, and let's face it, I didn't have many options for help at the moment.

So I swallowed what was left of my pride and allowed him to detach as much garbage from my clothes as was humanly possible.

"I can't believe my brother is such a douche."

Ben reached for something in my hair. His face came close to mine and his words tickled my cheek. "We all know being a douche is one of Sammy's better qualities."

I giggled.

"Think he'll really post the video?"

We stared at each other in contemplation. For a second, the world stood still. I tried not to flinch as his fingers brushed against the tip of my ear, but I couldn't help myself when my breath hitched.

Before either of us could figure out what was happening, the warning thrum of a group of kids heading our way hit our ears.

"Shit. They're all gonna know now." I sighed in defeat. Preparing myself for an onslaught of teasing.

"Follow me." Ben grabbed my hand. The spell between us broke when he pulled me toward a building I hadn't noticed before. The FAMILY BATHROOM sign above the door was a welcoming beacon of hope.

"Okay. I'll go wash, you keep everyone at bay." I fidgeted with my clothes. What was once a white shirt with thin black pinstripes now resembled a trash tie-dye.

"I don't think washing is gonna cut it. Here." Before I could stop him, Ben took his still miraculously white plain tee off and handed it to me. He was wearing a black ribbed tank underneath and I couldn't help but zero in on how cut his arms were becoming since he'd taken up boxing last year.

"You're going to get carded on dress code." I paused. Hesitant to accept anything that could get him in trouble.

"Nah. I'll blame it on the sun. Heatstroke. Now hurry. We're almost out of time."

He was right.

I hoped my smile truly managed to convey my gratitude.

When I returned after a quick sink-shower extravaganza that included fully rinsing my hair with hand soap, I was ready to face the world again. Yeah, the shirt fit a lot tighter than I wished it did. And yeah, there was a huge chance Frankie had failed her mission and I'd end up the laughingstock of the day anyway. But for some reason, right then, none of it mattered. Because Ben never left my side. And when I walked out of that bathroom he was still waiting.

And that was the day I fell for good.

Bam.

No turning back.

Sooooo . . . What do you think is the best way to ask if he'd be into an open relationship? Not only that, but one with our very best of best friends?

When you're going for greatness, shoot for the stars, right? Maybe I'll meet you there in the end after all.

Over and out—

Casey Jones

CouRage—

You can find it in liquid form
But beware, I heard side effects may vary
Words spew from the mouths of frothing teens
filled with hormones that clash
Together
A punk show, and we are the circle
Arms flailing, legs kicking
As we try to comprehend
Why
Everything in our lives feels so
Important
Immediate
Irreplaceable
We are eternal and we will never die
Until we do
So we take the biggest of chances
With the promise of little payoff
So we can get off
Behind the bushes of a backyard bbq
Or in the arms of another choice
Who cares who we hurt
All that matters is now
Here
With you
And you

And sometimes no one

Because when you're invincible

Is there really anyone out there

With the power to tell you no

To keep you from your quest

If that's what you want?

No.

We are young

We are invincible

We are eternal

So we go for it.

Even when we know it will break us down.

Because you only live once

Why waste any of the ride?

Hear us roar and get the fuck out of the way.

DEAR SAMMY,

Sooooo, yeah. I know I've been stalling about going into detail on a few important life events recently. The obvious one is my call to Ben. Which . . . hasn't *exactly* happened. Yet. Before you give me a big old *I told you so,* it's not like I haven't tried. It's just, between his work schedule and *all* the stuff going on here, our calls haven't been long enough for me to feel comfortable spilling my heart via a phone call. Yet.

Every day at Nonna's is emotionally draining to the point where I can't see straight. And *maaaybe* that has something to do with the fact that I'm getting loaded again. And maybe, more importantly, I don't want to talk to him when I'm high. As we both know, conversations while high are a lot different than conversations while stoned. Can't drop squishy love bombs on two Oxys and a Xanax. Believe me. I know.

And don't get pissed. I plan to stop taking them again once we get home. The stress has been too much lately and I needed something to settle my nerves. You think it's a weak excuse? Maybe. But you don't get to judge *me* on shit like *this* anymore. Besides, once this bottle is gone it's not like I can re-up anyway.

Now that we've graduated I don't even know if my hookup took off for college or what, and I'm not at the point of using where I *need* to go and find a new dealer. So sooner or later hopefully I can just detox for good or whatever. Will that need change when I'm sitting there without any pills? Maybe. Possibly. Hopefully not.

I'll jump that hurdle when the time comes, I suppose.

Then there's the *other* massive thing I've been putting off telling you. If I wait any longer I'm going to get to the end of the journal, wuss out, and burn it. That can't happen because I owe it to you . . . to me, to talk about something that went down earlier this summer.

Here's the deal, it's very difficult, almost impossible to write about this particular day. The day that was *supposed* to be *our* rite of passage into the big bad adult world.

Graduation.

But ever since Dad and I visited Nonno's grave I feel a bit braver about exploring my feelings. I'm going to try and tell you what graduation was like. Bear with me. I might not be able to once I start. But I swear, I'm going to try my hardest.

I think the most difficult part of the day was walking across the stage. If you were still here we would have been called up to walk one right after the other. Me first, of course, because alphabetical over age, braah. Except I didn't get to enjoy that because, of course, it was only me up there.

Grabbing my diploma.

Leaving school behind. Leaving you behind.

It's so weird, you know. I keep getting older and you're just staying the same damn age in my head. What's it going to be like when I'm thirty? Sixty? Will I still be able to talk to you like this or will it not work because I'll feel like I'm talking to a grandkid? Ew.

I can't even try to picture over forty years on this planet without you.

It's impossible to picture even two years on earth without you, even though it's coming up in a few months.

Holy shit. I cannot get over the fact you're not my older brother anymore. Like I'm almost two YEARS older. It's not right, Sammy. It's just not right.

So yeah, graduation . . .

"Bean, you're going to be late," Dad called from somewhere in the house.

Frankie wrinkled her nose and said, "You'd think he'd know by now you are irrevocably, perpetually, late to any- and everything that matters."

I threw a mascara-lined tissue at her.

"Time is made up. Maybe I'm early and everyone else is late."

"That . . . doesn't even make sense."

"Does to me."

"'Cause you're a weirdo."

I shrugged. "Maybe. Now help me finish my makeup before Pops sends in reinforcements." My meds had kicked in a little bit ago so I was finally able to get through most of the morning without crying. Ben and Frankie spent the night. It was nice. Almost normal. We hadn't really gotten to spend much time together lately. First I'd had the freak-out about FEELINGS and then I had the hospital stay and since I'd been back, well, as I told you before, Mom 'n' Dad thought it'd be best if I had a few days to recover by myself.

Which is unusual for them. They typically beg the Squad to hang out. It's less quiet when everyone is here. Less likely we'll slip and fall and not be able to get back up. The silences aren't as long when Squad is over. They still exist, just not in such an all-encompassing brain-and-body-shutdown way like what happens when we're unexpectedly reminded of you.

As Frankie and I got ready, Ben was somewhere in the living room waiting. Probably watching sportsball with Dad while Mom finished putting finishing touches on the cake she'd made the night before. Later on, we were all headed to Ben's house, along with Frankie's family, for a graduation dinner.

Frankie leaned in. "Close your eyes, I'm almost done."

My heart sped up as her breath tickled my nose. Peppermint. Always peppermint. Her favorite kind of gum. Her breath came in short bursts. I could picture her expression easily. The tip of her tongue sticking out as she concentrated with an artist's eye.

She can make anything beautiful, be it a scrap of fabric and a boxful of unmatching buttons or fancy silks and tulle, or even, in this case, a blank face and makeup. Everything she touches just seems to get a little brighter. Lovelier.

"Finished."

I opened a sliver of an eye and peeked in the mirror. Almost not recognizing the person staring back. "Wow, Frankie."

"I'm pretty badass, I know." The grin took over her face. "Can you believe we're graduating?"

She squeezed my hands and leaned in to put her forehead to mine. "It's finally happening. The world is our oyster and we get to start shucking."

"I don't think that's quite how the saying goes." I sniffed. My eyes were starting to water because in this moment, as amazing as it was, I really, really wanted you to be talking shit, teasing us, complaining about my slowness. Something. Anything.

"Oh. I'm sorry. I didn't mean to mess—" Tears ran down my cheeks, taking all of Frankie's delicate work right along with them.

"Oh, babe, don't worry. Here, easy fix." Frankie sniffed back a few tears of her own.

She grabbed a few more tissues and softly brought them to my face, dabbing the sadness away. "Can you believe Mom and Dad are in town for an entire month? I'm so happy they get to go to graduation. For a while there we didn't think Dad would get time off." Her lip quivered.

"That's so awesome. I'm super stoked they're here for you." I wrapped my arms around her waist and gave her a huge hug.

It was Frankie's biggest wish to have them in town for this moment. If they'd screwed it up I might have had to go seek revenge. They did that sometimes. Made promises, then bailed. In fact, Frankie wouldn't let herself believe they were coming until they'd landed in town the day before.

Now she could breathe.

Admission time. I know y'all debated moving to New York together after graduation.

No. I'm not mad. Really.

I don't think she planned to tell me since, well . . . but it slipped out one night when we were talking about how life's changed since you've been gone. And at first, I was furious you two would plan a future without me, but I get it.

I do.

You've always been looking for a way out of here, even when we were little. I've always wanted to stay.

Even now.

So who better to fly away with than one of your best friends. Like I said, I'm not pissed. I get it.

The future scares me. Always has. My perfect dream would be the Squad in our twenties all living together, going to the beach every day, living off bs jobs and having the time of our lives. Just the four of us.

And then we could grow up and have careers and maybe even families, and all the other crap that goes with being adults. But I wanted a few more years of Squad first, ya know?

By freshman year I understood it was a pipe dream. Ben had already started prepping for Harvard. Frankie had her top three list of fashion schools lined up and was creating her portfolio. And your plans for becoming a big famous DJ? You always said first you'd take over the Orlando clubs, and then? The world.

I bet you would have too.

Just so you know, Mom and Dad didn't get rid of your CDJs. Or your record collection. Or your turntables!

Maybe that's what I'll do. I've always found such peace when I dance. I haven't in forever. Maybe I should start again. When we get home, I'll dust off your CDJs and see if I can come up with a decent set. I think you'd get a kick out of that. Or you'd try to kick my butt for touching your stuff. Either way, yeah. I'm gonna do it.

Sooo. As I was saying, graduation. Ugh.

My fingertips brushed against the hundreds of iridescent sequins that made up Frankie's graduation dress as my hand traveled to the small of her back. When I let it rest there, it felt like there was no other place it could ever belong. A small chill ran through me. How had I not noticed this feeling until recently?

I let go. Confused. Curious.

"Thanks. You really worked your magic this time." I studied myself in the mirror.

"Well, I had a pretty spectacular canvas to begin with. But you know you're beautiful, dummy."

"Yeah, I know."

At that, she flicked my knee and stood up. "Come on, we really are gonna be late."

"Right behind you." I stood and pulled my dress down. It was a cream-and-gold mini with a flared skirt that took ages to find. But once we did, I knew there could be no other dress for this occasion. It hugged me in all the right places and the way the skirt swirled with every step I took, well, I felt like I looked like a princess. Which was good because on the inside I felt like a monster.

We locked hands, our fingers twining around each other, and started to leave my room. At the last second, I stopped. You weren't able to be with us in person but I needed to take a part of you along anyway.

I rushed back to my desk and snatched a pic of us that had made a home on the mirror since we were nine. You know the one. Yours is probably still on your mirror too. We all had a print. The four of us—the newly claimed Scar Squad—looking like run-over trash with bumps and bruises and casts and black eyes, sitting alongside the curb of our street.

It's my favorite photo.

We were cheesing hard, arms flung over shoulders. It's like you can hear the laughter, just looking at it. Of course, you and I were in the middle. Always sandwiched by Ben and Frankie.

You know what's loopy? I swear to God, Sammy, when I grabbed the pic, for a second, I felt the warm weight of your shoulder against mine, and it was like you never left.

"Hey, Frankie, can you give me just one sec? I promise I'll be right out."

She came to see what I was up to, looking over my shoulder. When she saw what I was holding, she let out a huge sigh. One of her fingers traced our faces in the photo.

She whispered, "Bet you would've done something so dang stupid today, broki. Like throw your hat at Mr. Walker or do a backflip off the stage. Wish I could've seen it, so I could beat you down for screwing up a perfect moment, dummy." She sniffed. Then mumbled something I couldn't make out.

I turned my head. We were face-to-face. So close. Before I could stop myself I quickly kissed her. It was almost nothing. Just a peck. Something we'd done a million times before. Still, in that moment, that tiny touch of her lips set me on fire. "He might not be with us, but he'll never be gone." Then I hugged her.

"Never." Frankie let go and walked to the door. Her face relaxed, losing its lost look. "Seriously, two seconds or they're all going to freak, k?"

"I won't even be that long."

The door shut, leaving me and a lifetime of memories alone. I lifted one corner of my mattress and pulled an almost-empty pill bottle from its hiding place. Carefully, I grabbed one pill and then broke it in half. I needed *something* to get me through the day but I didn't want to numb all the pain.

Not on a day like this. I deserved to feel whatever happiness I could gain from this event. Even when it was wrapped in anguish.

You'll be happy to know the rest of the day was perfectly uneventful. At some points it was even nice. For what it's worth, graduation is actually pretty boring. I think I told you that before, but I really want to emphasize you didn't miss much AT ALL.

It's a lot of sitting around and waiting and waiting and waiting and *then* they're calling your name after an alumnus delivers a forty-two-day-long speech, and *then* we get the valedictorian speech—which, by the way, Ben fucking NAILED it—I almost felt like I could go out into the world and be anyone by the time he said his closing words: "We can't edit our past, but with every new dawn we *can* revise our future. So never stop writing until you create the story *you* deserve."

I think he meant that part for us. Like we can't change what happened to you. But it doesn't mean our lives end with yours. Even if it feels like it often. And I mean, *come on,* if you couldn't be valedictorian then who else deserved to be up there? Right?!

But then it's more waiting, and name-calling, and *then* in less than two minutes, you're handed a diploma, a shake of the hand, and BAM.

You're an adult.

Officially free. So they say.

I had a small panic attack when I got back to my seat. The air was so hard to pull into my mouth. Like it was purposely trying to suffocate me. That's when I ate two Xanax. A few minutes later the pain numbed and I could breathe again. I could go back to paying attention while the rest of the class finished walking.

Sometimes you just have to push through in whatever way you can, ya know?

Ben could tell I was freaking. He was in the same row as me and he asked Patrice if they could switch seats. I think he saw how bad I was losing it. She said sure, and then he was holding my hand, telling me everything was going to be okay.

I believed him.

It was difficult to smile as the people behind us took their turns walking down the aisle. Until they called Frankie's name. Then I was standing, screaming until my voice was hoarse. She looked like a movie star as she grabbed her diploma, and when our eyes met, it was just me and her and Ben in the room.

No one else mattered in that moment. They never did.

Except for you. But you gave up that privilege, didn't you? Funny how you still take up the majority of our days. Our thoughts. Our feelings.

You loved being the center of attention at all times. Well, guess what, you still are.

But you didn't get to take graduation from us. Not all of it. That victory was ours. Different without you, for sure, but ours nonetheless.

I'm ashamed and guilty and proud and happy and depressed about it all at once. It's so weird to be happy *and* sad at the same time. Dunno if you ever got to experience a moment like that. Wouldn't recommend.

And then we partied until dawn. Everyone was so relieved to just live and celebrate without the guilt for once. We all wanted to squeeze out every single last drop of that normal and suck it down until there was nothing left.

After a while, Frankie and I ran off to roll a joint. The moment we lit it Ben appeared, it's like he's got nug radar.

The three of us passed it around. Telling our favorite moments from high school. You were in a lot of them. But also, you were missing from a ton of them. It was weird to discover how many good Sammy-less experiences I've had since you've been gone.

I won't lie, there are days when it feels like there aren't any. But when I really think about it, there are. And that's comforting.

By the end of the joint, we were well and truly toasty. Someone lit a bonfire and the remaining Scar Squad circled around it. Earlier that morning—before we got ready for graduation—we wrote to you. It wasn't a typical journal burning, but we knew you needed to be included, so we poured out all our secret dreams we'd had for you on paper and let you know you'd never be forgotten.

When the time was right, we threw the letters into the fire and watched as they burned away. I shit you not, the second they became ash, a gust of wind lifted the flames higher and I swear I saw particles float straight up into the sky. Heading right your way.

Then we stole a bottle of wine and got wasted. Trust me, wine sucks. And mixing wine and mojitos? Forget about it. I don't think I've ever woken up with such a bad hangover.

Anyway, that pretty much sums up what you missed.

Sorry it took so long to tell you. I guess I feel guilty because we had a good time. I know deep down you'd want us to, but it still feels wrong. Bad. Like I'm betraying you somehow.

It's difficult talking to you about these kinds of things. I wonder if it will ever get any easier?

Doubtful.

To be perfectly honest, I'm afraid of life getting easier without you. Does that make any sense at all? Maybe I'm just broken.

Hope I figure out how to fix myself before it's too late.

Over and out—

Casey Jones

DEAR SAMMY,

Why can't I ever get a break? I'd settle for a small crack. A fracture of good luck, if you will. Instead, I am showered with *sucks to be you* moments. Last night I pretty much had the worst phone call ever and now I'm on the flight from Hell. (SPOILER ALERT: I TALKED TO BEN!! But it didn't *exactly* go the way I hoped.) Now it's two hours before dawn, we're on a plane back home, and I'm fuming.

Here's the deal. I'm stuck in between a screaming baby and stressed-out mom (not their fault) and a super-nosy and very vocal businessman (totally his fault) and so my hopes of catching anything close to sleep were destroyed before we left the runway. Which is balls because after last night's call I didn't sleep a wink. My brain just kept processing the conversation, wondering what I could have said differently. If I should have even called in the first place . . . It's been about an hour since we departed, but before I tell you about the last of what happened at Nonna's, let me try to paint you a picture of what I've had to deal with so far this morning because I'm dying for some sympathy here, dude.

In a few hours I have to face both Frankie and Ben, and I feel so stressed that even my eyes hurt. Like what the fuck? How am I supposed to talk about important shit when I'm this frustrated? And on top of that I slipped into my stash about ten mins ago and now I'm super regretting my decision because what if they can tell I'm fucked up when I see them? Then I'll have to tell them. . . .

In fact. I'm gonna text right now and say forget about picking me up at the airport. Thank God Dad lemme get Wi-Fi for the flight home too. No way I want to see them at the luggage pickup. I'll tell them to get me at nine and we can go get breakfast and *then* surf instead of meeting earlier for a dawn sesh. That should give me a few extra hours to get my head together. BRB.

Okay. Done. I'm putting my phone on airplane mode because I don't even want to see their response yet. As I was saying, takeoff was chaos. I popped in my earbuds and pulled out my favorite book in the hopes I could escape reality for at least a few minutes, but I shit you not, this guy to my right felt the need to lean in with his late-night garlic breath just popping and stare at *my* book. He *finally* leaned away from me—so no more stinkbreath—but then the fucker opened his legs wide until his knee jammed into mine, because of course he had no comprehension of the personal space of others when his comfort was at stake.

And I did nothing about it, because it was a lot easier than doing something. Shocking? Not so much. I've been walking through the world as a girl for eighteen years, I know when to tread lightly even though it sucks to avoid deserved conflict. But it did make me wonder what the man would have done or said if you were here instead of me?

Anyway, that all happened in the first hour. Now the dude is passed out, snoring loud enough to shake us out of the sky, and here I am writing to you so I don't pinch his nose and get booted off the plane.

So where was I? Remember when I said calling Frankie was going to be one of the hardest things ever? Well, calling Benjamin was equally difficult. More so, maybe. In fact, I didn't quite build up the nerve to call until about an hour before dinner last night.

It couldn't be put off any longer. In retrospect, I probably should have waited until we saw each other to explain what I was stressed about. A talk like this deserves a face-to-face conversation. With both of them. If I had to do it all over again I'd wait. Especially because I don't know if I've totally screwed up any chance Ben and I had to be together. Maybe I'm reading too much into it. Ugh. I just wish I knew where I stood. Guess I'll find out soon. Heh. ☺

It basically went like this:

"Heeeey, Benny boy, how's it been?"

"New phone, who's this?" He chuckled but it was strained.

I cringed. If he only knew why I'd be stalling. I rolled my head once to try and relieve the tension in my neck and mumbled, "Yeah, I know. I've been the worst friend ever."

"Absolute garbage."

"Trash."

"Yesterday's leftovers."

"Hey now, that's going too far." Okay. So far, so good. Maybe he isn't upset that I've been sorta ghosting him after all. I can work with this.

"My bad. Besides, it isn't *all* your fault. Work is slammed now the summer rush is hitting. I can't wait until hurricane season is in full swing, might finally get some days off. Haven't been out in a heartbeat."

"Yeah, *still*. I coulda made an effort to find time for more than a three-minute chat when we *did* connect." My free hand slid from tapping a drumline on my thigh to picking at the stray thread on Nonna's quilt.

"Eh, it's all good. Anyway, you're home tomorrow! Want to see if we can get a sunrise sesh in? I can hit up Frankie if you're down and we could swing by, grab your board, and meet you at the airport?"

I pictured us seeing each other for the first time after asking if they'd be down for a poly relationship. Heat hit my cheeks. What if he says no? Fuck. Crapnuts. This is so difficult. How do I find the right words to say I like you, let's date, *annnd* can I date Frankie too, by the way. I can't keep stalling. I need to find out if he likes me enough to share. Which did not make this conversation easy, Sammy. At all.

My pause as I tried to figure out what to say next was becoming infinite so I inhaled and just blurted, "That would be sweet. Um. Before that can happen, I think there's something we need to talk about."

"Yeah? I know you've been going through hell. Don't worry, I haven't stopped thinking about you, and I can't wait to ask if you want to—"

"Benjamin, before you ask what I think you're about to ask, remember when we promised we'd never lie to each other? Always tell the truth? Even when it hurts?"

"Yeah, Case. That's what I'm trying to do."

I reached for the drawstrings of his hoodie, which I'd put on for courage, and pulled them tight. As soon as the fabric closed around my head I could smell the faint scent of him and my nerves settled slightly. "Hear me out, because there's been a glitch in our scheduled program. When we kissed, it rocked me. Like I'd been dreaming of that moment forever . . ."

"Me too."

My palms felt clammy as I searched for the right words. I'd never done anything like this, and Benjamin wasn't just anyone. He was one-third of the Scar Squad. My Best Friend Forever. Someone I loved unconditionally.

If I wanted this relationship to work I needed to be as truthful as possible in that moment. There was no way we could become a healthy couple—regardless of whether it ended up including Frankie or not—if I kept hiding how I feel. Because left unresolved, those feelings were going to fester and infect all the love building between us.

I prayed he wouldn't hate me forever and said, "It *was* pretty perfect. But there's a problem."

"Uh-huh. I see what you're doing. I mean, I *suppose* I could find some time to practice with you. Make sure the next time is *actually* perfect." There was a chuckle in his voice.

Before I could stop myself I said, "You'd do that? Make time out of your booked schedule just for me?" I bit my lip. It was so easy to fall back into simple teasing and flirting, which was exactly the opposite of where this conversation needed to be. Serious conversations deserved serious intentions.

"I'll always make time for you, Case."

Why does he have to be such a gem? A true fucking jewel, and here I was possibly turning him into a piece of coal. I didn't want to snake his luster, but in the end, I knew asking him to share his heart might make his shine dim. I didn't want to, Sammy, I swear. But I *needed* to.

"Benjamin Dean, I like you. A fuck-ton. More than you probably even know. But . . ."

"But?" For the first time in our conversation he didn't sound so sure of himself.

"But I *think* I also like Frankie."

"*Whaaat?* Did I just hear you right?" Ben's voice rose like two octaves.

My shoulders crept up to my ears. "Shit. That's a lie. I *do* like Frankie. I don't even know how or why or when. Well, I do know when. I noticed things were changing for a few months now, but I really figured it out like five minutes after you and I kissed at the spodie, and I saw her all arms-and-elbows-deep with Raine . . . and the two of them were sucking face, and I swear to God I've never been so angry and it was just. Bam. I knew. You know?"

"No. I don't know. What exactly are you trying to say right now, Case?"

"I like you both. That's why I'm trying to explain even though I'm *apparently* not doing a good job of it. And I hate telling you like this because the last thing I want to do is hurt you and cause tension between all of us, and the most fucked thing is that I still like you *SO DAMN MUCH*. I do. It's just—"

"You like Frankie too. Yeah, I clocked that the first time you said it." His voice definitely had a rough edge to it. One I didn't recognize.

"I get you're angry. You must hate me. I sorta hate myself right now and if there was any way I could change things or, like, make myself not feel this way, then I would in a heartbeat because, I mean, let's be honest, I've crushed on you for almost a lifetime and never in a million years did I ever think you'd like me too. And now this? But feelings. Heh. What do they say? You can't control your heart or whatever . . ."

"Case. Let me get this straight. For a while you wondered if you liked both of us but you definitely knew after we kissed the first time, and then again when we kissed at your house? And it didn't once cross your mind to tell me *waaaay* back then?"

"My nonno died. I—"

"Okay. I'll even give you that. Maybe. But it's been weeks."

"I know but . . ." I paused because nothing I said in the moment would be a good-enough excuse.

Ben didn't wait for an answer. "Like, you've had more than enough time to process this. You do realize you've been stringing me along, right? Since we last saw each other I've pictured us turning into something more, which is obviously *not* what you had in mind."

"No, Ben! I still do have that in mind."

"Doesn't feel that way."

"It's true, though. I want us to be more."

"But you like Frankie."

"Yes."

"So how exactly can we ignore that?"

"Well, we can't. But I do think this can still work if you just trust me and hear me out."

There was so much silence between us at that moment and it was *deafening*.

Sammy! I felt like I was betraying him. Even right now, a whole ten hours later, I still feel like I fucked him over and I'm pretty much the worst friend ever, much less possible future girlfriend. If he never wants to talk to me again I'd understand. Guess I'll find out sooner than later. What if he doesn't even show up with Frankie? Holy crap, I wouldn't be able to handle that. I really really hope he comes over.

Damn, I can already feel this pill. Shit. This morning is going to suck so bad. I just know it. Where was I? Oh yeah. The worst part of the call . . .

Tears welled in my eyes. I was totally the bad guy here.

Ben sighed. "This is a lot to take in. I gotta go."

His voice already sounded distant. Like he was mentally preparing to pull away. Crap.

"Yeah. I get that. Just don't disappear on me, k? I need you in my life, Ben. I swear. I don't know, but what do you think about an open relationship? I've had some time to think it over and that's what I want."

"Must be nice. I haven't had any time to think."

Ouch. that hurt. I tried one more time to make some sense. "I'll give you all the time you need to consider, as long as you give me that. Don't pull away. I want you *and* Frankie. And that's probably the most selfish thing I've ever said, but I can't picture it working any other way."

"Case, you're killing me here."

"I'm not trying to. I mean, do you want me to lie? To pretend? I don't even know if things will work out with Frankie."

"So you've already talked to her about this? Of course you have."

"Well, not *exactly*. Some. I mean she didn't say she *didn't* like me, but she hasn't actually said she *does* either. In fact, she wants to talk in person about it later too. Ugh, I'm rambling. Sorry. With my luck it will all blow up in my face and I'll lose both of you." My voice caught in a sob as my deepest fear broke the surface. "I just don't think I could go on without you both. It's already so difficult without—I—"

"You're not losing me, Case. I just need some time to process. I'll talk to you later. Swear."

"Ben, don't kill me, but if you aren't still totally pissed tomorrow, why don't you pick Frankie up and meet me at the airport like you wanted, and then we can talk about this in person."

"Shit, I dunno. If you're scheming, we're all in trouble."

With that one small jab, a little bit of our old easiness fell back into place.

"I think it will be good."

"That's what you always say."

"And I'm usually right."

"Ha."

I waited for him to say more. Something. Anything. Just when I thought that was it, he said, "Okay. Fine. I'll see you tomorrow. But don't expect me to like it."

I kept the cell to my ear and sat in the silence as I processed everything. He'd be there. Frankie too. And that was all I could ask of them. Hopefully I wouldn't destroy the last ten years of memories we held together just because I couldn't make up my mind.

In all the years we'd known each other, Benjamin had never broken his word. So why for the first time did I not one hundred percent believe him? Nonna's advice swirled into my thoughts, her voice a salve on the open wound that was my heart. *It doesn't have to be one or the other. You're young, cara, this is the time to find yourself. Try dating both of them and see what happens. You might even surprise yourself.*

After the initial shock fades, will either of them be up for a poly relationship? Will I?

I think I am, Sammy. I can picture dating them at the same time, and it fits, ya know? My biggest worry is will I be okay if they want to date other people too?

I know, I know, I'll have to learn to temper my own jealousy first.

I'm not ready to give Ben up. Not even for a chance at Frankie's heart.

When we hung up, the cell dropped out of my hand to the bed and I walked over to my suitcase. It sat empty beside the dresser. Well, almost empty. Nerves hit me, and I flew to the door and locked it. No way did I want any uninvited guests peeking in on me at this moment. Once I felt a little safer in my surroundings, I rummaged through the hidden zipper in my suitcase and grabbed my emergency stash. A half-filled pill bottle rattled in my hand. Carefully, I opened the childproof lid and pinched the answer to my stress.

Before I placed the pill on my tongue, I closed my eyes and made a wish. *I wish I was strong enough to get through life without a crutch, but I'm not. Not yet.* The pill went down my dry throat uncomfortably.

Carefully I hid my stash back in the secret pocket and sat on the edge of the bed to wait. Soon my worries would feel far away. By dinnertime I'd be riding a synthetic wave, all the sharp edges dulled as the high took over. My worries and stress would lessen to an annoying pulse, a reminder that nothing I did would ever fully take them away, but at least they wouldn't be center stage.

Is that how it started for you? I think the first time I stole the bottle I'd found in your closet after . . . was just so I could see what all the hype was about. What had pulled you away from us. Back then, I promised myself I'd never take more than one, but sometimes the urge to go even further hits in a way that can't be denied.

When the effects finally kicked in, my shoulders relaxed and a sleepy smile hit. Double vision played with my sight, and my fingers trailed along the comforter, all senses on alert, albeit a slow-motion alert.

"Casey, dinnertime," Mom called out as she passed in the hall.

She would be devastated if she knew. I straightened my shirt, stood up, and unlocked the door.

It's been scarily easy to pretend to be sober. Then again, maybe everyone else is so neck-deep in their own pain, they refuse to see what's right in their face.

If you were here, you'd know what to say. How to help me. Do I have a problem? AM I becoming an addict? I can't follow you, Sammy. I'm scared.

I'm so alone. Even if you didn't know to help, at least you'd be by my side. And we could suffer together. Guess I'm just going to have to learn to do all this on my own because I'm not sure I can find the courage to tell Ben and Frankie whether we start dating or not.

Telling you this stuff is exhausting. I think I'm going to try to take a nap. Wish me luck!

Over and out—

Casey Jones

DEAR SAMMY,

Okay, I'm sorry I shut down sometimes. I don't mean to. It's just that every once in a while when I'm writing I forget we're not talking. Like, I'll sit there and wait for you to answer and it hurts so much when there isn't one.

I bet you understand.

Anywho, it seems like all I talk about lately is doom and gloom. I hardly ever invite you to see the good bits of our family. I was so busy telling you the fail of my call with Ben earlier I forgot to tell you what else happened with Nonna and Aunt Sofia. I've got half an hour until we land and right now I'd rather not think about Frankie and Ben so lemme fill you in on some epic TEAM CARUSO moments. You would have loved every second. We had a wonderful adventure on our last day. We decided to go explore, so of course Nonna packed a picnic lunch to feed a small army, and we all piled into the rental minivan and set off for Great Smoky Mountains National Park.

Obviously, the almost-one-hundred-mile drive was filled with a thousand unimportant arguments—or as Nonna always calls them, *discussions*. But the *mostly* tongue-in-cheek fights became background noise to calm my nerves as I watched the scenery fly by. Every once in a while, I even joined in, but only when the conversations revolved around harmless things. Now that I'd made my decision to date both Frankie and Benjamin I felt somewhat protective of my choice. Also, I didn't want Sofia and Nonna getting into it again.

After a long hike, we sat at the base of a waterfall and Dad fanned out two massive blankets for us to sit on. I helped dish out the Tupperware full of antipasti, placing all the meats, cheeses, and olives on a tray. You know it doesn't matter if we're in the woods or in her dining room, Nonna's always prepared for a feast, lol.

Dad dragged a rectangular Tupperware close to him, a grin pulling up the side of one cheek.

"Whatcha got there?" I asked, leaning over his shoulder for a proper look.

"Keep your paws off my cannoli!" Dad frowned in an attempt to appear intimidating.

"I'll catch you slipping. Just wait."

Nonna *tsk*ed, as if we'd personally affronted her. "Stàtivi! There's enough for everyone."

Sofia huffed. "Have you seen Alesandro eat, Momma? He could easily pack in half that tub before you finished your first cannoli."

"As could you, sis."

They both stretched across the blanket to give each other a fist bump.

"I suppose it's our burden in life to always finish the meal, then." A sly light gleamed in Sofia's eyes as she continued, "How else are we going to keep these cushions so fluffy for times like these? I'm sure you don't mind the Caruso caboose, eh, Madison?"

Mom reached for a paper plate. "Well—"

"Mo-om, Sofia, ugh!"

Sofia smacked her butt jokingly, head tilted back as a peal of laughter left her lips. "The Caruso behind is a gift. Who wants to suffer needlessly on this uneven ground? Madison should consider herself lucky her man comes with a portable backrest!"

"I admit, Alesandro makes for an extremely comfortable pillow, among other things."

Dad winked at Mom. "Ah, see! I supply the softness to protect all your pointy bits. That's how we work so well together. Might have to test that theory later, my dear. Make sure it applies in all situations."

"Gross." I pretended to gag, but between you and me? It was refreshing to see them being so carefree again. They used to flirt and kid with each other all the time before . . . well, *before.* Now it's a rare event to even hear them laugh at the same time. This felt nice. Simple. Normal.

"You're lucky your genes lean toward our side, Casey," Sofia interrupted. "Could you imagine trying to sit on these rocks without some natural padding? Eh, not for me! I think this is why I'm a city girl. I'm in it for the furniture." She snorted as she laughed. Aunt Sofia's low throaty laugh is a balm to the soul. The kind that encourages others to join in. So of course we laughed along with her.

Remember how Nonna always says, *You have everything you need if you've got shelter, a good meal, good conversation, good company, and the joys of acquiring a great ass through such a lifestyle.*

Or Sofia's go-to, *With all the bullshit that comes at you in the world, there's nothing wrong with a little cushion to soften the ride.*

Our family dishes out some pretty good advice, if you ask me.

When we got back to Nonna's we spent some time packing. Then of course Nonna had to present us with her biggest feast yet. She made your favorite, butternut-squash-and-mushroom risotto with a mountain of Parmesan piled on top. Roasted an entire sea bass and a chicken. As well as her homemade arancini, and meatballs and gravy, and all the sardines you could eat.

After dinner, she took me aside and handed me a small square of silk. Something hard was wrapped up inside, but she'd tied it with ribbon and when I started to open it, she stopped me, closing her hand over mine.

"Not yet, cara. Save this for a rainy day. And then? Think of me, eh?" She reached up to pat my cheek, her eyes glistening with unshed tears.

I nodded, trying not to cry. "You gonna be okay up here? You could always come stay with us, you know."

"Oh, I know. But for now, I'd like to live in my memories a little while longer. I feel Stefano here. He's in the furniture. The air. I'm not ready to leave him just yet. Soon, though. I promise."

I understood.

"That isn't to say I won't be ready to make new memories soon. We cannot stay stagnant. That is how we lose our purpose. You and me? We are part of the field, not the castle. We are destined to bloom again. That is my promise to you, cara." She nodded to the painting that hung over the couch. The sepia one with the crumbling castle and fairy flower field.

"I hope so. I forget what it's like. Moving on."

"It's time, my dear. That's what Sammy would want. Deep down you know that too. You won't ever forget him but you cannot pause your own life. You just can't."

That's exactly what I've been doing since you've been gone. I don't know how to let you go . . .

She's right, though. At the time I didn't want to hear it, so I sighed. "I'll go see him when we get home. Promise."

It's been almost two years since I've returned to your grave. No one has pushed me. Not even on the anniversary of your death. But the time has come. I'll visit soon. Swear.

Nonna held my hand and squeezed. The silk felt cool against my palm.

Later on, when we were all saying our goodbyes and piling into the minivan, Aunt Sofia wrapped me in a ginormous bear hug. "I'll see you in a few weeks, kiddo. Remember, protect your heart, but do not hide it. K?"

"K. I didn't know you were coming for a visit!"

"Yup, big bro decided it's been way too long. So we booked my ticket after dinner. You can introduce me to your boyfriend. Or girlfriend, or whichever you end up with."

"Uh, first of all, you've met Ben and Frankie like a billion times. Second, what if I end up dating both?"

Sofia clucked her tongue. "If you do follow Momma's advice then I suppose you'll just have to reintroduce me to both. Whatever makes you happy."

And this is why I love our family so much. They just roll with it, ya know?

"Sweet! We'll all have to go to a show while you're out." We hadn't been to a concert in ages. Since music's her lifeblood, just like you, it never felt right asking her to go without you. For some reason it did then.

"Already looking up events," she said with a wink.

Nonna came by and kissed me on the cheek. "Did you pack your gift carefully?" She eyed my bulging backpack with uncertainty.

"I did. Thanks again, Nonna."

"Remember, don't open it until a rainy day."

"I won't. Are you coming out with Sofia next month?" It'd only been a few hours since she'd declared that she wanted to linger in the past for a while, but that was before Sofia had booked her ticket.

"She will be if I have anything to do with it." Sofia's voice held a note of authority.

"We shall see." Nonna nodded and blew me a kiss.

I'm happy that it was as close to a perfect day as I've had in forever. Especially after the anxiety-fest of last night's call.

Oh crap. Guess it's time to face reality again. The pilot just told us to prepare for landing. We're almost home. One way or another things between the Squad are going to change when we land. I'm terrified of what's to come.

Over and out—

Casey Jones

DEAR SAMMY,

Yeah. I know. I know. It's been almost an entire month since my last entry, but yo, there's been a lot going on.

Like so much that until today I didn't even know where to start.

I . . . I think I know where to start now.

This is the part where I'm supposed to tell you everything worked out perfectly. Like it does in a rom-com movie. You know, we all would live happily ever after with no more hiccups as the closing credits played. Maybe we'd high-five on the football field or take turns sharing super-romantic kisses at the next party while all our friends passed by in slo-mo. No one would leave, we'd all move into an apartment together, and the world could think whatever they wanted to.

No matter what, we would be absolutely happy. Together. All our issues would turn to dust.

Except coming home was nothing like that at all.

Nope.

Not even close.

And the worst part of what's been going on since my last entry is that Ben leaves for Harvard in less than two weeks. I'm devastated. And yet, also weirdly optimistic. The truth of the matter is I've got all the feels right now and I don't know how to process any of them.

But before I get to that MAJOR detail about Ben leaving, I guess I need to first explain what happened after we landed.

Shit, Mom's calling me. I'm supposed to go pick up Sofia and Nonna at the airport. I triple-dipple swear I will finish telling you what happened as soon as I get back.

But before I go, I just wanted to say that when I *did* see Frankie and Benjamin again nothing went like I expected it to.

And honestly?

Maybe that was a good thing.

Over and out—

Casey Jones

DEAR SAMMY,

I don't think I say this enough, but in some ways I'm pretty lucky. In other ways, there's a very real possibility I'm cursed. When I asked Nonna if she thought I was cursed she said, "Back in the homeland, curses hold a lot of power, so always have some olive oil, salt, and holy water at your disposal *juuust* in case. You never know when someone will come for you."

I'm not sure if she answered my question because she didn't *exactly* say I wasn't cursed. Who has it out for me anyway? Maybe Raine, I suppose.

Either way, after that horrific flight back (cursed), I felt pretty lucky I'd rearranged our plans so I could actually sober up a bit before they came over to our house.

The moment Frankie and Ben's faces came into view (not cursed) as they came into the house, I also felt hangry, nervous, excited, and overwhelmed. So I did what I do best. Concentrate on breathing.

Let me just say here and now, I am so sick and tired of paying attention to breathing; however, this time it was the only thing that kept me from running as far and as fast as I could away from the both of them.

Inhale. Exhale.

Step.

Inhale. Exhale.

Step.

When they walked in Dad mumbled a groggy hello and goodbye. Mom hardly waved, and said with a huge yawn, "Night, all. I'm hitting the sack."

"Sooo, no breakfast then?" I asked, trying to stall the inevitable.

"Babygirl, you're eighteen. You figure it out." She patted me on the shoulder, leaned down, and whispered, "Good luck," before wandering off to bed. Dad grabbed her hand, following alongside.

And then it was just the three of us.

Scar Squad.

My heart beat double-time at the sight of them. Until they stepped over the threshold and I saw with my own eyes that they were there, I still doubted if Ben would show up.

They both leaned in for a hug at the same time, tumbling onto the couch with me, which of course ended up with us all awkwardly tangled, arms and elbows, and something we'd done for forever now felt . . . weird.

Or maybe it was just me?

I kept wondering, was Ben holding me a little bit too tightly? Was Frankie's grip a little too loose?

"Case, you look good." Ben grabbed the back of his neck with a hand, head tilted as his eyes locked on mine, a slow half smile lifting his lips in a way that said he meant every single word.

Does he forgive me? He doesn't look pissed . . . or is he just trying to hide it? I peered at him to see if I could figure it out.

"I think she looks tired." Frankie frowned.

"She can look tired and good at the same time, dude."

"I suppose you're right."

Well, at least the news hadn't ruined their banter. Maybe I was the only one who was off. "Thanks for the observations, guys, so glad you care. Since Mom isn't cooking, can we grab breakfast before we hit the beach?"

"Cranky," Frankie said.

"Hangry," Ben said at the same time.

Sammy, in the ten years we've known each other I don't think there's ever been a more awkward silence than the one that kept building up around us that morning. It sucked. I really, really didn't want things to be weird between us. We needed to get back on track to figure out what our futures held now that *feelings* were involved.

So, of course, I did the opposite of getting back on track and pretended we were only friends, because ignoring reality seemed way easier. Especially at nine a.m. after a night of no sleep.

I know. I know. But I swear I'm not a wuss. You'll see what I mean in a few, promise.

I knew if we didn't go somewhere soon the silence was going to swallow us, so I pretended everything between us was copacetic and said, "Yes, I'm tired, cranky, and hangry, all while looking absolutely stunning because I'm one hundred percent that bitch. And you're both very lucky to have me back in your life. No, no need to thank me. I know my presence is a gift. Now let's get something to eat." I threw both arms around the Squad and dragged them in the direction of the door.

If I was acting stranger than usual hopefully they'd blame it on my nerves, not the pills.

"Okay, okay, we're going," Frankie giggled.

"Your wish is our command."

"Well then, I wish we could go to Langley's Diner over on Second Street because their waffles are calling my name." I cupped an ear. "Shhh. You hear that? *Casey Jones. Caaaaaasey Jooooonessssss Carusooooooo.*"

"All I hear is your stomach." Frankie patted my belly.

"True, she's definitely talking. Don't worry, girl, I've got you covered," I whispered down to it.

"Did you wake and bake or something?" Ben's eyes narrowed.

"Or something," I mumbled. Then I cracked a super-cheesy grin and said, "The question is, shall we smoke another before we feast."

"Always," Frankie and Ben both said at the same time.

When we reached Frankie's car, Ben rushed to the back door, yelling, "Shotgun!" Then he grabbed the handle, and upon opening the door he bowed, waiting for me to take a seat.

"Rude," I huffed as I crawled in.

"Not rude. Fast."

"But I've been gone over a month, I feel like that supersedes all claims of shotgun for at least a week."

"Um, nothing tops calling shotgun. Nothing." He eased into the passenger seat and turned to wink at me.

"Not fair. Frankie!"

"Nope. I gotta agree with Ben on this one. Calling shotgun trumps all."

"You both suck."

"But at least we suck up here." Ben high-fived Frankie.

Sammy, I couldn't tell if it was just his usual banter or if he was actually being more of a smartass than usual. Maybe they both were? Perhaps I was just being sensitive because I was a ball of raw nerves.

"Whatever." I let my head fall back on the headrest. My eyes closed as either Frankie or Ben adjusted the music. This was familiar. Normal. I think I even took a quick catnap because the next thing I knew Frankie was shaking me gently and saying, "We're here, Case."

"I'm awake. I'm awake." I sat up in a flurry.

"How about them waffles?"

Whatever sleep still lingered faded as the promise of waffles lured me out of the car. Remember how we always stopped at Langley's Diner? I'd get waffles and a coffee with two creams, one sugar. You'd get the Cali omelet with extra avocado and a hot chocolate, and Frankie and Ben would switch back and forth between blueberry and chocolate pancakes and chamomile tea.

And we'd all share a plate of covered and smothered hash browns.

This was the first time in about a year we'd gone back for breakfast. For the briefest of seconds, I couldn't get out of the car.

My hands curled into fists and my tongue felt thick. It was hard to swallow.

Then Ben grabbed my hand. "You've got this."

Frankie peeked over his shoulder. "Come on, babe. Easy-peasy."

Ahead of us stood an old converted metal Airstream trailer. The Langley's Diner sign glowed in a pink fluorescent haze that fit my mood.

Ben held the door for us. A comfortable chatter filled the air. The scents of freshly brewed coffee and hash browns hit my nose. I was home. We always found our way here for big life events. Breakups, makeups, family arguments, epic surf seshes . . . losing you.

Good or bad, Langley's was where we talked about it. I suppose it was only right, then, that this would be the place where we tried to figure out how to tackle our new predicament.

We ordered the usual and chatted bs while we waited for the food to come. Frankie and Ben told me about the last month here, and I tried to talk about my time at Nonna's. When the food came out, I won't lie, seeing the hash browns made my eyes sting. I knew they were going to be absolutely perfect. Brother dear, some things just don't change. You know me. ☺

This would be the place where we figured out our best step forward because Home is where the Heart is, and directly across the booth from me, *my* heartbeats were staring me right in the eyes, waiting for an answer.

HOME IS—

Home is

A place to hang your hat

A moment in time where you couldn't imagine being
anywhere else

A person

A feeling

Home is the scent of safety and good conversation

Memories, good and bad

A place to hide

To love

To sleep

An abstract, a wish, a dream

Home is where the heart is

Where the heartbreak is

The hurt

The pain

The hope

Home is the what-ifs, the maybes, the sometime soons

The goal

Home is you

Home is me

Home is we

We are home

Oh shit, doorbell. Ahhh, 1 hear Frankie talking to Mom. BBlAB.

Over and out—

Casey Jones

DEAR SAMMY,

Okay, okay. I know I left you hanging. Frankie stopped by and said things were kicking off at the beach. You know the deal, waves before words.

The best thing about August imho is hurricane season. I live for it! Some clean nine-footers kept ripping, and well, I got sidetracked. My bad. I know you would have too if places were switched.

Okay. Back to business. Where was I? Oh yeah! After a full belly of waffles and extremely bitter coffee, we finally started talking about the big storm cloud hanging over us. Time to truly listen to my heart and plunge in, awkwardness and all.

Awkward is an understatement.

I stumbled over my words at first. To this day, I'm not quite sure if I actually said anything even remotely close to a complete sentence. But bless their hearts, Frankie and Ben let me ramble until I finally gathered myself enough to blurt out:

"Okay, so as we all are aware, I owe you both an apology."

"Understatement," Ben mumbled.

"No way," Frankie declared.

"Assholes," I replied.

Ben's lip lifted in a snarky smirk as he said, "You love us."

"Adore us, even."

"I do, God help me. To the point where I can't imagine being with only one of you. I know. I'm selfish but there it is. I probably should have done this way differently but I didn't. And the super-screwed thing is, Ben, I know you're going to Harvard in like a month. And Frankie, I'm still not even sure if you like me back, but . . ." All the courage drained right out of me. Here I was, finally being honest, and it could all be for nothing.

But I went for it.

"The fact of the matter is, regardless of how much time we have left, I think it's worth a shot. If y'all do too, I mean." I stared at my hands because I couldn't look either of them in the eye. My fingers moved quickly, demolishing the discarded paper wrapper of my straw. I was surprised it hadn't crumbled into dust.

Ben broke the silence first. "Well, not that I wouldn't be down for a throuple, but, um, I don't think Frankie swings that way."

I peeked through my bangs to see Ben laughing. Great.

"Oh, trust me, I don't." Frankie cringed dramatically before continuing, "*And* even if I *did,* who's to say I'd ever consider you in the first place, Benjamin Dean? I'm not really okay with the whole *I'm-so-ahmaaaazing* type. *Annnd* the fact you have a dick doesn't really get the heart pumping either." Frankie shrugged.

Ben grabbed his chest and winced. "Ouch. You must be looking at a skeleton because I think I'm officially dead."

How could Frankie and Ben be so lighthearted while I couldn't stop thinking the entire world might stop turning?

Then again, that's who they are. And why I love them.

Just because there isn't romance between them doesn't mean they don't love each other. They do. A lot.

I sighed. "Okay. So no throuple action. But you know, it would have made things *soooo* much easier."

Frankie rolled her eyes.

"Jokes. Anyway, since that's off the table—" I stopped mid-sentence to remember to breathe. What I was about to say next could change everything. I inhaled and let the words rush out: "Would you two be open to a poly relationship?"

Their features changed as the teasing atmosphere morphed into something serious enough for them to mull the thought over.

Before they could respond, I continued. "And while I'm laying all my cards on the table, regardless of if we *all* date, or just two of us, or none of us, like, I don't want to settle down. With anyone. At least, not for a long time. So I'm not asking y'all for a forever and always, I just want you both as my right now. And yeah, I know I'm asking for a have-your-cake-and-eat-it-too moment, but I've always liked cake. . . ."

Oh my God, Sammy. I could not stop the word vomit. I ran my fingers through my hair in an attempt to pull back all the thoughts pouring out of my mouth. It didn't work. So I said, "Shit, I *still* don't even know how you feel, Frankie. Or, for that matter, what you feel now, Ben. Fuck."

Benjamin held up both hands and said, "Driving that train high on cocaine?"

"Casey Jones you better watch your speed," Frankie finished with a laugh.

"I've changed my mind. I hate you both equally."

"I mean, your parents *were* pretty brilliant with the name game." Ben tried to look serious as he joked.

Frankie didn't even try. She barked out a laugh. "Psychic, maybe, even."

"You both suck." I took another sip of coffee. "Here I am, offering you my heart, and you're both dissecting it like I'm some seventh-grade biology experiment."

"Sorry."

"Our bad, continue." Frankie dipped her head, giving me the floor.

I wasn't certain, but Frankie actually appeared to be a little bit serious for once. Honestly, it was hard to tell. I mumbled, "I'm out of words."

"A first." Frankie held up a hand with a wink to stop my preloaded retort. "Okay, so here are my thoughts about this. Last time we talked, I said we needed to have a face-to-face, and here we are doing so. But honestly, I didn't imagine our conversation would involve Ben. No offense."

"None taken," Ben said solemnly.

"Appreciate that. I still want to have a talk alone with Case before I make any decisions." She smiled softly in case Benjamin secretly did take offense at being left out. Even though we both knew he wouldn't, because he's Ben.

"Fair enough. At some point we should probably have a private chat too, Case. Why don't we hit the beach and I'll take all the beasts while y'all talk feels? Don't worry, I'll leave some ankle-slappers for you to ride when you're done."

Frankie and I looked at each other.

I couldn't help but ask, "Does he think he can *outride* us?"

"That's what it sounds like."

I leaned back as my heart slowed to a steady beat. Maybe we could work this out after all. "So what's the plan then?"

"The beach," they said in unison.

"Duh." I giggled. *So far, so good. They want to keep talking. No one's told me to go fuck myself (at least not yet). I've totally got this.*

(Sammy, I did *not* quite have this. But you'll see. I'll fill you in later. First, let's finish this moment.)

"Hey, Ben, why don't you warm the car up with Case, I'll get the check. You got it last time."

"You two have been eating out without me?" I pretended to pout.

"Only about three times a week." Ben started to reach for my hand and then let his drop.

It pained me to see his indecision, so I linked my pinky around his. And yup. Same warm fuzzies as always.

For the first time this summer, I allowed myself to believe this was going to work. We walked to the car side by side. When we stopped, Ben kissed my forehead. "Case, I can't speak for Frankie, obviously, but I want you to know I've thought about this a lot since we talked . . ."

Oh shit. He was waiting until we were alone to tell me to go fuck myself.

I KNEW IT.

I told you, Sammy. I never get what I want.

Well, when he started talking I leaned back. I wanted to see the resolve in his eyes as he essentially broke up with me. This was it. The end.

Ben and Casey, never.

A whole year of prepping and all for nothing.

And then he said, "I'd like to give it a try."

My mouth opened slightly. "You would?"

Wait.

What's that, Sammy?

I didn't hear you.

You TOLD me so?

Well, asshat, I guess I deserve it. Now we can pause a moment so you can gloat—wherever you are, I'm sure you're gloating if that's even a slight possibility. Or we can finish this damn entry.

Ben squeezed my hands before dipping his head until the tip of his nose rested on mine. Instead of letting myself go cross-eyed to keep eye contact, I closed them instead as his next words sank into my soul. "Casey Jones Caruso, *you're* willing to try to make this work even though *I'm* the one taking off next month. It'd be a dick move to keep you all to myself. And an even shittier one to not try at all. Besides, if you have to like anyone else in the world I *suppose* Frankie isn't a horrible choice."

I opened my eyes and tilted my head because I really wanted to see his face now. "How did I get so lucky to have you in my life?"

"I ask myself that all the time."

Ben's pupils dilated. The sweet scent of maple syrup lingered on his breath and when we finally kissed his tongue tasted like blueberries.

It. Was. Perfect.

Guess we weren't going to need that private talk after all because I think we just agreed to date. Squeeeee!!! But don't get too excited, bro. I still needed to finish my chat with Frankie.

A cough brought me out of the steamy cloud I was floating on.

"Don't mind me, it's not like I have anything important going on," Frankie grumbled playfully.

"Sorry, we were, uh, just working some stuff out." Ben blushed, but he didn't pull away.

"Yeah, yeah. I can see that. Well, climb in, mano. We've got people to do and things to see. And now it's my turn to, *uh, work some stuff out.*"

The smugness of her smile when she said that? It was a level ten, Sammy. You would have been proud.

This time Ben did step aside. He even let me ride shotgun. I contemplated what had just happened, chewing my lip to keep from losing my train of thought. Ben kissed me! And Frankie was still ready to talk!

Score. Score. Score. Maybe today was turning into a win after all.

I snuck peeks at Frankie and Ben, trying to suss out if there was any underlying tension from our kiss. If one kiss could bring bad feelings on either end we need to acknowledge it to make this work. This whole dating-multiple-people thing definitely had a learning curve. Well, I might be a bad student, but that didn't mean I wasn't a quick learner. If we were going to do this right, we would have to set boundaries and respect each other's limits.

To be fair, Frankie didn't seem bothered by the kiss. But I still didn't want to throw it in her face. If it had been Raine, well. I don't even need to go there, do I?

And with that, my hand is cramping. I'll write you back in a bit. Besides, you always loved a good cliffhanger. Muwahahahahah. 😜

Over and out—

Casey Jones

HOME—

A million grains of sand
Rushing in and out
The water pulls and pushes
Footprints fade, forever
Ephemeral marks
A kiss of the past
Present
future
the grains tumble together in perfect harmony
Building castles of daydreams
Nightmares and thunderstorms
Baked to perfection in the sun
Under pressure
glass forms
A million years
A million grains
And still there's nowhere
I'd rather
Call
Home

DEAR SAMMY,

I could sit here and tell you our whole conversation word for word.

But I'm not going to. Some things aren't meant to be shared.

Instead, I'll tell you how the sound of Frankie's voice made me feel. It's like I was simultaneously floating and drowning all at once. How when she grabbed my hand and never let go—not even when we brought up the hard stuff—I knew then and there I'd accept her choice no matter what, as long as we didn't lose our connection.

When we got to the beach Ben wandered off to catch all the good waves (ha) and gave us our privacy. Frankie and I opened our hearts to each other as the world passed on around us. The salty air revived me whenever I felt at a loss for words. Then once, in the middle of a particularly difficult moment, Frankie asked, "Want to take a quick swim?"

I nodded, and together, we dove into our place of solace, letting the ocean renew us from our aches and worries. Without any spoken words, we instinctively knew to swim to the sandbar. My arms stretched out as long as they could, my legs kicked in a controlled rhythm, and I ate up the distance without getting winded.

Frankie matched me stroke for stroke.

Once there, we kneeled. The higher ground gave the illusion of shallows, but we knew a few feet in either direction and the water would be above our heads. Here, though, we were safe.

Far in the distance I saw Ben line up for a set. It made me smile. Then I put all my concentration on Frankie. On this moment. On us.

Light played off the ocean. It illuminated our skin as salt-water drops ran haphazardly down our faces and hair. I fought an impulse to reach for Frankie, and instead let my fingers play in the sand around my knees.

And then she said:

"... I think I might like you too. A little bit. But I'm scared. I'm not very good at relationships, and I mean, it's not like you aren't aware of that. As for Ben, I'm not the jealous type, so I don't think an open relationship would be a problem for me. Course, why you like that goof, I've got no idea."

She rolled her eyes, but a small smile played on her lips. When I tried to answer, she held up a hand. "I'm not done yet. If you hadn't said anything while you were in Asheville I would have been happy to keep dating Raine, even without a label. Who knows. Maybe I still will. I'm not saying this to hurt your feelings." Her lip twitched when she saw my hands flex. "You know this works both ways, right?"

"I do-ooo. No. I do. I just, um. Does it *have* to be Raine?"

Frankie folded her arms over her chest.

"Okay, okay. If you want to keep dating Raine, that's *fine* by me." I narrowed my eyes. "Just make sure you bring your toothbrush when you see me after because I don't even want to think about—"

"What the fuck, Case?"

"No, no. I was just playing. Seriously. Jokes. If we do this, I won't continue to talk shit. Out loud. I can't make any promises for what I think, though."

"I guess that's fair, for now. Besides, that's not what's bothering me. I know you two have beef, and that's between y'all." Frankie shrugged. "You don't need to be jealous, though. She doesn't want a serious relationship, which is actually a good thing. We both know I tend to screw those up in the end."

"Maybe you just haven't found someone to keep you interested." I waggled my eyebrows.

"*Maybe*. But fair warning, my natural avoidance for relationships could be absolutely apocalyptic for us. I can't promise you I won't try to run at some point. Like if we got serious. What then? Do you really want to deal with the fallout because I got bored or whatever? I don't know if I can do that to you, Case. To me. To us. Is this worth it? I like you too much to lose you."

She likes me too! But is it enough?

I sat silently for a long time before I answered. "Yes? No? Maybe?"

I wasn't entirely sure. I didn't want to think about if we didn't work out. Even if I should. "Look. I can't read the future," I added. "But I can promise you this. If we don't work out, I swear *I* won't blame *you,* as long as *you* don't blame *me.* I know how scary this is, I'm fucking terrified. Even so, I still think it's worth a try."

Frankie let out a massive sigh and wrinkled her nose. "What am I going to do with you, Casey Jones Caruso?"

I bit my lip before saying softly, "Whatever you want, Francesca Graciela Romero."

"Be careful, I might take you up on that offer."

"Is that a threat?"

"A promise."

"Yeah?" My voice wavered. *Is this really happening?*

"Yeah." The word left her mouth as a barely formed breath. Frankie tucked a lock of wet hair behind her ear and leaned in closer.

WARNING, big bro. I'm laying out all the mushy stuff right here. These journals are as much for me as they are for you and I want to relive every second of this moment with Frankie because it was a freaking long time in the making. So if you don't want to hear all the best bits (IMO), just look away.

Or, well . . . shit. You know what I mean.

I don't think I've ever seen Frankie more beautiful than at that moment. I could make out every freckle on her face. My hands felt numb and my back was on fire as the sun beat down on us. Little cold waves splashed around our thighs and I opened myself to all the sensations happening around me. I didn't want to forget a second of it. My skin grew goose bumps, simultaneously cold and hot.

The earth could be dissolving around us and we'd never even notice. We could only focus on each other as we slowly moved together.

Her full lips landed on mine. At first it was soft, questioning. Then we pressed ourselves even closer and my hands wrapped around her waist as she threw her arms over my shoulders.

It was like time stopped. Nothing mattered anymore except that moment. I closed my eyes so I could let myself completely go, and I swear we molded together until I couldn't say what was me and what was her. We were fire and ice. A million sensations all rolled into one. Stars, explosions, a galaxy of possibilities that all began and ended with each other.

And then she bit my lip playfully, pulling me out of space and back down to Earth. She tilted her head and said, "Well, I *suppose* I could get used to this. I mean, it's not *entirely* awful."

"Oh, not entirely?"

"I could think of worse things."

"Enlighten me?"

"Double cheeseburgers. Five free tickets to a sold-out show. A shopping spree—"

"None of those are bad. So that must mean I'm a pretty good kisser. Ha. I was expecting homeless kittens or world hunger or something."

"Well, I did say not *entirely* awful. But I dunno about pretty good. Average, maybe." She covered her mouth with a hand to keep from laughing.

"Average?" I tried to keep my voice light when really all I wanted was to pull her in for another kiss and show her how *average* I was. But we had time. There was no need to rush. So I leaned back and let my hand run through the water. When I angled it just right, I sent a plume of water straight for her face. "I'll give you average."

Frankie leapt to the side, rolling off the sandbar and into deeper water. I followed with a laugh. We continued splashing as we floated up and over the gentle waves. The tide was moving in so we let the ocean take us back to shore at its own pace. Before we could stand and touch the sandy floor completely, Frankie leaned in lightning-quick and planted a sweet short kiss on my nose.

"I'm not saying yes, but I'm not saying no. How about we take everything day by day and not put a label on it. K?"

"Yeah, I'm cool with that."

"And if it gets weird between the three of us at any time, then we need to swear we'll talk about it."

"Swear."

"All right then. We'll need Ben's swear to make it official."

"Scar Squad official?"

"Yup. What do you think Sammy would have to say about this?"

"A fucking mouthful. And then some."

Frankie cackled. "I'd give half my heart to hear even a few words."

"Me and you both." My toes gripped the sand. It was time to leave. Ben was definitely waiting for us.

All my life I'd read about love triangles and could never understand why anyone would want to be part of one. And now here I am, in a love infinity loop. Me in the middle and Ben and Frankie on each curve, existing together and apart all at once. Not forever, but for right now. Forever is a long freaking time. Regardless, Scar Squad for life.

I like that we don't have to go behind each other's backs and hopefully the jealousy (let's face it, *my* jealousy) can be kept to a minimum.

I made a promise to myself that day with Frankie that I'd work on it.

Don't laugh. I really am working on it. Every day, I get a little bit better at controlling it.

Dude. I know you're laughing. You're such a dick.

Yes, there's going to be a lot of mistakes and sometimes even hurt feelings, but we're the Scar Squad, and *you* know better than anyone we can pull through anything. I mean . . .

Well, it's safe to say we've survived the worst-possible scenario ever, so I think we can figure out an open relationship.

When we left the water, Frankie wrapped her arm loosely around my waist as we trudged to shore. I was tired of thinking about the future, and I'm sorry, Sammy, but I was exhausted from always living in the past.

And as we grabbed our boards and headed out to where Ben was waving us over I decided that for just a little while, I wanted to live in the here and now. Just the three of us.

I'd tell you how the rest of the day went, but I guess some things you just don't need to know.

Except for this: you can never call me a pussy again!

And I know you can't, technically, but even if you *could,* you couldn't. :p

The reality is this *entire* journal is full of things we'll never say to each other. And that kills me, dude. But if I have even the slightest chance of living a full life without you, I need to push past the pain and live. For the both of us. Then your death won't be in vain. A part of you *will* keep on living, because I am. We come from the same DNA, might as well make that count, right?

I'll be back, swear, but for now, I just need some time to explore being a twinless twin. Don't be mad. There's still a few pages left, and I won't leave you hanging.

Only you get to do that.

Over and out—

Casey Jones

DEAR SAMMY,

Summer is well and truly over. It's officially fall as of today. Which is fitting because the last two weeks I've definitely felt like I've been plummeting. Ben left for Harvard a week ago. And I've been swimming in a sea of confusion ever since.

Mostly because my brain is full of what-ifs:

What if he gets so busy he forgets about me?

What if being surrounded by smart people all the time makes him think I'm stupid?

What if I can't bring myself to ever leave this town?

What if he falls in love with someone else who wants only him?

What if he falls out of love with me?

What if I fall out of love with him because he's so far away . . . (Yes, I realize I've been saying I don't want forever, but I've been crushing on the dude for a decade and we've only been together for like ten minutes. So I'd like this part to last a *bit* longer, thank you very much.)

What if he gets so busy he can't ever fly home to visit?

What if phone sex sucks? (Screw you, Sammy, these are legit concerns. Deal with it!)

What if he loses his wallet and goes to find it in the lost and found only to be abducted by aliens and they take him away for two years, and when he returns it's him, but not really, and I only find out after we try to say our Squad Vows and he screws them up, but we've already made out and now I'm carrying some freaking strange alien baby and it pops out of my stomach and I die?

Whatever, I am not responsible for my imagination and sometimes my brain wanders, okay? I mean, it *could* happen. After all, the government *finally* admitted aliens are real. I'm not saying it will happen, just that it coul—OH HOLY SHIT! YOU DIED BEFORE THEY ADMITTED ALIENS ARE REAL. Damn, Sammy. Do you remember the amount of times we argued over whether they were or not??!!!

Damn.

For all I know you're up there hanging with some Martians right now, laughing at how slow the rest of us were to catch on. . . . I can't believe we finally have an answer to one of our biggest ongoing debates and you aren't here to appreciate it. Frankie and Ben are going to trip out when I tell them.

You were wrong, dude. Sooooo wrong. THEY EXIST! Man, I won't lie, I started writing this entry bummed out. But right now I feel pretty dang vindicated. Guess sibling rivalry doesn't die just because the sibling does. I have no idea why that makes me feel better. Weirdly, it does.

Not going to dissect it, just bask in the glory of being a winner. Don't mind me as I don my BITCH WAS RIGHT ALL ALONG hat. I'll be wearing it for the foreseeable future.

Anyway, where was I?

Oh yeah, Ben leaving. It was inevitable. We've known it since like the sixth grade so no shocker, out-of-the-blue, slap-me-in-the-face decision here. And come on, it's Harvard. Not like he's going to choose me over school, nor would I want him to. That would be universally stupid. So we decided to enjoy every moment we had until the day he left and then . . . well? I guess we'll see what happens from here.

Before he took off we had some pretty stellar dates, though! We've been taking it slowly. Sometimes we hang out as the Squad, sometimes we go on for-real dates.

My favorite date had to be when Ben and I went to Crystal River so we could kayak with the manatees. You would have LOVED it. Not sure why Mom and Dad never brought us but it's super sick. So peaceful. I felt infinite as we floated. We rented see-through kayaks and since the water is as crystal clear as the name implies, it was like floating on liquid glass. Everything below me moved around like I was part of a real-life snow globe or something.

Much different than when we're out surfing. In the ocean I always have adrenaline pumping through me. Never know what's underneath my board. Under me. But this place? Absolute zen.

And the manatees? Dude. I am a sea cow fan for life. In the summer while the resident population is smaller, you get to see the newborns! It was pretty much perfect.

To be fair to all involved, I've spent a lot of alone time with Frankie too. It's not like we could just put whatever's simmering between us on hold until Ben left, ya know?

It's been interesting, to say the least. I never expected how some things would change between us. Like I find myself feeling shy at the weirdest moments. In situations where normally I'd be super confident, but now? All the feels get in the way. And that makes for some awkward moments. I'm happy to report there are more chill moments than awkward, though.

I think my fav date with Frankie was when we went down to the Keys for the weekend with Tita. We swam around in the Dry Tortugas and found Jesus somewhere off the coast in Key Largo. Okay, not like the real Jesus. There's a nine-foot underwater statue of him off the coast, and well, we weren't saved or anything, but we did see some great fish. Afterward, I packed us a picnic and we went to the beach for a sunset dinner. Tita Shirley managed to find a local bingo game, so it was just the two of us.

It was a blissed-out day.

See. That's the thing. I keep having these quality moments with both of them, and I'm starting to see what Nonna was talking about. Life is short. There's nothing wrong with testing the waters.

Also, I'm proud to say, I can get through an update about Raine without cringing. In fact, lately she's been . . . well, not nice. But not a total bitch either. Maybe one day we'll even be friends.

Okay, okay, that's bs. Hahaha. But hey, like I said, baby steps. If she makes Frankie happy too, then more power to her. I know she can't come between what Frankie and I have.

So things have been chugging along without too many speed bumps. Even on Ben's last day at home I felt more hopeful than depressed. I mean, one of us is actually following their dreams right on time. I always knew it would be him first. It's hard to be sad in a moment like that. Like, all I've ever wanted for the Scar Squad is happiness and I would never get in the way of that. I now know deep down our friendship can outlast anything. I suppose I'll find out soon enough if our romantic one can. Since I'm not sad, I suppose the falling sensations I mentioned earlier lean more toward my fear of what comes next now that he's gone. In the spring Frankie leaves for her school and then it will just be me.

Maybe it's time to follow my dreams too.

For now, I'm taking it day by day. Enjoying every minute. Every second. And they breeze by, let me tell you. Now with Ben at school and Frankie and me working full-time, we're all super busy. Another reason why I haven't written to you lately. But like I said in my last entry, I needed some time to just be Casey without an *and*.

I will admit I've been slacking on sending this your way. There's a few reasons. Since I've been home it just didn't feel right ending this journal without a resolution and leaving you hanging for who knows how long. And I wanted to tie up some loose ends about other things too. Like the pills. I've got only a handful left.

I swear to you on my life (and your death) that I will tell both Frankie and Ben what I've been doing . . . when I eat the last pill. I'll need their help if I want to try and actually stay sober this time. I know you know when I aim to eat the last one. Sorta serendipitous, right? As I said, I'm always down for some drama.

Plus I can't burn a journal until the Scar Squad is together. But! While Ben won't be here in September, he is flying down to visit for the first week of Oct. He'd never leave you hanging and you know this, man!

I plan on building the biggest bonfire in the world. I think you deserve it if you're about to read a journal as . . . what did I claim this thing was going to be in the beginning? God, that seems a lifetime ago. Lemme check real quick.

BRB. AHA! Found it, first entry. I declared this was going to be *the* Mount Everest of journals. Whew, I wasn't lying, was I? What A Climb. I think I'm psychic or something. Makes sense since Nonna swears we come from a long line of witches. Must remember to tell her next time we talk.

K, mio caro fratello. There's not much time to wind this up and create an anniversary of epic proportions. Something to remember forever. As if we could ever forget you in the first place.

Get ready, 'cause in a week and five days we're gonna burn baby, burn.

Over and out—

Casey Jones

DEAR SAMMY,

I've reached the end of my journal. Which, in a way, is sort of serendipitous because I've also reached the end of my constant worrying about whether things would work out between me and Frankie, or me and Ben.

Because, honestly? Who knows.

Speaking of being busy . . .

Benjamin arrived early yesterday afternoon and came straight over to our house. Since Frankie was working late we spent time catching up and then had a sunset sesh and then . . . well, you don't get to know everything anymore.

Once Frankie got off work we all curled up on the couch and had a movie marathon with Mom and Dad. Watched all your faves, even *The Big Lebowski,* how's about it nowski. Mom and Dad tapped out when we put on *Dazed and Confused.* Wusses. Then it was just the three of us.

We stayed up until sunrise and sat on the roof smoking a blunt. Frankie on my left, Ben on my right. A Scar Squad sandwich, just the way I like it. Oh, get this! Can you believe it's the first time Ben's gotten high since he left?!?!

He said he can barely swing his workload sober, much less stoned. Makes sense, I suppose. Anyway, as the first rays of sunlight turned the purply-blue sky into fiery shades of oranges and reds and pinks I held up *the* pill bottle. It'd been sitting in my pocket since the night before and I'd been waiting for the perfect time to come clean. I thought, what better time than the dawn of a new day.

Especially a day like today.

There was one lonely pill sitting at the bottom. It rattled as I shook it. Frankie lifted an eyebrow, her lips pursed tightly. Ben ran a hand through his hair and mumbled something like "Ah, you sure it's that kind of party?"

To be honest I think he was kinda cracking a joke but my nerves were strung so tight I snapped and said, "Could we be serious for like a second? This is important."

"Clearly." Frankie said it slowly. Like she was talking to a caged animal.

Ben blushed. "I'm sorry. Not sure what I did wrong."

I looked left to right, trying to keep eye contact with both of them and failing. So I scooted away until I could turn and face them both. I raised the bottle, the clear orange plastic catching the new light and filtering it onto the pill. When the two could see it clearly Frankie frowned.

"What the hell is that, Case?"

Right as Ben said, "I hope that's not what I think it is."

"You both know exactly what this is. But hear me out. Since Sammy died I haven't been honest with you. I found his stash a few months after . . ." I inhaled and tried again. "And at first all

I could do was look at them. Wonder how something so small could destroy someone that was unbreakable."

I bit my lip as they nodded. I'm sure they've wondered the same thing as often as I have. "Anyway, after a while when shit got too hard I'd open the bottle, break a small piece off, and eat it. And then one day, I ate a pill. That's when I understood. It took all the pain away. Shoved it so far into the shadows that I could breathe again, and let me say, I haven't been able to breathe right since Sammy died." I looked up to the sky. "No offense, dude."

"Oh, Case." Frankie's voice carried barely over a whisper.

Ben reached out and placed his hand on my knee. The touch was so light and so heavy all at once. I could have stopped right there, but if I really wanted a chance at quitting I had to tell them everything.

"Once those pills ran out I found someone to hook me up an—"

"I swear to God I'll fucking kill them. Tell me who." Frankie pushed up on an arm like she was about to jump off the roof and go avenge me or something.

"The who doesn't matter. Besides. I haven't seen them since graduation. Sit *dooowwnnn*." This time I was the one reaching out to comfort. I tucked a stray lock of hair behind her head. "It's cool. I swear."

Frankie huffed but stayed where she was.

"Okay. So I planned on eating this pill this morning so I could get through the day, right?" I opened the bottle and dumped it into my waiting palm. It really was such a small insignificant thing. Which only made me furious. HOW DARE IT ruin you,

Sammy? The audacity of it. Well, it'd already taken one Caruso. I refused to let it take another. "I'm not going to eat this." I dropped the pill back in the bottle, tightened the cap, stood up, and shoved it in my pocket. "Come on. I've got an idea."

Frankie and Ben looked at each other. I could tell they were DYING to say something, dude. But today—of all days—I got a free pass to be, um, chaotic, if you will. And they knew it. So instead of picking a fight (which if I was honest they had every right to pick) they stood with me and followed me down to the house. I grabbed a few things I'd packed the night before and then asked Frankie to take us to the Squad's home. Your favorite place in the world.

I reiterated we had somewhere we *needed* to be and it couldn't wait. They know I *never* want to go anywhere on your anniversary, which, in retrospect, is probably why they came along without asking a million questions. Frankie grabbed her keys from the kitchen counter right as Mom walked in the room.

She stood there in her bathrobe, hair all tousled, and gave us a small, sad smile. "Heading out, babe?" Mom kissed my forehead. She had huge circles under her eyes. Guess we weren't the only ones who'd been up all night.

"It will only be for a little while."

"Take all the time you need. Dad and I plan on going over there later. Maybe we'll meet up." She turned to pour herself a cup of coffee. Her shoulders low. This day sucks so bad for everyone, I hope you know. And we get to experience it every year for the rest of our lives. Thanks *a lot* for that. Ass.

"Where's Dad?" Usually he was the early bird in the house.

"He finally fell asleep a few hours ago so I decided to let him rest." She walked back over to us, steaming cup in hand, and gave each of us a one-armed hug. "I am so pleased that you could all be here. Love y'all."

"Love you too, Mrs. C.," Frankie and Ben said at the same time.

I grabbed my purse and kissed Mom on the cheek. "See ya soon?"

"You bet."

I paused in the hall. No turning back now. Always forward, never straight. I made a promise at Nonno's grave that I would see this day through to the end and I intended to keep that promise to him, to you, and especially to me.

"K, everyone jump in. Can I drive, Frankie? We gotta go now or we'll miss it!"

"Sure, just don't speed like usual."

"Miss what?" Ben asked as he sat down in back. He knew there was no point in fighting for shotgun this time. LOL can you picture Frankie trying to be convinced to ride in the back of her own car? Bet that image made you chuckle.

I buckled up and said, "I don't mean to be a bitch but you'll see when we get there. Just trust me for now."

"We trust you, Case."

"I know." The car ride was silent for a few minutes and then Frankie turned on your playlist. Yeah, dummy, we made you a playlist. You're that cool.

My left leg kept bouncing as I drove, waiting for the inevitable assault of questions about the fact that I'd been taking pills and keeping it on the DL.

Eventually Frankie's voice broke the silence. "Chillax, we aren't here to stress you, babe. We'll talk about it, but it doesn't have to be today if you don't want to."

"I appreciate that."

She blew me a kiss. "Look!"

Out the window, I could see small waves breaking on the shore as I pulled up to *our* spot. It was pretty packed, so I angled into an empty spot far away from our usual place. The sun slapped us with its heat. None of us were even dressed for the beach, so I hoped they didn't freak about what I had planned.

They followed along behind me faithfully, trusting me. Every time I looked out at the water, I thought of you. Massive thunderheads were forming out on the horizon. Every once in a while, a bright streak of lightning hit between the dark clouds and highlighted the waves. A brilliant sun behind us and a storm in front. Fitting. Even Nature couldn't decide how to act today.

She's got a good sense of timing when it comes to you.

The wind picked up a bit onshore, cooling down our sweating bodies as we walked toward the pier. It would be a while yet before the storm hit.

The change in the weather reminded me of that *one* morning. How it stormed like a hurricane was coming in. How all I could think about was the surf and the epic waves that were about to hit. And then the world exploded.

I stopped walking. It was too hard to breathe. My hands pulled at my shirt as I tried to suck down air. The people echoed around me, my ears felt fuzzy and my vision grew dark. Then hands gently lowered me to the ground while I tried to not faint.

"Easy, Case."

"We got you, babe."

I let myself fall back against the sand and looked up at the sky, trying to find my calm in the clouds overhead. To find you.

I can never find you, Sammy.

Not even now.

Not even today.

Ben sat down next to me, letting his feet dig in to find the cool spots. "Breathe through it." He let his fingers travel over the sand until they found mine. Then he slowly trailed his thumb along the back of my hand. The sensation calmed me a bit. We sat in silence. I never took my eyes off the clouds. For the first time in my life, I couldn't bear to look at the ocean. It would've killed me to admit it out loud.

So I didn't.

Instead, I tried to make out as many animals as I could while I tried to pull myself together. "There's a giraffe," I whispered. "I miss these kinds of moments with you, bro. So much."

Someone sniffed. We were all crying, it seemed. After a few minutes, the panic eased. When I could breathe again, I pulled myself together somewhat and managed to say, "Sorry. I needed a sec."

"'S'all good. Take as long as you need." Ben rubbed my back and Frankie held my hand. I stood and the three of us walked to the shore. The water slid over our feet as we sank into the sand, gluing us in place. The wind lifted my hair. It tangled around my face, almost as if you were taunting me or something.

I dug into my pocket for the bottle and then flung it into the sea. "I refuse to drown, Sammy! Do you hear me? I refuse. I won't be like you. I won't." My voice cracked as I cried, "I can't!" We stood there for years. Decades. Eons. Until I felt strong enough to look up.

The bottle was gone. The last pill still inside. Lost to the ocean. Hopefully it would give it a good grave because I never wanted to see it again. I wiped my eyes. "Guess I didn't need a pill to get through today after all."

"Not when you've got us." Frankie leaned her head on my shoulder.

"That was brave of you, Sammy would be proud." Ben released the saddest sigh ever. "I'm sorry we didn't see sooner how bad you've struggled."

I shrugged. "I mean, it's not like you two weren't struggling too. And I tried to hide it. I think you guys came close to sussing it out a few times."

Frankie laughed sharply. "I knew you had to be more than stoned when we were at the spodie. There was this look in your eye and I couldn't place—"

"Ah, that might have been more because I was tripping about . . . Well, never mind, maybe I was high. I can't remember. Anyway, If I have any chance of quitting these pills I need y'all by my side. Maybe I need to find a hobby or something."

"Quilting?"

"Wax figure collecting?"

Frankie clucked her tongue. "Paint by numbers!"

For the first time today I laughed for real. "You guys suck so bad."

"There's always surfing." Ben smiled.

"Yeah, but that's not a hobby. It's a lifestyle."

"Speaking of, how are those waves treating ya, Mr. Ivy League? Catching some killer sets?"

"*Haa haa,* Frankie. You'll be happy to hear Case and I did manage to slide in a few last night."

Frankie stuck her fingers in her ears. "Gross. I mean, look, there are just *some* things better left to yourselves, alright? When we said open relationship, I didn't mean like—"

I punched her arm. "You are such a dork."

"At your service."

Now that the panic had settled I found my bag and pulled something out of it. A small glass bottle. "Here, y'all, bend down and scoop. Like this." I dropped to my knees and let my fingers run through a million grains of sand. Maybe one of these small pieces of our world had touched you at some point in the past, Sammy. Maybe you rode a wave that sent this particular part of the beach far into the ocean, and it only washed back up onshore today.

I'd like to think that could happen. In any case, I let my fingers close around the wet grains and watched as they trickled from my hand into the bottle. Ben and Frankie each scooped up a handful and poured theirs in too. Once the bottle was halfway full I filled it with the ocean and then stoppered it up. When I lifted it in the air, the water swirled around as stormy as the sea. Fitting, if you ask me.

(I'm not the only one of us who enjoyed a bit of drama, am I?)

I stood and tried to brush the wet sand off my pants, figured it was pointless after a few seconds, and just laughed. "Welp, if Sammy can't make it to the beach anymore, looks like it's time to bring the beach to him. Ready?"

Ben shook his head. "Never ready."

"Me either."

"Me either. But for once I plan on showing up. It's been way too long. Let's go or we'll be late." I tried to calm myself as we walked back to the car. Inhale. Exhale. My hands still shook a bit and my neck hurt from how tense I'd kept my shoulders.

Are you proud of me? I'd like to think so.

Before I got to the driver's seat I tossed Frankie the keys. "Shotgun." We all climbed in and Frankie took off. I didn't close my eyes. There was no point. I knew without a doubt where we were headed next. Nowhere else to go, ya know. So instead, I tried to brace for what was about to happen.

Need a breather. BRB. No. For Real. I swear . . .

. . . Okay, I'm back.

As I was saying, I bet you made a deal with Mother Nature to kick up today because whew, it's been storm city. A few hours ago the air felt thick. The bad weather had moved inland, and it felt like the entire world was made of static electricity. My hand brushed the door handle and little zaps hit my palm.

I didn't know if I could get out of the car.

"You got this, Case." Ben's whisper brushed my hair.

"Do I?" I whispered back.

"We can sit here forever, if you need us to." Frankie turned off the ignition.

Ben wasn't lying. They really would sit there all day and night if that was what I needed. But I had a promise to keep. So the only way to honor it was to get out.

I climbed out of the car, not waiting for either of them. They knew the path. Probably better than me.

Admitting that, even to myself, hurt. Admitting that to you is devastating.

I promise, I visit in my dreams. Almost every night.

Tall pine trees swayed in the breeze, blowing the scents of roses and gardenias around, filling my nostrils and making me want to vomit. I kept on the path, refusing to step a foot in the grass. The whole place skeeved me out. By the time I arrived at the spot, I couldn't see clearly anymore. I couldn't even remember when I'd started crying, but by then, I was a lost cause. Snot and sorrow spilled down my face, companions to grief, traitors to the heart.

The gravestone still looks new, by the way. Whoever's been visiting lately has gone through a lot of effort to keep the area clean. Fresh pink peonies were set in a low vase. I'm guessing Mom and Dad must have made it before us.

I'm the only asshole who could never find the nerve to show up, after all.

The grass crunched as I sank to my knees. "I'm so, so fucking sorry it's taken me this long, Sammy. I'm—" A fit of hiccups stopped me from saying anything else to you. It was hard to tell if it was raining or if my tears were soaking the marble underneath my hands. All I knew is I was finally there. I made it. I kept my promise to you.

I won't lie. I was a little scared. You—at least a part of you—were six feet below me and there I was, basically sitting on your remains. I tried to push the thought away because it was just too much to handle. Still is.

Instead, I remembered the time we got lost in the current. How you held my hand and promised to never let go.

So here's what I said: "I can't figure out how to let go, Sammy. I don't even know if I want to. I promise, I think about you all the time, even when I don't come here. I write to you constantly. You'll find soon enough what, because today is a burn day. The *biggest* burn day. Since I've been filling my journal up since MAY, and whew, it's going to be a bumpy ride." I laughed through the tears.

In that moment I pictured you actually reading this cluster-fuck story of my life and how your eyes would grow wide, all the WTF moments you'd remark on. All the parts you'd love. Or hate. But you would be there.

And actually, if you were still here you wouldn't even know half this shit. Maybe not even a quarter. I'm finding I'm a lot more open with you dead then I ever was when you were alive. Interesting.

Anyway, hope you're happy because I totally lost it back at the graveyard.

My emotions were all over the place. I remember going from laughing one second to crying the next. After a few moments I pulled myself together enough to say, "Life is so fucking hard without you." I sobbed. "I'm so sorry. I miss you, dude. So much." My entire body was breaking in half. In a way, I've been broken in half ever since you died.

It isn't fair.

Eventually, as time passed, the sobs slowed. My river of tears turned into a trickle. And my nose was so stuffed I didn't know if

I'd ever be able to breathe through it again. I swiped at it, trying to get all the snot off my face and failing miserably.

My knees ached, so I settled into a cross-legged position and let out a deep sigh. "It's okay," I said to Frankie and Ben. "You guys can come over here if you want."

The Scar Squad had been waiting patiently this entire time. Allowing me and you to have some privacy.

"Love you." Ben squeezed my shoulder. "You too, Sammy."

"Always," Frankie said, and nestled down by my side. "Here." She shyly pushed the bag with the ocean in it my way.

I slowly took it from her. "I thought you two might want to honor Sammy with me today, and I figured the best way to do that is to leave a bit of our souls with him. Then he'll never be too far from our hearts. Not that you ever could be, dickhead." I looked up to the sky and glared.

I grabbed our stoppered bottle of the Atlantic Ocean from the bag. Next, I pulled out a Tupperware full of sand, and from underneath that, a pocket knife.

Frankie and Ben looked at the offerings with curiosity.

I sobbed again, this time because I had the best friends and lovers in the world next to *me* to celebrate *you*. To mourn you. My eyes filled with happy tears. "You two are the best. You know that?"

"I mean, duh." Frankie chuckled.

"Of course," Ben agreed.

I held up the knife. "Ready for this?"

You woulda been proud, Sammy. Neither of them looked scared. Just curious. Frankie did ask, "What's that for?"

"Oh, well, remember when we all became blood siblings?" I pulled up my sleeve and stuck out my palm. "Figured we could anoint the sand. Renew our vows and give Sammy some protection since we can't always be here."

(Hope you're down with a lil spell therapy, dude. I told you. We come from witches. ♡)

Without a word, I opened the knife and quickly drew it across Frankie's palm. Then Frankie grabbed it from me and drew it across Ben's. Then he took it from her. When he reached for my hand, his touch was gentle. He drew the knife across in a precise and fast manner so I didn't feel the cut at all.

We chanted, "Forever and always, we swear to God, nothing will shatter the Scar Squad."

"Not romance. Not books. Not school. Not TV."

"Not moving, or growing up. Together we'll be. Scar Squad for life and longer!" We finished our vows and held our hands together; the three of us letting our blood drip into the container of sand before we whispered the creed again for good measure.

When we released our grip, my hand lingered over the sand until one more drop fell. I said, "There's some Band-Aids in the bag if someone wants to grab em."

Frankie pulled out three Band-Aids and passed them out. "You know, we really should rewrite our vows. We didn't have a lot of faith in the lasting power of our squad. Not school? Not TV?" Frankie giggled.

Ben laughed with her. "I mean, you never know when a good show might ruin a friendship forever."

I thought about what *you'd* want and said, "I dunno, I sort of like it as is." I hugged my knees to my chest. "Besides, if Sammy isn't here to help us come up with new ones, we can't change the words without his permission." I placed the bloody sand and bottle of water next to the flowers.

When I sat back, my soul felt lighter.

Ben nodded. "True."

"Okay. Then we'll keep our vow as it is."

"Yeah, I think you'd like that, huh?"

We all looked up to the sky and waited for your answer. Right at that moment, I shit you not, a huge thunderclap rattled above. Two seconds later a brilliant burst of lightning rocketed across the sky. I'm not saying I totally believe in the afterlife, dude, but you couldn't have answered any louder if you were right in front of us, screaming in our faces.

We burst out laughing. "Welp, looks like the Squad vows aren't changing."

"Love you, Sammy."

"Love you, bro!"

"Screw you, buddy. Oh, *and* I love you, and shit." Frankie waved a fist in the air.

"You ready?" I stood. Much as I wanted to stay longer, even you aren't worth getting electrocuted over.

"Whenever you are, babe." Frankie winked.

"You lead the way, we'll follow."

"I know." I smiled at both of them. My squad. Our squad. Scar Squad. We may have cuts that will never heal, but the scars will make sure we never forget the good times either.

Our forever and always. Because even though you're gone you will never be forgotten.

As we piled into the car, the sun was getting low and the storm had fully come in off the coast, close enough that you could smell it. Nothing like a summer storm on a hot afternoon when ozone seeps into your nose and makes you feel like anything can happen.

So we left.

And now I've got a few preparations to get ready so this evening is perfect for you. Don't worry, Sammy. We aren't finished saying goodbye just yet.

Over and out—

Casey Jones

UNTIL TOMORROW—

Goodbyes are so final

An ending to a beginning

And I'm not ready to go

To let you go

Instead it's going to have to be

See ya later, alligator

In a while, crocodile

Peace out

Talk soon

BBIAB

TTFN

But know that in my heart

I'm holding on to this goodbye

Until I can say hello

Until tomorrow

When we meet again

In a time and place

Where words

Are the illusion

And we all return

To stardust and daydreams

Farewell,

For now.

Over and out—

Casey Jones

DEAR SAMMY,

I want you to know even though you're gone you'll always be my big brother. My twin. My *and*.

I promise to visit more often and believe me, expect more journals. In fact, I'll be sending this one your way in about five minutes.

You'd laugh so hard if you could see us right now. We didn't make it home before the storm hit. Which makes sense, I suppose, considering how this all began in the first place. But when we went into the house I couldn't find Mom and Dad anywhere. Frankie pointed to the backyard. That's when I noticed the glow playing on the windows.

When I opened the sliding door, there they were, holding umbrellas over their heads and halfway over the bonfire. Just waiting for us to show up. Even in the downpour they managed to keep the fire raging. They must have poured a gallon of lighter fluid on it.

I need to be quick as I write, because if I don't make it out there before the wood burns down, all their hard work will have been for nothing.

I love them so much.

They miss you hard. Nonna too. Everyone does.

But I think you know that. Give Nonno a hug for me, will ya?

I hope when the ashes of this journal reach you, wherever you are, that you absorb all the love I'm putting into these pages. I mean, Dad says we're all stardust, right? So eventually this has to find you. I know these are all things I'll never say to you in person, but they still matter. Because *you* still matter. You always will.

And remember, as the great Jerry once said:

If you should stand, then who's to guide you?

If I knew the way, I would take you home . . .

Find your way home, Sammy. Be free. And if you can't, wait for me until I find my way to you. Might be a while, but I promise, one day we'll meet again.

Over and out—

Casey Jones

ACKNOWLEDGMENTS

To lose someone and mourn their loss is to know that you've loved completely, and that is one of life's most magical gifts—which is ironic considering you don't experience the full depth of that love until there's a death. I think, in a way, that's how we become immortal. The memories your cherished ones carry of you and pass down through the generations keep you alive long after you're gone.

I feel honored to be a part of that tradition and humbled to share the stories of those loved ones who have passed away any chance I get.

Although all the characters in *Things I'll Never Say* are fictional, they were born from experiences with my own loss, and this story is a tribute to those no longer with us—especially the ones who died of an overdose. Writing this book was part of my own grieving process that was a long time coming. Something I've learned over the years is that grief never ends but it does evolve, and that's how we survive. I hope that any of you looking for validation for your own feelings and solidarity with others who are grieving a loss can find some comfort within these pages.

There is no wrong way to mourn. So feel your feels and ride the wave of those emotions, because that's the only path to healing.

There are so many people I'd like to thank—because just like raising a child, it takes a village to make a book.

First I want to thank my parents, CJ and Belinda Catalano— without y'all I wouldn't exist and neither would this book, so double high-fives for being the creators of this story's creator. Both of you gave me the tools I needed to enjoy life to the fullest, to follow my dreams, to imagine, travel, and make the most of every day. Also, the skills to play a mean game of poker, and a love of reading. I love y'all.

And to my parents-in-law, Gerry and Caroline Newbould— I'm forever grateful for how much you've made me truly feel part of the Newbould family over the years. Love you both!

Maxwell—you are the peanut butter to my jelly. Sure, we could make a sandwich without one or the other, but WHY? Thank you for being my best friend, for exploring all the side paths with me on this winding road, and for letting my stubbornness be an asset instead of a hindrance ;). I am so grateful I get to experience this journey with you—always forward, never straight! LuvLuv forever.

Neeks, KC, Xanda—you are the blood that keeps my heart beating. I live for the three of you, and all I want in this life is to see you thrive. Whatever that path may look like, I am here and will be cheering you on every day. Thank you for loving me. I hope you find magic in the small things, knowledge in the big things, and the time to pause and take it all in. Make every day count. I love you!

Jamey Catalano—you are the best sister I could ever have wished for and my forever friend. Most of my memories include you, and I wouldn't change a minute of them. Let's settle it here and now: you may be better at dancing, but I am the best card player :p. Love you!

Ashley Hearn—where do I start? You freaking get me, man. Working with you over these last months has truly been an author's dream. I so appreciate how well we flow and cannot put into words what this entire journey has been like except to say that I wish every writer could experience the support and skills you bring to the table. Not only are you an epic editor, but your passion for life is true motivation. Keep climbing those mountains, because I live for your nature pics.

Peachtree Teen—THANK YOU for believing in me and my story. I am so happy that *Things I'll Never Say* found a home within your walls. To all the amazing people who worked to bring this book to life, I appreciate you SO MUCH—Lily Steele, Sara DiSalvo, Barbara Perris, Zoie Konneker, Jamie Evans, Keara Watkins, Mya Bailey, Terry and Michelle, Bree Martinez, and the entire marketing team at Peachtree, I am grateful for all the work y'all put into making this story a book!

Hokyoung Kim—thank you for giving me the most beautiful cover I could ever hope for. You made *TINS* a piece of art.

Ernie Chiara—my dude, you are a dream agent. Thank you for believing in *Things I'll Never Say*. You have repeatedly shown me how kickass a partnership between an agent and author can (and should) be in a multitude of ways. I cannot wait to bring more books into the world with you. This may be the first, but it will not be the last! And a huge thank you to everyone at Fuse Literary!

To the three awesome peeps who beta read *TINS*—

Kelly deVos—you were the first of my friends to read TINS and give feedback. I love you and all you bring to this industry. You are AMAZING. Dante Medema—you were the second to read *TINS,* and I am forever grateful for your thoughtful feedback. Thank you! Alicia Sparrow—thank you for helping me polish before I queried *TINS.* LOVE you!

TEAM ERNIE—Katharine, Lex, Asia, Meredith, Aman, Fen, Julia—it's so cool to share this experience with you, and I'm happy to call y'all my agent siblings. Can't wait to celebrate all the wins with ya!

Better Than Brunch Crew—I don't know how I'd survive being an author without you. Denise Williams, Charish Reid, Taj McCoy, Alicia Sparrow, all my Sundays belong to y'all :). I love watching your publishing careers THRIVE and am here for it always! LOVE YOU!

To all the authors, writers, daydreamers, and publishing people in my life, may you always keep creating.

Special thanks to Rebecca Sky, Alechia Dow, Harper Glen, Kelly deVos, Irene Reed, Kristin Thorsness, Destiny Rae, Diana Pinguicha, Kim Johnson, Ashley Schumacher, Rebecca Sky, Maura Jortner, Catherine Adel West, Julie Murphy, Chris Baron, Shauna Holyoak, Lori M. Lee, Cindy Baldwin, Rosiee Thor, Julie Artz, Sona Charaipotra, A.J. Irving, amanda lovelace, Rachel Griffin, Kristin Dwyer, and Shari Green for your constant support and checking in. It's so awesome how much we writers can rely on each other.

To my friends and family—it would take many pages and an obscene number of words to describe my love and show how grateful I am for each and every one of you. Since I don't have that much time or space on the page, know that you are my world. I do need to shout out those who've been a constant influence in my life: Heather, Tiana, Wanda, Cindy, Gretchen, Faith, Andy, Catie, Mason, Ashlyn, Dov, Erik, Hayley, Johnny, Leah-Lani, Kassie, MaryBeth, Anne, Rachel, Whitney, Kelly, Jody, Katherine, Leslie, Mickey, Britton, Rochelle, Monique, Sam, Rex, Annie, Scott, Bella, Lily, Rupert, Imogen, Spencer, Jay, Kimmy, River, Ashton, Holmesy, Stacie, Krystal, Ryan, Jenny, John, Mac, Jimmy, Ginger, Will, Noopy, Joe, Adam, Ant, DJ, Toby, Ben, Mary, Paavo, Slime, Maya, Allison, Ruby, Maddie, Dani, Zoe, Cosmo, Lynda, Suzie, the rest of my Runion, Catalano, Catches, Newbould, Cove Point, Jupiter, Florida, Cali, Vegas, New Mexico, Colorado, Pine Ridge Reservation, Washington, and UK family and friends, and my mIRC-DOAEOTAD crew—this would have been a lonely adventure without you in it.

And to my beloved friends who I miss daily—Adam, Scott, Cory, Mike, Brennan, Easton, Sarah, April, Josh—you died way too young, but the memories of y'all will live forever, and holy shit, are they epic ones!

Our country is suffering from an opioid crisis and we are losing too many of our loved ones to addiction and overdose. Here are some resources if you or someone you love needs help, and please know, you are not alone.

https://www.directrelief.org/issue/opioid-epidemic/

https://opioidresponsenetwork.org/

https://www.ruralhealthinfo.org/topics/opioids/
organizations

https://www.asam.org/advocacy/coalitions

https://nam.edu/more-than-100-organizations-
join-the-national-academy-of-medicine-in-
countering-the-opioid-epidemic/

https://nam.edu/programs/action-collaborative-
on-countering-the-u-s-opioid-epidemic/
network-organizations/